D1462559

"While most depictions of Italian American life are like Olive Garden commercials, Tony Romano sets us down in the real kitchen and the old Latin Mass. His story of the Peccatori family is a profound exploration of what it means to be a hyphenated American. Family members are bound by obligation, reassured by ritual, but left alone to wrestle with what this all will become. In clear and sensual prose, Tony Romano maps the topography of our yearning."
— Daniel Ferri, National Public Radio commentator

"Tony Romano pays a rare attention to the human heart in *When the World Was Young*. As he takes you from the new world of Chicago to an old world at the foot of the Apennines and back again, you will follow his characters into backrooms and backseats—through their sins and kindnesses—like sneaky cousins, to find in the end that the journey was a personal one. For Romano's characters—like his readers—neither sin nor love, neither confess nor forgive without question. He reminds us all that we are fed on more than the milk and bread of our mothers and fathers. Their sins, too, have grown us."
— Billy Lombardo, author of *The Logic of a Rose: Chicago Stories*

"Little Italy lives again in this mythical tale of love, life, and death. Romano has concocted a new brew from an old-country recipe that reminds us all of the humanity inside the shared emotions that transcend time, nation, and culture."
— Fred Gardaphé, Director of Italian American Studies SUNY at Stony Brook

"[Romano's] characters are granted complex, ambivalent motives, and he manages to evoke tenderness without ladling on the treacle. . . . A low-key, compelling look at family love and betrayal, set against an old-style immigrant drama."
— *Kirkus Reviews*

"Romano finds a rich vein of material in a place and time buffeted by changing mores, insularity, and tenuous ties to the old country." — *Publishers Weekly*

"[A] tenderhearted novel about an immigrant family during the 1950s. . . . Romano describes the mourning process in heart-wrenching passages even as he relays the love and the secrets . . . that bind and separate family members. In addition, he offers a finely detailed depiction of the Peccatoris' west-side Chicago neighborhood, from its Italian beef stands to its majestic Catholic church."
— *Booklist*

© 2007 by Alyse Liebovich

About the Author

TONY ROMANO has been nominated for two Pushcart
Prizes and is a two-time winner of a PEN Syndicated
Fiction Project award. His fiction has appeared in many
publications, including the *Chicago Tribune*, and his stories
have been produced for National Public Radio's *The Sound
of Writing* series. He lives near Chicago, Illinois.

WHEN THE WORLD WAS YOUNG

Tony Romano

HARPER PERENNIAL

NEW YORK • LONDON • TORONTO • SYDNEY • NEW DELHI • AUCKLAND

HARPER ● PERENNIAL

A hardcover edition of this book was published in 2007 by HarperCollins Publishers.

FIRST HARPER PERENNIAL EDITION PUBLISHED 2008.

Designed by Lorie Pagnozzi

Library of Congress Cataloging-in-Publication Data is available upon request.

ISBN 978-0-06-085793-6

08 09 10 11 12 ID/RRD 10 9 8 7 6 5 4 3 2 1

To my girls
Maureen, Lauren, Angela, and Allie

Part 1

1976

NICHOLAS PECCATORI

❧

Though Mama may not have seen this as consolation, Papa didn't fall in love with Sophia Loren until about a year after poor little Benito died. At least that's how I'd always understood it, Papa's grief giving way to obsession. The one thing Mama and Papa did agree on was they'd never use Benito's room ever again, at least not for anything as functional as a bedroom.

How I know all this is still a mystery to me since I was born a full two years after Benito drew his last breath, two years to the day. On birthdays I'm keenly aware of the somber glances at Benny's photograph that sits atop the china cabinet shelf in the dining room, along with the raucous laughs and the slaps on the back that seem too exuberant. In the photograph, Benito stares clear at you from his high chair, his dark saucer eyes showing no signs of the fever that would soon ravage his body.

I know I've taken in much of our family history on my own, away from the pitying stares of my older brothers and sister, who look at me as the one who came after, the only innocent one. Yet innocence isn't what I feel. I feel instead that I was there when Benito died. He lifts his infant arms to me, I touch his hands, and they are like fire. I see the mourners file out of St. Columbkille behind two pallbearers and the tiny casket, then the awful lowering.

Two years later, before I had the words to know him, Benito was by my side. He was there when I nuzzled on Mama's grief. I have been in her arms at the precise time of Benito's passing, and in her innermost thoughts, she has noted it. My twisted mouth sucking became his. I have seen him in Mama's eyes on my first day of kindergarten, and picture day, and anytime I refused to eat or showed the slightest sign of fever. I have seen him when a certain light flashed through the curtained window on a lazy Sunday afternoon. I am the living marker of what could have been.

Benito should have been the last, I know. And I am an afterthought, bittersweet and haunting. On those rare afternoons, never at night, when the house is empty, I amble into Benito's old room, Papa's sanctuary now, and lean on the edge of the bed until my head stops reeling, until the walls stop whirling. Papa's smell steadies me, an attic scent that speaks of ages and reminds me always of oil and church. And behind that, wafting up from a drawer in the blond dresser in the corner, the fragrance of baby lotions.

If you push aside the Sophia Loren memorabilia—the poster, the records, the videocassettes, the news clippings, the heart-shaped ashtray embossed in red, white, and green, showing Sophia blowing a kiss—you can still find signs of my brother. The tiny bed of course. That's what hits you first, what you always come back to. His dresser. The mitt-shaped night-light. His powder-blue rosary draped across another photo of Benny as an infant with cheeks too red that sits on the nightstand, angled toward the lace pillow.

When I sit on that bed the world is transformed. Benito is finishing college, majoring in medicine. We look like brothers, everyone says—short spark-plug frames with round faces, dark, with Papa's thick hair and Mama's broad shoulders. We ride the back of the CTA bus together to Wrigley Field and sit in the bleachers. He teaches me the nuances of the game, what pitch should come next, where to place the ball. He loves the game almost more than he loves me. And when I take stock, there are six brothers and sisters in the Peccatori family, not five. Six there are, and always will be.

1

1957

At the first glimpse of her stepping off the westbound Grand Avenue trolley, Santo Peccatori clutched his shirtfront in longing. He looked on from the silver-tinted storefront panes of Mio Fratello, where he worked for his father and uncle on weekends wiping tables and washing cocktail glasses, duties his younger brothers, Anthony and Alfredo, would soon take on now that school was out, while Santo, having just graduated high school, would busy himself stocking liquor and wine, pouring the occasional drink when his father was out and the men couldn't wait for Uncle Vince to wrest himself from a table of patrons, and positioning himself in this very spot so he could spy Sylvia Gomez descending a trolley at 4:05 P.M. after an eight-hour shift at Illinois Bell.

She had on a sleeveless, floral-print dress splashed in mari-golds that reminded him of the dresses his mother wore when he was a boy. She waited while the bus, a pale green-and-cream metal grasshopper, pulled along by hundreds of crackling volts of live cable overhead, swept past her and blotted her from view for several seconds. The trolley poles clanked along the wire, zapped twice, and the bus disappeared. As she waited for traffic to recede so she could cross Grand and circle behind Mio Fratello to get to her apartment, she stretched and turned as if she'd just been awakened from a long slumber. Santo gazed at her bare legs. She wore her black slip-ons, the ones with the small heel that made the slide of her leg tilt ever so slightly. On her right calf, the result of sitting too long in one position, was a blushed circle, the size of a peach, the size of Santo's palm.

Santo's father, Agostino, unloading bottles of Gallo wine from crates behind the bar, glanced also at the bus stop where Sylvia Gomez now tucked her grand rivulets of thick dark hair behind her shoulder and pulled on the strap of her purse, ready to cross. Agostino set down a mug-handled gallon and strolled outside to the back of the tenement. The ground floor of the flat was a combination liquor store–bar — some called it a club — where the same twenty or thirty men shelled out sweaty dollars for shots of liqueur or schnapps and then retreated to the back lot on hot summer nights such as this to wager on bocce. Agostino picked up the wide rake and worked at leveling the fine stones in the bocce alley, one of the varied tasks he left undone each afternoon until this time so he could step outside with a degree of nonchalance and appear busy. He and his brother, Vincenzo, who lived in the apartment above the bar, had framed the stones with two-by-tens and lag bolts seven summers ago. Each year they added a fresh coat of pine-green paint to the boards and darkened the red foul lines, so that except for a few dents from errant tosses, the lane looked untrodden.

He whistled a slow aria, each note precise and assured, until he spotted Sylvia Gomez out the corner of his eye.

"Signora," he called, leaning an elbow on his rake, wiping the back of his hand across his forehead, as if he'd been at the stones for hours. He had to work at keeping his left eye still—his father used to call him *sinistra*—and that combination of the wandering eye and the subtle tightening needed to steady it made him seem vaguely pensive. Though average in height, Agostino still appeared lanky, his khaki trousers hanging modishly, supported by a thin brown belt. His dark mustache, peppered gray, bristled with perspiration.

"Señor," she said, and nodded.

"Another hot day, no?"

He marveled at the sound of the words in his head before he spoke, pure Midwestern, and what happened to those sounds once they were pushed into the air, revealing the sharp accent he worked to soften, even after twenty-two years in America.

She slowed her steps and finally stopped. "Not as hot as yesterday."

Their eyes remained fixed on each other. She slung her purse onto her other shoulder and Agostino scratched at his chin. They broke their gaze and one after the other glanced at the adjacent brown brick flat. Tucked away along the side of the building where the sun blasted each morning was a patch of dirt that served as a vegetable garden: tomatoes and cucumbers and sprigs of parsley.

Inside, Santo peered out and calculated that Sylvia Gomez, who at twenty-seven or twenty-eight, was no closer to his father's age than his own. Santo, eighteen in a month, sourly concluded that Sylvia Gomez anticipated these meetings as much as his father.

Agostino waved her toward a table. "Come. Sit. A glass of vino."

"I need to start dinner," she said.

"A small glass." He moved to one of the white, wrought-iron tables and pulled out a chair. "Please. Sit. In the shade here it's cool."

Santo knew his father would not bellow out his drink order to him, not with Mrs. Gomez. He was tempted to bring out drinks anyway and remind him that Mama wanted him home for dinner tonight. Mama, who would be cooking all day because her sister, Zia Lupa, would be back from her travels. Except for Uncle Vince, who would need to mind the store, the whole family would be there, together for once. Zia Lupa at the head, Agostino across from her. Mama next to Zia, though Mama would barely sit. Anthony and Alfredo on one side, sharing their private adolescent jokes, Santo and his sister, Victoria, a year younger, on the other, who would pout all night about being treated like the youngest, though she was sixteen. She wasn't allowed anywhere near Mio Fratello. And baby Benito, of course, squeezed in near Victoria, who would watch over him.

Santo waited until his father glided in and out with the wine, then began wiping down one of the four bar stools, a spot that afforded him a partial view of Mrs. Gomez's back. Off her right shoulder a tiny portion of an ivory strap had slipped out from her dress. Santo pictured her putting on the brassiere this morning, imagined how she held it in place somehow while fastening the clasp. How she stepped into the marigolds, pushing her arms into the holes of the sleeves. Or did she lift the dress high and let it cascade around her like so much water? These bedroom gestures were a great mystery to him. Santo couldn't quite make out what they were saying, but he heard their frequent laughter. After each laugh his father would glance at her small round breasts, then cast his eyes down the alley toward her apartment.

Santo stepped closer, straining to hear. Agostino was telling her about the Great War, recounting the familiar story of his father in Italy getting shot by the Germans. He told her what he and Vince were doing when they received the telegram from overseas—smoking a cigarette in their bar of course. On top of that, Roosevelt took great pleasure in lambasting Mussolini every day, causing hardworking Italians in America to cower like dogs. Santo wondered why he would tell her such stories, other than to evoke pity. For any other listener, his father would have added the part about naming his youngest son Benito, how he wouldn't allow a madman like Mussolini to tarnish such a beautiful name, but his father must have determined that such defiance would not charm her and perhaps even push her away. And he certainly wouldn't add that Benito was named after his wife's grandfather, a kindly old man who had split his time on this earth farming and painting frescoes on village walls in Italia.

There was still a certain formality to these afternoon meetings, which suggested that his father was not yet sleeping with Mrs. Gomez, a thought that emboldened Santo. But his father's affairs were shrouded always in deception, so Santo could not be sure.

He pushed open the screen door and stuck his head into the bright afternoon. "Hey, Pop. Is Uncle Vince upstairs?"

Mrs. Gomez put down her glass and flashed a broad smile at Santo. Agostino stared openly at her breasts.

"Non lo so," Agostino told his son.

"Hello, Santo," Mrs. Gomez said.

"Hello."

"Why?" Agostino asked.

"Why what?" Santo wanted to know.

"Why do you need *Zio*?"

"Oh. I just wanted to know if he ordered any more JB. We're low."

Agostino leaned toward Mrs. Gomez, pointed to the store, and said, "He think he own store." He shrugged and conceded, "He can do by himself."

Santo felt his chest swell. If he were three years older, he *could* run the place, a prospect that filled him. Maybe they would even rename the store Mio Fratello e Figlio. "Can I get you anything else, Mrs. Gomez?"

She took one last swallow, pulled a scalloped napkin across her mouth, and waved away his request. "No, no, I need to go."

"Some coffee maybe?" Santo pleaded.

"No."

"Water?"

She shook her head.

"A toothpick?"

Santo got the laugh he expected. He wasn't the best-looking of his brothers — his protruding ears were dented at the top and his friends at one time called him "walnut" because of the shape of his head — but he breathed confidence. As a boy, he was the one who pranced around on his heels at parties offering kisses to Zia Lupa and Uncle Vince and all the other guests while his brothers cowered in Mama's lap.

He was the one who, when asked if he had a girlfriend, would flash even teeth and offer a school snapshot of the lucky girl for the week. Girls saw in him someone who was assured and harmless, which, when he began dating at sixteen, allowed him to get much farther up their blouses than the girls might have originally intended.

As Mrs. Gomez walked away down the alley, father and son looked on. Agostino ran a pocket comb straight back through his thinning hair, his free hand trailing with delicate precision, a gesture his son secretly admired. His father's sinewy arms, bulging with each greasy swipe, reminded Santo of the graceful sweeps of a bodybuilder. Santo turned and went inside, the screen door slapping behind him. He felt an ache of anticipation in his chest, not unlike the ache he felt as a boy sitting on the front stoop, waiting for the mailman to deliver the prize he'd won for selling candy tins for St. Columbkille. But he was no longer a boy. He was through with school forever. And summer's heat was just beginning.

Santo knocked on the window of Uncle Vince's back door, three hard raps. He knocked again and again, peering into the green-and-gray, checker-tiled kitchen. His uncle lived alone in the second-floor apartment above the bar. His wife, Gloria, left him in 1934 after a year of marriage, claiming he spent more time at his bar than with her. She was big and blond, and Vince still carried pictures of her in his wallet he liked to show. A real lulu, he told everyone. Shortly after she left, Vince sent a telegram to his brother, Agostino, in Italy, offering him partnership because he'd already begun his drinking and knew he'd lose the business without help. Agostino balked at first. He'd just completed a long apprenticeship with the tailor Lucca Strazzi in Naples, but the prospects of a thriving shop were slim in his small village. He'd need to move elsewhere, either to Naples or to America. After increasingly urgent telegrams from his brother, Agostino settled into the second bedroom of his brother's apartment atop the bar they renamed Mio Fratello.

Santo turned to the Singer sewing machine behind him on the enclosed porch. His father's. He took in the aroma of the A-1 oil can on the machine's table sleeve. The black, cast-iron pedal, wrought with leaves, brought him back for a moment to his father's lap not so long ago, a place he suddenly missed with such force that he felt himself begin to sway. The pedal made a sweet, rhythmic click when his father worked it, causing a leather belt to rotate iron wheels that pushed the needle like a greased piston. A single black thread dangled from the spool at the top of the machine.

He had a vague memory of the sewing machine being in the basement at home, his mother mending a collar, but this seemed more dream than real, which confirmed an idea he'd been obsessed with lately—that, because he and Mama were close and little had changed between them over the years, nearly all memories of his mother were cloaked in the same soft haze. All their days blended together. They were still affectionate with each other, his mother pinching his cheek, adding a light slap as a reminder to behave, Santo responding with a hurried hug or a squeeze of her hand. He could still make her laugh and coax her into singing at night on the porch, Benito cradled in her arms. And neither of them tired of the little tricks he played on her, Santo sneaking into her kitchen to dip a piece of warm bread in the red sauce, blaming the missing piece on Anthony and Alfredo—or stealing a meatball and spreading the rest around the pan to conceal his deceit. Which also explained the vividness of sitting on his father's lap, since this contrasted so sharply with how they got along today, like two men working side by side, bound by blood but unwilling or unable to confide in the other. Maybe they didn't have the shared language to do so, both of them barred from conveying satisfaction or loss or yearnings deeper than the surface hungers that dictated their exchanges. The sandwich is good? The customers are fine? The shelves are full? Yes, Papa. *Tutti e buona*. Everything is good. How could he begin to tell his father he missed him? And did his father feel the same?

Uncle Vince finally stirred and shuffled to the door.

"Come in come in, Santucci. But not so loud, hey."

Although it was June, Vince, claiming always to be cold, wore a flannel, long-sleeved nightshirt, boxer shorts, and slippers. He was the lone Peccatori to stand nearly six feet tall yet seemed much shorter because of his hunched shoulders and severe limp from a degenerative hip that he swore he'd let a doctor look at soon.

He rubbed his eyes and settled into his overstuffed couch, the flattened cushions outlining his usual position. "What is the news, hey?"

Santo gazed over his shoulder out the porch window, wondering if he could spot Sylvia Gomez's house. "Did you order the JB?" he muttered.

Vince ran a hand through his tangled thatch of black hair and yawned. "JB . . . AB. You think bar will close if we no have? *I patroni*, the old men, they drink most anything."

Santo sat across from his uncle in a hard-backed chair and leaned his head against the plaster wall. He didn't much care about the JB. Uncle Vince belonged to a different time, a bygone age, and Santo enjoyed being there, listening to him spin his grand view of the world. "Careful with the three Cs, hey," Vince liked to tell him. "The three Cs — the Coin, the Car, the Cunt — they ruin everything. Kill you." Santo gazed at his uncle's ruddy complexion and wondered if cognac would ever be added to the list.

Vince pulled out a smashed pack of Pall Malls from his shirt pocket, picked out two cigarettes with his fingertips, and flipped one to Santo, who lit both with his book of Mio Fratello matches. They leaned back and blew smoke over their shoulders, as if doing the other a favor. A light breeze curled the ivory curtain at the only open living-room window in the apartment, and pale light fell in misshapen squares on the gray carpet.

"This is *primo*, hey?"

"*Primo*, Zio."

"Hey. Santo." He cocked his head and considered his cigarette. "Vittoria, she no smoke, hey?"

Santo put up his hands and shrugged. "I don't know anything about that, Uncle Vinny."

Santo's younger sister, Victoria, had been stealing cigarettes from her father for a year before Agostino caught on. He wanted to forbid her from smoking, but he knew she was strong-willed and would only smoke more. So he never said a word, other than to let on that he knew the cigarettes were missing.

"So tonight. Zia Lupa, hey?" Vince said. "She come back?"

"She come back."

Aunt Lupa had won a monthlong trip to South America through a raffle at her church.

"I should marry that Lupa, hey. She take good care of me. She lucky."

"Then you'd be my uncle twice. Double uncle."

"One time is enough. No?" He puffed on his Pall Mall. "But your mama. She help. Yeh, yeh, Angela Rosa she talk to Lupa. Make arrange. You know how sister, they talk, hey?"

Vince carried on the same conversation regarding every unmarried woman he knew, as well as a few married ones. He acknowledged that life was hard and he was weak and constantly looked for ways to even the scale some, always with a grin.

"Find someone to watch the store," Santo told him. "Everyone'll be at the feast anyway. Come to dinner tonight. Lupa can sit on your lap."

Vince feigned a look of terror and sank down in the couch as if he were being crushed. "No no, the store. I must keep the store."

There had been a few serious attempts to find a wife for Vince—a trip to Italy was even arranged, the same way his brother, Agostino, had met his wife, Angela Rosa—but he always retreated. Now he had Carmel, whom he visited once a week, he had his cleaning woman who took care of the apartment, what little needed to be done, and he had his bar. He saw enough of his nephews and niece and didn't pine for children of his own. Why complicate his life now with marriage?

"What about Mrs. Gomez?" Santo asked.

Vince fanned his hand as if it were ablaze. *"Elegante."*

"What if you met someone like her? Would you marry her?"

"Too young."

Santo couldn't hide his smile. "And too married?"

Vince shrugged, indicating this wasn't such a big concern, and scratched his prickly chin. "Ehh."

"How old do you think she is?"

Vince, amid putting his feet on the coffee table and his hands behind his head, suddenly stopped. He remained frozen for a moment. *"Santucci! Mio Santo."* He put his feet down and stood up, suddenly alert. "So, Mrs. Gomez, hey?" He smiled and turned. Making his way to the bathroom, he laughed heartily, shaking his head and muttering, "Just like his papa."

Victoria Peccatori, sixteen, with sweater sets that hugged her too snugly and ruby lipstick that shined too brightly, hated her aunt Lupa. And bulky Zia Lupa, her dresses stiff and seam-tight, her chalky pink rouge caked thick and punctuated with carnival-red dots on each cheek, didn't hide her disdain for Victoria. *"Miserabile,"* Lupa would lament to her sister, Angela Rosa. *"Quella li ucciderà,"* she'd add, which meant, roughly, "That daughter will be your end," though Victoria didn't need a precise translation. The fierce eyes and the biting tongue were enough.

On the night of her return from South America, Zia Lupa greeted her niece with the obligatory kiss on each cheek, which Victoria promptly wiped away. Lupa took her by the shoulders. "How big," she said, the only English she would attempt all night. She pushed past Victoria, her pungent perfume trailing her, patted Santo's chin, offered quick hugs to Anthony and Alfredo, and marched straight to Benito on the floor, who was drooling over a hard biscuit. She picked him up, smothered him with wet kisses, burying him in her substantial bosom, Benito squealing with delight at first but then twisting away. *"Caro, Benito. Bello."* She wouldn't loosen her grasp until she sat down minutes later.

Victoria noted with satisfaction the great pocket of air her aunt produced when she settled onto the plastic-covered couch cushion. Victoria enjoyed watching her try to push away the thick clear plastic from her legs, noting how the plastic left blotchy pink patches. Victoria sauntered past the living-room window of the apartment to catch a glimpse of her shoulders. *How big*, she thought. She tried to convince herself that she needn't worry. Fortunately, her waist was still slight and her legs slender. And her thick hair softened her shoulders some. She gazed beyond her reflection toward Zia Lupa, then back at herself, and even in that slanted light she found the resemblance uncanny. Zia Lupa had turned bronze in the South American sun, and Victoria had to admit she looked vibrant, like some Amazon.

Victoria couldn't help identifying with her barren aunt— which is why she hated her. They had the same Tamburi shoulders, square and solid, that Victoria feared would thicken with age. They were both doggedly stubborn and not easily pleased. Victoria prayed that the lines at the corners of her eyes would not converge and harden like her aunt's.

She crossed the living room and put her arms out to Benito to rescue him from all that perfume, but Zia Lupa turned and waved her away. Annoyed, Victoria slipped off to her room at the far end of the apartment and pored through her latest copy of *True Confessions*. She would lie on the bed and wait until they called her for supper so she would spend as little time as possible with her aunt. That's what she liked about their apartment. They lived on the second floor of a three-story brownstone. The main passageways from living room to dining room to kitchen, though narrow, seemed to go on forever. If she kept out of these main rooms, privacy was never a problem.

She hoped that Zia Lupa, after her long trip, would insist on going home after dinner instead of joining them at the feast. Each year St. Columbkille celebrated La Festa di Madonna, a three-night feast stretching across four blocks of West Ohio Street that marked the beginning of summer. Victoria planned to spend the first hour pushing Benito in his buggy, raising him high over her head at the shrine of the Virgin Mary, passing him around to all her friends, who would smear lipstick over his blush cheeks. Taking care of Benito made her feel older, filled her with purpose in a family where she felt increasingly detached. What difference should it make to them how late she stayed out or what car she hopped into or how much lipstick she brushed onto her lips? She tried to impress upon them, even her younger brothers, Anthony and Alfredo, who at thirteen and twelve had become surrogate fathers, that she could take care of herself. Besides, whatever illicit activities she might do could just as easily happen before ten o'clock as after. When she tried to explain this, they'd all shake their heads, Anthony and Alfredo doing their utmost to appear stern.

After watching Benito tonight, she'd slip off behind Jimmy's beef stand, one of the vendors at the feast, where she and Darlene would drag down the same cigarette that Jimmy's nephew, Stick, would supply. Darlene and Stick had been going steady for a year now, but Victoria got the feeling lately he was interested more in her than in Darlene. She still hadn't decided what to do about this, which unsettled her. Which got her thinking about what it means to do the right thing. She doubted there was such a thing. She'd heard a story on the radio about a mother who'd been arrested for killing her son by holding his head underwater. The mother said she wanted to teach the boy not to be afraid of water. What kind of God would allow this? Victoria wondered. And if God didn't exist, how would that mother ever be punished? She prayed then, for justice, for hell with all its lapping flames, doubt spreading through her like ragweed.

Her brother Santo knocked on the casing around her door, though the door was open. She knew better than to close it, and Santo knew not to barge through.

"Hey, Vick. Dinner."

She rolled her eyes.

"What," he said.

Zia Lupa's shrill litany pierced through the passageways like an air-raid siren.

"Oh. That." He picked at a crack in the paint around the doorjamb.

"If she says one word about my sleeves or the slit in my skirt or—"

"Ah, forget it. C'mon."

"Yeah, right. She doesn't give you any crap. That's why, *forget it*. What? Does she expect me to wear one of those old-lady black shifts?"

"No, really," he said. "Forget it. What's she gonna say?"

"Aw, cripes. She's gonna say my sleeves are too short. 'Cover those shoulders.' That's what she's gonna say, Einstein."

Santo looked out the window, knowing if he stepped near it he could see the pulsing neon arrow outside Vince's apartment and the roof of Mio Fratello. The smell of night was coming on, and the bar would be crowded soon. He heard what he would say next and told himself not to, but the words kept forming, and just thinking about them made them into a thing he couldn't contain.

"Maybe you should, you know, cover your shoulders," he said.

Her eyes became fiery slits. "What's it to you? Father number two." She whisked past him. "Where's Father number three? And four? Jesus H. Christ." She took long strides, hoping to hike up her worsted skirt to highlight the slit. "Four fathers I got. Christ."

Victoria didn't utter a word through dinner.

As usual, Agostino insisted that Zia Lupa sit at his place, at the end of the long dining-room table. She filled that spot, weighed it down like ship cargo, everything—the chairs, the crystal water glasses, the rose-tinted bottles of Chianti—tilting toward her, it seemed. Agostino sat next to Lupa so he could pour her wine and fill her water glass. Lupa directed most of her remarks to her sister, Angela Rosa, at the other end of the table. Victoria studied the seldom-used table leaf before her, its gray flecks darker than the rest. Anthony and Alfredo sat across from her, conspiring. Next to her, Santo slurped down minestrone soup. She nudged closer to Benito's high chair on her right and spread small portions of food across his tray.

Out of the corner of her eye she could see them reaching, a tangle of arms, as if they'd never eaten before. Reaching, shouting, signaling. She wanted to do her own shouting, tell them to slow down, that there was enough here for the whole neighborhood. Chicken cacciatore. Garlic chicken baked with sliced lemons. Fresh gnocchi and meatballs that she'd rolled and fried. *Baccala*, codfish to Americans, with red vodka sauce. Potato wedges with golden-crusted edges. Buttered asparagus. Steamed broccoli. Tossed salad she'd rinsed and sprinkled with olive oil and balsamic vinegar. Homemade bread she'd kneaded and sliced. Water. Wine. Soda for the boys.

To no one's surprise, Zia Lupa did most of the talking during supper. She had been to the university, the only woman in her village, the only woman in her province to do so, and spoke precise Italian, unlike the Neapolitano dialect the Peccatori children were used to hearing. Victoria was able to make out about half of what she said, which was half more than she cared to hear.

Lupa told them about the shrines she visited in Peru with Father Emil and Sister Ernestine and the rest of their small entourage of parishioners from her parish in Berwyn. "The Peruvians are fine people. They welcomed us into their houses with heads bowed like we were dignitaries. When we broke it to them we were vacationing and not on missions, this put them at ease and we all had a great laugh. But look at me, I must have gained fifteen pounds. They use lard for everything. They would put lard in cereal if they could. And everything is eggs. Eggs for breakfast, eggs for dinner. Agostino, be nice to Lupa and pass me that small piece of steak. I need meat. And the dirty stink from those kitchens nearly suffocated me. Peruvians, pff, such dirty people. One night a deaf boy and his brother came into St. Basilica, a fifteen-hundred-year-old stone church we were visiting just outside Lima. A colossal Virgin Mary is painted on one of the walls and every spring she weeps. Not when we were there, of course, but the smaller boy, the deaf boy, as old as Anthony or Alfredo maybe, he knelt down and prayed, then spoke to his brother with his hands. My throat was scratchy. I wanted to cry. The older one, tall and thin and dark like my shoe, went around with a cup for pesos, and no one could resist. Later, when we were strolling through the village, I saw the deaf boy and his brother handing the cup to a woman, their mother maybe. The deaf one—the younger one I should say, stupid me—was not using his hands. Do you hear what I'm saying? He spoke. With his dirty mouth the deaf boy spoke. If they had been laughing, mocking us, and hadn't appeared so desperate, I would have marched up to them and knocked the cup right out of their filthy hands. Such a poor people. Full of disease. I never want to go back there again. Not if you give me—"

Zia Lupa began coughing, a hacking, crouplike cough that went on for some time. Her sister, Angela Rosa, racked her solidly on the back and offered water. Victoria understood enough of Zia Lupa's story to offer rebuttal but thought better of it. Sarcasm wasn't so effective when someone was choking. Maybe there is a God, she thought, who caused people to choke on their own words.

After Zia Lupa wiped her eyes and settled back in her chair, breathing evenly through her mouth, she looked spent. Agostino raised his glass and offered a toast to Zia Lupa's safe return. Victoria thought he meant her safe return from choking, but everyone, even Anthony and Alfredo, had a glass raised and seemed to know what he meant from the start. *"Salute,"* Agostino said. When Benito raised his cup, they all broke out in laughter.

Victoria blushed with shame. She alone had hesitated in raising her glass. Sometimes meanness so dark streaked through her that she couldn't explain it. Where did it come from? Certainly not her father. More than anything, Agostino was starry-eyed, always looking slightly beyond the current crisis to some minor reprieve — a glass of wine, a plate of pasta, the morning sun. Victoria was getting to an age where she understood that much of her father's composure was probably anchored in his manhood, that much of it was show. Still, she'd seen him distracted with worry only once, after Mama had broken three bones in her pubic region after delivering Benito. This was when the lines around her father's eyes had begun to fan out in tight folds, as if they'd been sculpted there. He would stroke his chin in that contemplative way of his and put Santo in charge, then trek the fourteen miles to visit Angela Rosa and the baby at Loyola Medical.

It would have been easy for Victoria to blame her mother for her own meanness, but Angela Rosa was like every other mother Victoria knew, strict with her sons, stricter with her daughter. In Victoria's estimation, her mother had married too young and resented the narrowing of choices in her life, though Mama would never admit as much, not even to herself. But how could she *not* harbor resentment? She'd been plucked from her home, brought to America, and made pregnant. Just thinking about the ten-day trip across the ocean and the twenty-four-hour train ride from New York to Chicago made Victoria's stomach turn. She vowed never to be led about like that, like a woman-child. And whatever bitterness resided in Victoria would remain within her, not directed at a daughter.

After her grueling labor with Benito, Angela Rosa had softened some. Victoria gave her that. Her injury, it seemed, had crippled not only her body, but also her fury. Her words became more deliberate. She had to look at you then. She couldn't race from one end of the kitchen to the other, wiping a face along the way, picking up an onion skin off the linoleum tile, all the while cursing about the pants Victoria better not be wearing outside this apartment. And the words became more precise as well, meted out in quiet sternness. The effect was startling to Victoria—Angela Rosa's calmness held more power than her ranting. Victoria welcomed the reprieve and hoped her mother would notice this irony herself. But as Angela Rosa's strength gradually returned, her voice became increasingly louder, more shrill, her movements more flurried, and Victoria felt ensnared once again.

Victoria gazed at her mother at one end of the table, then at Zia Lupa slumped at the other. She tried to imagine them as girls, one chasing the other down a dirt field, kicking a ball, pulling each other's hair. But the images seemed all wrong. Preposterous. Zia Lupa was an aunt but not a sister. She had no past. Even the stories of Zia Lupa chaperoning Angela Rosa and her new husband, Agostino, on their voyage across the Atlantic seemed difficult to imagine. Lupa returned to her village after a month, only to find her own prospective suitor gone. Angela Rosa convinced her sister to rejoin her in America, where husbands grew like figs on trees. Lupa, skeptical, reluctantly agreed, but year after year found no man suitable.

Victoria finished the last of her water and wondered if her future nieces would one day view her in the same narrow band of light, if they would bother to look at her at all. She pushed herself from the table, brought out the fruit—a bowl of red apples, oranges, pears, a separate bowl filled with grapes, cherries, sliced melons—and began clearing dishes. She was glad to be alone in the kitchen, dipping her hands in the hot soapy water, listening to the steady rinse of the faucet.

"Where do you want these, Vicki?"

Alfredo? Clearing dishes? She turned. "What are you doing, Freddy?"

He shrugged and set the plates next to the pile of unwashed ones.

"Dessert will be out later," she said.

"I know." He picked up a dish towel and began drying.

"You heard enough about Peru?"

"I guess." He kept drying, studying each dish.

"Anything wrong, Freddy?"

"Nuh-uh."

"Just feel like drying?"

"Uh-huh."

"You and Anthony fighting?"

"No."

She went back to the soapy water, biding her time, lulled by the sound of dishes clanking.

"The thing is," he said.

She didn't turn for fear he'd stop.

"I heard Mama and Zia talking."

Still she wouldn't turn. "Oh, yeah?"

"About you."

She sidled closer to him. "About me, huh. What else is new?"

He peered toward the dining room. "They said you couldn't go to the feast unless you changed."

"Both of them said that?"

"Sort of." He scratched his chin and glanced at her shoulders. "So, I don't know. Maybe you should change?"

Anthony was usually the peacemaker, but she'd had harsh words with him over something she couldn't remember, so he probably pulled rank and sent Alfredo. They meant well. She'd give them that. But the evening had been long, with Zia yapping, and—"You know what, Freddy?"

With his dish towel he circled the plate. Stocky Alfredo. Eager to please.

She reined in her anger, touched his shoulder, and whispered, as if they were bound by what he'd confided, "When Zia shuts up for thirty seconds straight, that's when I'll change my clothes."

Alfredo grinned.

Before heading for the feast, Santo stopped by Mio Fratello to check on Uncle Vince. That's what he told himself anyway, while the real reason lurked like electricity in the cellar of his mind. He strolled along Grand Avenue, stopping at Battiste's fish store for a handful of salted pumpkin seeds. Farther along, Russo the barber sat in front of his shop with two older men donning faded fedoras, the red and white stripes on the barber pole swirling skyward untiringly, making the men appear more still than they really were. The scent of witch hazels cut through the summer night.

"*Buona sera,*" they said, nodded lazily, then went back to gazing after traffic that streamed by. Some of the men had dirt under their fingernails.

"*Buona sera,*" Santo answered, and followed their gaze. Scores of two-door sedans with grinning grilles, some with badges on their hoods, whisked by in either direction, their tires whining and scratching. It was a Friday and everyone had somewhere to go. Even Crazy Willie, the big oaf, now turning onto Grand from Damen Avenue, who circled the neighborhood endlessly each day, muttering to himself, even he had a destination, it seemed. Santo bent down and cuffed his jeans and pressed the fold to form a neat crease. A delivery truck with LLOYD J. HARRIS PIES emblazoned on the side plodded by, the driver leaning on the huge wheel, a cigarette dangling from his mouth. He'd put in a full day. Santo stood up, pushed a pocket comb smelling of Brylcreem through his wavy hair, his other hand trailing, then wiped both hands along the sides of his blue jeans. He decided, right then, he needed a car, a thought he'd never had before. His family had gotten along forever without an automobile, his whole life was within walking distance, the buses could take him anywhere he wanted—but the image of himself behind a chrome-inlaid steering wheel took hold. Once that happened, Santo knew, acquiring the car was inevitable, a small step really. He didn't much believe in fate or destiny, but he believed that thinking about a thing more times than not made that thing happen.

He looked ahead a few blocks toward the orange and yellow pennants strung around Grand Autos, a white gravel lot with thirty or forty Quality, Dependable, Guaranteed Used Cars that Santo had barely noticed before. His pace quickened. He imagined himself driving around in a midnight-blue Bel Air with bullet-nosed fenders and whitewall tires with chrome-cone hubcaps. He pictured someone next to him in the car—not a girl; not Becky or Vera or Karen; he was tired of girls—but a woman. A woman who smiled easily, someone who would appreciate a ride home from work maybe. Someone who wouldn't have to scrunch up close to him every time but who would rest her arm along her open window and let the wind take her hair. Later, while parked along Fullerton

Beach, both of them gazing out toward Lake Michigan, white-capped waves crashing against one another like children, she'd curl her fingers around his and whisper something that would make the two of them smile.

But there were no Bel Airs or midnight-blue cars at Grand Auto. Only SKY BLUE and CHERRY RED and PEARL WHITE. The dealer had swirled these descriptions across the entire length of the windshields with chalky-white paint stuff. Beneath this, in smaller print, the year and the price were blocked in yellow. Shocked by the numbers on the first few windshields, Santo stopped looking at the cars altogether and scanned only the prices. He found two possibilities: a '47 Studebaker and an even older Mercury with its front end accordioned in. But when he actually calculated, he figured that even three years of tips would barely cover half the cost. He had forty-five dollars put aside for a new Zenith transistor radio with leather case that his mother could get at discount, even though she hadn't worked at the factory in years.

Had the dealer been out there to hound him, Santo might have spent more time gaping, maybe taking the Mercury for a test ride, license or no license — Zio Vincenzo had given him a few lessons last summer in his cream Caddy — but the lot had been closed for hours, and dusk was fast giving way to night, so he left.

As he thought of ways to buy the car he took in the vastness of the molten sky before him. Mercury ash. He loved this time of night, the tallowy moon in place, stars striving to blink through the haze of day. He was always struck by the clarity of thought during these moments. Striding down Grand, one hand in his pocket jingling change, the other swinging at his side, he realized that his desires on this day represented less than a pinprick in the forces that pushed the world along. A thought which, instead of causing him to brood, never failed to evoke in him a warm physical surge that began in his feet and laced its way into his sternum before finally lodging itself in his throat. He breathed through his mouth for a second. He played a part in the vastness, however fleeting. That's what struck him. That's what took his breath. This was his turn.

"Mio Santo!" Vince said. He wiped his hands loosely on a dish towel and draped it along the edge of the utility sink. He'd changed into one of his silk shirts, the gray one with the two wide swaths of beige running vertically along the front. A folded white apron covered the top of his town-and-country trousers. "You checka me, hey? No worry, I make business."

"Yeah, yeah, I checka you, Uncle Vinny." Santo grabbed the inner part of his thigh and said, *"Right here* I checka you."

They both let out a kind of laugh, and Vince cuffed his nephew on the back of the neck, his fingers still damp from the soapy water in the sink where he'd been washing out quart carafes.

"No action yet, huh?" Santo said.

From where they stood on the enclosed porch they could view most of the bar out front and part of the bocce lot behind them. Not a single person in sight, which wasn't unusual for early evening. By eleven o'clock, when the feast began to wind down, the club would be filled with rumbling laughter and loud debate, the men assuming their usual places. Out back the serious ones would stand huddled, laying down bets on bocce, cheering, each lob creating a halting silence, followed by shouts and contortions designed to tilt the earth and guide the ball just so until it came to rest. On the sidewalk in front, men would straddle chairs they'd pulled from inside, checking for women in every direction—in cars, on buses, on bicycles, on foot. If they *were* walking, especially if they were perfumed and decked, the women were barraged with questions to stall them. But they were never offered a drink or a chair—in fact, it was Santo's job, though no one had ever assigned this, to take in any abandoned chair. This way the men would not seem rude. And if the women didn't sit, the men had nothing to deny to their girlfriends and wives, who also might be passing. Inside sat the heaviest drinkers, though they showed few signs of this. They were calm, their movements measured, speaking to one another in baritone evenness through thick smoke. They played checkers and cards, studied racing forms, but mostly they talked, Uncle Vince joining them, weighing in on neighborhood news and religion, gas prices and mortality. Santo loved weaving about each group, wiping tables, anticipating their needs, ready with matches and an order pad in his back pocket. When the store got busy he'd do what he could to ease the rush, surreptitiously pouring a glass of wine for a regular, who would wink and lay down cash as Santo, too young to serve, slipped away.

Santo plopped down on a wicker-backed chair near the sink, his right foot tapping the cast-iron plate over the floor drain. When he started tagging along with his father many years ago, this porch was his favorite room. Next to the sink, shelves formed a long narrow aisle filled with crates of liquor and wine. He'd throw a rubber ball toward the far wall at the end of the aisle and count how many times he could get it to return straight back to him without ricocheting away. On the other side of the shelves near the outer wall was a bathroom with a pull-chain toilet and a curling strip of waxy brown fly-paper hanging from the ceiling, and beyond that the slate-gray steps that led to Vince's apartment. There were many nights when Santo would climb the steps to watch the bocce matches from the window next to his father's sewing machine. He'd rest his chin in his palms and stare at the tops of heads, the old men's arms flailing, their bodies lunging. Beside the bocce pit a circle of men playing *scopa* would slap down their cards. Dense smoke would rise past the porch window and curl into the inky sky. Santo imagined the men's voices doing the same, wafting over rooftops and falling into chimneys.

"I want to see something," Santo said. He jumped up and climbed the stairs two by two. He slid open the porch window and poked his head full out into the night. The sweet aroma of fried bell peppers sailed up from one of the houses on Marshfield Avenue, where Sylvia Gomez lived. Beyond that, an arc of light outlined the stand of maples that ran along Ohio Street, where the feast blazed a full block away. Santo could hear the din of high-pitched voices cutting through the still air.

After a while Vince joined his nephew at the window.

"Where you look, hey?"

"Nowhere, Zio. I just wanted to see if you could see the feast from here."

"Ah . . . why you no go?"

"I will," Santo said. He looked for the moon but couldn't find it.

Vince pointed west. "Look."

Over the top of an elm the uppermost car of the Ferris wheel came into view, then disappeared and another took its place.

"Hmm," Santo said. They watched three complete cycles without a word. "You know," Santo said, "I need to . . . do something. You ever feel like you just have to do something?" He glanced at his uncle, who seemed not to be listening.

"Zio?"

"*Che?*"

"You think I can borrow one of your shirts?" A silk shirt would make him look older.

Vince stuck a cigarette in the corner of his mouth, where it would hang unlit, Santo knew, until Vince reached for another, forgetting the one in his mouth.

"Hrrrm . . . do some *thing*," Vince said. "Ha . . ." He peered across the rooftops on Marshfield, single peaks in a row with brick chimneys, nothing to distinguish one from another. That row took up just a tiny portion of the wider grid of similar peaks, interrupted now and then with two-story and three-story apartments. A smokestack punctuated the sky to the east. Vince nodded as if deciding, pressed his lips down on the cigarette, and rolled it with his tongue. He shrugged and put out his palms. "He gotta do," he said. "*Mio nipoto*, he gotta do some thing." He turned to Santo. "I no tell you before 'bout the three *C*s?"

"I know the three *C*s, Zio."

"You know, hey?"

"I know, hey."

"Then I tell you. Some *thing*. Some thing else. Because you want I know."

"Because I want *to know*. Not *I know*."

"What I say?"

"You said 'Because you want I know.' It should be 'Because you want *to* know.'"

Vince slapped Santo's right shoulder with the back of his hand. "You want! I know! *Si?* Or you want—"

"Know what?"

"Shut up. I tell you. I tell you because I'm your *zio.*"

Even with the ridges in his hair brushed flat, his knit shirt hand-washed, and his trousers creased—washed and pressed and hung in his closet by his cleaning woman, Louise—Vince still looked disheveled. He missed a spot under his chin with his long-necked razor, and his collar needed adjusting, but mainly it was his goofy half-hitched step and the way he hooded his eyes even in dim light that conveyed disorder. Because of that, because he appeared so harmless, everyone spoke freely around him. So Vince knew everything.

He told his nephew about Sylvia's husband, Henry Gomez, who had connections with the State Department, though what Henry Gomez actually did for a living Vince didn't know. Henry heard about a woman in Cuba who had grown up in Chicago. When she was twelve her parents were killed in some sort of accident, in a boat maybe, and she was sent to live with an uncle in Cuba, who passed away himself about eight years ago. A woman now, she needed a situation, a life. Henry was forty-two, maybe older, never married, and Sylvia was twenty. So with little fanfare, he flew to Cuba, met the family, married her in Havana, and brought her back to Marshfield Avenue.

"Hmm," Santo said.

"What? You look, how they say, disappoint. What's wrong, hey?"

"Nothing. Nothing's wrong."

"Good," Vince said. He clapped his hands together several times as if removing particles of dust, then wiped them along the sides of his apron. "Now you forget. You no need, hey."

Santo thought about his father, who had a similar gesture to dismiss matters. Agostino would clap once, hold his palms together as if in prayer, then rub them back and forth a few times. Each time, Santo imagined grains of sand slipping through those leathery fingers and disappearing onto the ground, lost forever. He wondered if what a man did with his hands was passed down somehow from one generation to the next.

He had to admit he was disappointed, but he couldn't say for sure why. He felt like he'd heard too much and he'd heard too little. He knew Sylvia was married, but he'd never really considered it before. And capsulizing her past like that made her seem older somehow. He would have preferred to have her story unfold before him in paper-thin layers.

"I think I'm gonna split, Zio. I'll stop by later."

"Yeh, yeh, you split. Be good boy, hey." Vince cuffed Santo on the neck and offered a half grin and a sidelong glance, then shuffled down the stairs, searching his pockets for a match. "No forget shirt, hey."

Santo felt a flush of embarrassment sweep over him. Every time someone referred to him as a good boy, he felt like a twelve-year-old again. Beaming. Hair slicked down by Mama's spit. He wondered if maybe he was pursuing a woman ten years older than he was to counter all that, to help him feel like a man. She could be the one to initiate him—since he never really counted the fumbling that went on behind St. Columbkille. She could be the one to teach him the intricacies of—what, he didn't fully know. But that wasn't it. He was chasing her, he finally had to admit, because his old man was chasing her. Since Sylvia Gomez seemed within Agostino's grasp—her breath filling the same pocket of air, her lips brushing the glass that held the same red blush wine—she seemed a possibility for Santo as well.

Whenever Victoria Peccatori considered her name, she alternated between fury and amusement. Most often she gave her parents the benefit of the doubt. They must have been unaware of the singsong nature of the name, she concluded. Or they couldn't have known that in elementary school her name would be chanted in retaliation whenever a scuffle ensued at the schoolyard. "Vic-TOR-ia Pecca-TOR-ia . . . Vic-TOR-ia Pecca-TOR-ia." The chant was always the last dig, sung as she walked away. Which she did often enough back then. Not out of cowardice or admission of defeat, but because she knew this was the right thing to do. Even as a girl, Victoria Peccatori believed she possessed a heightened sense of what was fair. Forget law, forget religion, forget the rules of parents. She felt she could strike with razor precision at the heart of a matter. But no one wanted any part in that; they just wanted to get their way.

So when Zia Lupa uttered the inevitable, warning her niece to cover her shoulders, Victoria took off with Benito. Pushing her brother's long-spoked buggy down Ashland, she hummed the old singsong taunt, hearing it now as a nursery rhyme. Vic-TOR-ia Pecc-a-TOR-ia. Even the extra syllable at the end didn't bother her. Why hadn't she heard it like that before? She crooned. She sang louder, all the rancor and mockery gone from each note. Her name became a lullaby. When she realized Benito was listening, she replaced her name with his. "Benito Pecc-a-TOR-ia . . . Benito Pecc-a-TOR-ia." He kicked his feet and twisted his little neck to see her but couldn't turn fully around.

She stopped and squatted down before him. "You like that, kiddo? You like your sister's singing?" She poked him in the chest, nudged his neck, squeezed his cheek, and got back a squeal each time. "How 'bout a pinky, kiddo." Her other brothers had taught him to poke out his little finger and hook it with theirs early on, and even now, at sixteen months old, Benito complied, his round pasty face lighting up each time.

"Victoria take you to the feast?" she said. Victoria. Too many syllables. Too long. Most people shortened it to Vick, which sounded harsh to her ear, metallic. Some of her friends at school called her Tori now and then, but that wasn't her. She'd gone through a Vicky period back in seventh and eighth grades, but that struck her now as bubbly—she couldn't help but recall the little circle she used then to dot the *i* and how the tail of the *y* snaked across to underline her name.

"Let's go, kiddo." She pondered why the pitch in her voice rose higher when she talked with Benito. "Victoria will take you to your first feast."

"Tawya."

"What! What did you say?"

He grabbed at his shoe, white and polished.

"Did you say Toria? Toria? Say it. Tor-i-a."

"Tawya."

She laughed like she hadn't laughed in a long while and looked around to find someone to tell.

"Tawya," she said. "That's it." Hi, how do you do . . . my name is Tawya. Tawya Peccatori. "Can you say Lupa?"

"Papa."

"No, not Papa. Lu-Pa."

"Lupa."

Victoria clapped to show her amazement. "Now, can you say Witch?"

Just before they turned onto Ohio Street, Victoria stopped, adjusted her calf-length red skirt, and brushed her shoulders with two precise flicks of her fingers. She smoothed down her sleeveless white top and pulled at two thick strands of her ponytail to tighten it, then drew in a deep breath, letting it out slowly and evenly.

"Say Tawya."

"Tawya."

"Good boy."

They turned the corner.

"There it is, kiddo."

Ohio Street ran from Lake Michigan to the western border of Chicago, and on any other night, there was little to distinguish these four blocks from any other—row after row of frame bungalows with plastic awnings, red-and-brown brick apartments with flat roofs slathered in tar, and the occasional five-and-dime corner store like Casey's that sold milk and bread and candy and cigarettes. But tonight, strings of bare bulbs stretched from one side of the street to the other so that they formed a canopy. Inevitably a string or two would flicker off as someone's fuse burned out, but for now everything was illuminated, a pack of tiny night flies swarming around each smoky yellow bulb. The lights may have been too bright for Benito because he glanced down at his pudgy fingers, then gazed skyward at a constellation of stars directly overhead. Victoria squinted to spot someone she knew, but there were too many faces, too many legs. Did the crowds grow thicker each year, she wondered, or was this one of those tricks of memory?

On either side of the street, just off the curbs, vendors had erected makeshift stands with ropes and tables and tents.

"Lupini beans here. Get your lupini. Ceci beans."

Victoria bought a small bag of lupini and broke one apart for Benito, who chewed with trepidation on his brow. They strolled over to the African Dip, where for twenty-five cents you got three chances to dunk a Negro into a tank of water. The man sat on a metal chair that swung out from under him whenever a baseball hit the bull's-eye next to his head. Someone had thought to add a metal grate to shield the man's face. The white proprietor of the booth, an older, fat man with a thick cigar wedged in the corner of his mouth, quietly collected bills while the Negro egged on the crowd. He had a tight handful of singles.

"Just laughin' and prayin' and singin' and hopin'," the Negro sang, "he will be there." He flashed a wide grin with the biggest teeth Victoria had ever seen. "Now, now, you can do better'n dat," he cried to three young boys sharing a quarter's worth of tosses.

The African Dip turned out to be a game of peekaboo for Benito, who laughed each time the man crashed into the water. Victoria remembered a time when she'd been amused by the game herself, but this time she stayed for Benito's sake. Something about the whole thing tugged at her conscience, though. And after a while she knew why. Standing there, gazing blankly—at the splash, the laborious readjustment of the metal seat, the heavy leap back onto the chair, water dripping from those broad blue lips, and that grin, especially the grin — the irony slowly dawned on her. She thought, *If this Negro were out of that cage and walking down Ohio Street right now, minding his own business, he'd get the living crap beat out of him.*

And she knew the guys who would do it. She liked some of them. They were older, closer to Santo's age. They hung around a social club with no name on Erie Street. One of the boys' uncles had a candy store in the space before his wife died, but the aisles had been pushed aside now for card tables. Every time she passed the club Victoria couldn't help but glimpse inside. The storefront windows were painted a rich burgundy, but the great glass door was usually wedged open enough to spot someone pulling in a poker pot or taking a drag off his cigarette or bending down to tie a shoe. She was ashamed for them, for their narrow scope, for their rage, but she was drawn to some of them like lightning heat. Guys like Dominick Pacini and Eddie Milano. Even Pooch with his rounded shoulders. They were just trying to protect what they thought was theirs. They didn't know better.

A thin strain of an Italian ballad her father liked to hum blared from one of the apartment windows behind Victoria. She turned the stroller and walked toward the music, the record's needle scratching out rhythmic pops and hisses, the sound turning more warbled with each step. On her right a man who looked like her father curled a sledgehammer behind his shoulder, lifted it high to where it seemed suspended in midair, and brought it down on the rubber pad of the Hi Striker with such torque that she felt the thud in her tailbone. Still, he missed hitting the bell. On the other side of the street a man with hairy shoulders threw weighted balls at a trio of tin milk cans, knocking down all but one. Beyond the stand two boys with cutoffs and dago tees darted out of a gangway with shoulders hunched and hands over their ears. They crouched and waited and seemed disappointed when only two or three firecrackers on their string popped.

The charcoal aroma of Italian sausage nudged Victoria along. She craned her neck trying to spot Jimmy's beef stand, hoping she'd find Darlene or someone she knew. She was beginning to feel that isolation of being at a party full of strangers. She passed St. Columbkille, where the flashing lights from the carousel in the back parking lot spilled onto the street. Father Ernie, the young priest, bending over a stroller, patted the soft tuft of an infant's head that pulsed red, then orange yellow from the lights. Father Ernie spoke to the mother briefly, then touched her arm at the elbow, a light, reassuring grasp. He leaned his head toward hers and whispered something. The mother gazed down at the asphalt and barely nodded. The two of them appeared to be in confession. As he backed away from her, Father Ernie held his gaze and offered what Victoria called a funeral smile. Genuine, full of compassion, but tinged with pity. The mother tried to muster her own version, but her gaze landed just beyond him, the pity directed more toward herself. She raised a hand in Father Ernie's direction, as if to wave, but scratched at her shoulder instead, her gray, woven wool sweater, too heavy for June, crimping at the edges.

Victoria headed straight for the woman, thinking the two strollers might give them pause to exchange a few words, but the woman, worry lining her face, barely noticed her. Even Benito, who pointed to the baby and muttered "Bino" couldn't pull her attention.

"That's right, kiddo. Bambino. Just like you."

She tried thinking about what could be wrong, but she didn't get far. Under a streetlight between Tony's Clams and a booth that sold Vienna Red Hots stood the boy who could complicate her summer if she gave in to her yearnings, Eddie Milano.

For Santo, the feast was like a holiday that had lost its magic. The same gray men sat on the same flimsy folding chairs on the same corner at Ohio and Damen, slapping knees and shouting about presidents and politics and the latest soccer scores from Europe. Their faces became so intensely flushed when they drilled home a point that Santo couldn't help but laugh. He recognized many of the men from the store, so he had to stop while they hurled questions and talked about him in Italian. Two summers ago, during such an exchange, one of the men, who couldn't have known the impact his words would have on Santo, the remark delivered in such an off-hand manner, said, "The church gets its cut." He was talking about the feast, of course, and now, every game, every ride Santo passed, every dirty dollar bill exchanged for a hot dog or beef sandwich, Santo would think, *The church gets its cut*. He couldn't see any wrong in this, but the unadorned truth pulsed before him like a gaudy Christmas light.

He'd already run into Fran and Karen, who insisted on walking with him, but he sidestepped them easily, telling them he had to look for Victoria. Which was more or less true. He had to get her home by eleven. He talked with Eddie Milano for a while, who wanted to know what Santo had been up to and how his sister was. Suddenly everyone wanted to know about his sister.

The first time he spotted Sylvia Gomez that night, across the street, walking hand in arm with a man who could have been her father, Santo felt feverish. She wore the same dress she had on that afternoon when she sat and sipped wine and smiled at him, all some faded memory now. Rather than envy he felt sorry for Henry Gomez. He was too old for her. He should have been kicking back with the gray brigade on Damen, hollering about taxes in America that didn't fund health care, not strolling the streets with a woman nearly twenty-five years younger.

Sylvia dipped her head to the side to move the hair from her face, then tossed it behind her ear. *I could make that*, Santo thought. The line was a running joke with his friends, delivered always in deadpan earnestness at the most unlikely moments. But all irony was drained now from the line and replaced with a more guttural groan, a slow yearning. Santo continued in their direction, casually glancing across now and then. The last thing he wanted was to catch their eyes.

Why would a woman allow such an arrangement? Santo wondered. She'd been more or less sold to Henry Gomez. There couldn't have been much passion there, not enough anyway. Santo felt that given half the chance, he could be an expert in passion. What else was there? He trailed them awhile longer until he realized what he was doing—following them—and circled back toward the church.

Women from numerous sodalities and auxiliary societies in the area gathered around the statue of the Madonna, making last-minute adjustments for the procession. Barefoot, draped in black, lace shawls spread delicately over their shoulders, they were professional mourners. Their hands worked in a flurry, nimbly pinning pale lilies and irises at Mary's feet. They lighted rose-tinted votive candles. They unlatched the strong-box. They provided the required solemnity, without which the feast would simply be another carnival. A handful of local chapter members from the Knights of Columbus milled about, their royal-blue blazers and gold-cloth shoulder cords gleaming against the night's black. Once the procession began, they would form a flank around the regiment of women.

The street began to thin as people jockeyed for position near the curb, waiting for the Madonna to pass. They were mainly older, louder. What did the young ones know, they said. *Giovanotti ignoranti. Tutti.* But soon the younger ones, the mothers and fathers, did join them. And one day they would be the ones to complain. Santo wondered if the generation after that, his generation, would someday follow step. He could do without the sodalities, their graveclothes and solemn bows, the incantations under the breath. He could do without the ceremony. He wondered if the rituals would hold some particular fascination for him in the future. Was that a natural part of aging, like balding? Along with a bulging gut came an obsession with rosaries? The procession did nothing for him but evoke memories of past processions, memories so sweet his throat sometimes ached. But that couldn't be enough to sustain all this, could it?

He backed out from the tight throng that had built up like moss around him and studied the backs of their heads. He wasn't of them. And never would be.

At ten o'clock the bell in the church tower clanged, a majestic peal. As soon as the reverberation from one bell crash rippled out, another took its place, creating something like a hush in the street. A reordering of attention. Six women on either side of the stretcher that held the Madonna—Santo counted them, twelve in all—hoisted the makeshift altar to their shoulders and began their crawl down Ohio Street. The rest of the women, fifty or sixty, maybe more, fell into place behind them. The women looked at no one, their eyes downcast throughout the entire march. They weren't worthy. No person was worthy enough, their gestures implied. They clutched their black bead rosaries, their fingers traveling around the circle of thread like they were doing piecework.

As these graven women and their escorts carved their way through the tunneled street—men, women, and children clamoring on either curb, a canopy of lights blanketing them from above—the regal Knights floated toward the outstretched arms to receive the wave of dollar bills, stuffing some of them into the black strongbox, pinning others at the Madonna's feet. Though he hadn't seen her, Santo knew Zia Lupa was among them. *If you're stingy with God*, she said, *God will be stingy with you*. Some of the older men and women at the curb, the ones who could recount stories about the grand feasts in their *paese*, sauntered toward the altar, pinned their gifts, then retreated into the tangle of pressed bodies.

Santo inched along the sidewalk, keeping pace with the procession. A half block ahead of him, not more than ten houses away, Sylvia Gomez pushed out from the crowd. Santo stopped, waited for a husband to slip out behind her. But no one did. She strolled ahead of him, toward Damen, nothing between them but segments of sidewalk. He picked up his pace some.

Nice night, isn't it? Sylvia?

Ah, Mrs. Gomez, nice evening.

Signora. Cooled off some, didn't it?

Long time no see.

Come here every year?

Is this your first time?

Without breaking stride, Santo swiveled left then right, searching for a husband. The poor guy couldn't make it past ten. That would give them something to talk about. Weather. Feast. Husband. There was plenty to talk about.

He came up on her right.

"Hey, uh—" He stopped himself when *Hey, ma'am* fell thick on his tongue. *Hey, ma'am* would have ruined everything.

She turned. "Santo!" A slow smile overtook her surprise.

He took a step in the direction they'd been moving and she moved with him.

"Can I get you that water now?"

Confusion registered on her brow.

"This afternoon . . . I offered . . . never mind. Dumb joke. How are you?"

"Fine. And you?"

"Never better." He'd heard someone say that once and remembered feeling better himself.

"You're not working tonight?" she asked.

Up close, her nose sloped straighter than he'd recalled, and her coffee-brown eyes were set too close together. The imperfection excited him.

"Everybody's here," he said.

She glanced around as if to confirm this. "I guess you're right."

"I'm always right."

"You're always right?"

"I'm always right."

"What about when you're wrong?"

"Well, that's different."

"Ah."

They came up on two girls with Hula Hoops and had to squeeze around them, Sylvia's arm brushing against his. How easy it would have been to take her hand then.

"What do they call those rings?" she asked.

He knew exactly what they were called—his brother Anthony had one—but he decided that a man with a silk shirt, borrowed or not, didn't say things like *Hula Hoop*.

"Some kind of hoop," he said. "A fad, you know."

"I want to try."

"I don't know. It looks kind of dangerous."

"You're right."

"I'm always right."

A faint grin. "I know."

A man with a red beret selling pinwheels stepped in front of them. Santo wanted to ask the man what he was thinking. What he saw. A man and a woman—together? Did the man expect Santo to pull out a quarter and present the pinwheel to the lady? They shook their heads and swung around the man, not even pausing. A good sign. They were together and couldn't be bothered.

Trying to appear nonchalant, Santo poked his head around, still waiting for a husband to emerge. Well behind them, the marchers had stopped at the church, the midway point, to pray with Father Ernie. *Say a prayer for me*, Santo thought. He supposed he believed in sin, had probably committed sin during their short walk. Coveting they called it, which sounded innocent enough.

He glanced across the street. "Goddamn," he said. "That frickin—"

"What?"

"That no—"

"What. What happened?"

He thought he'd been muttering under his breath. "Nothing. Nothing happened."

He craned his neck trying to track his sister and Eddie Milano as they slipped in and out of view between pockets of neighbors. No doubt Eddie was searching for a dark gangway they could duck into.

"I . . . uh—" *Santo, forget it*, he told himself. *Just forget it.* "I think I have to go." *What the hell am I saying?*

"Is everything okay?"

He stepped away from her. "Yeah. It's nothing."

She peered beyond him. "All right. Take care of what you need to take care of." She tried to suppress a smile. "What's her name?"

A surge of panic. "No, no, it isn't that. It's my sister."

Before he crossed he stopped and leaned back. "You sure you don't need me to walk you home?"

"You go. I'll be fine."

That brilliantined prick had his arm resting along Victoria's shoulder blades. Just his arm. One stiff arm that you could have hung a winter coat on. More than a head taller, he had to stoop considerably, though he still managed to strut, a loose-kneed, bicycle-pedaling sort of strut that Santo once thought was something. But now those limber-kneed legs looked as if they were tromping through so much muck. When Santo came up on them he would call out Milano's name, and the prick would turn and offer that shit-faced grin, slide his arm off Victoria's shoulders, and never betray even a trace of alarm.

"Hey, Milano."

And there it was. The easy turn. The slow smirk. But his arm didn't move, not until Victoria sidled away from him. Then his hands dropped to his sides. Long creamy fingers. A girl's hands.

"Santo, my man."

Santo stared down his sister.

"Where's Benito?"

She rolled her eyes. "I left him on the corner—in the middle of Ashland."

"Uh-huh." The only comeback he could think of was *her* tired line: *You're so funny I forgot to laugh*. So he waited.

"They're here," she said. "Everyone's here. Zia's got him."

Santo considered this while chewing on his lower lip.

"So, whattya up to, Eddie? Doin' a little babysitting?"

Victoria folded her arms and turned away from him, shifted her weight abruptly to one side. Eddie put up his hands. "Just walking, my man."

Santo had seen those same hands balled into fists. He'd seen the damage done by those white knuckles. Seeing his mitts out now in resignation, Santo realized with sudden clarity that Eddie never mixed it up with anyone unless he had two or three friends behind him. Santo felt his own hands tightening.

"Just walking, huh?" Santo said.

"A little walk."

"With my sister."

"With your sister."

"You were probably gonna stop at church, right? Say a few novenas. Light a few candles."

Eddie couldn't conceal the slow smirk that he must have believed made him appear harmless but never did. Except maybe to one sixteen-year-old.

I'll wipe the sidewalk with that smirk, you prick.

Santo moved one step closer to him. He straightened his back. The procession had started up again, and Santo figured that by the time each of them got three or four shoves in, the Madonna would be glaring down on them. He thought about blood on his uncle's shirt. He thought about one of the women in black pulling the two of them apart, yelling *Basta, Basta,* kicking them with her black-bottomed feet. He thought of a dozen reasons to step back, but he just wanted one swift crack at Milano's chin. One little swipe.

As the Madonna passed, the three of them stood fixed there. Waiting. The streets were once cobblestone, Santo thought. The stones were still there, buried beneath years of asphalt, which was a mystery to him, all that blackness. Cobblestone he could understand. A portion of the domed roof of the church loomed over the sidewalk trees. How they built the spire, he couldn't even begin to imagine. He scratched at the back of his neck and peered around for the moon. This was one of those moments, he thought, when the moon should have been there, waxy white against the blue-black night.

Later, when he tried to recall what finally drew his attention away from his rage and his scattered thoughts about stone streets and domed roofs, Santo couldn't decide if it was the stricken look on Victoria's face or the first caplike pops of the closing fireworks behind him.

He turned. Bricks of firecrackers had been unraveled and threaded along someone's chain-link fence, and starbursts of light fired in rapid succession. Eighty packs of firecrackers blazing one after the other. Down the street at the corner his father, Agostino, stood nose to nose with a bulldog of a woman—her teeth bared and body coiled. When she spoke her one hand slashed the air while the other remained poised outward toward Agostino, fingers splayed, like she wanted to choke him. She jabbed at him with a finger, the bun of steel-gray hair at the back of her head loosening with each poke.

Agostino was one mass shrug, shoulders so tight his neck disappeared. His head angled sharply to the side, he put his palms out toward the old woman and eased them apart, like he was drawing open a lace scrim. Santo had seen that gesture before, a gesture meant to calm the woman. His father glanced behind him, his eyes darting, searching, then faced her again.

A cherry bomb exploded. Then another. A spatter of five or six more. The smoke thick and rising in ash clouds, black pollen, the sulfur bitter and metallic.

His father backed away and began to turn from the woman. There was nothing else to do. He wiped his hands along his trousers.

The blast from an M-80 rocked Santo on his heels. The sidewalk shook. He moved to cover his ears, then let his hands drop to his sides. He needed to take this all in. His eyes burned, but still he gazed through the smoke.

The enraged woman stepped closer to Agostino, still ranting. There was no pacifying her. She poked at his chest. Another woman appeared then. Much younger. A stroller at her side. She tapped on the old woman's shoulder, mouthing *Mama*. Pleading, she pulled on the old woman's shoulder.

Come, she motioned. Come. Please. She seemed pinned for a moment between the old woman and the infant, grasping firmly at her left and rocking gently on her right. She teetered there, struggling, then suddenly turned and marched away, pushing the infant, her gray wool sweater too hot for June curling behind her.

2

ike the dust that collects at the tops of doors. That's how I feel sometimes, thought Angela Rosa. So when the butcher Larry with the Polish last name suddenly started paying attention after years of waiting on her, Angela Rosa didn't complain. He'd lumber out from the back room with a fresh cotton apron, wiping his soapy hands across his chest and flashing a snaggletoothed grin. "Rosa," he'd say. "What's cookin'?" No one but her mother had ever called her Rosa, but *Rosa* sounded right coming from this fair-skinned butcher with the scrubbed fingernails. Hands offered glimpses into a person's private world—she'd discovered this soon after arriving in America; studying hands was safer than meeting the eyes—and clean hands, especially on a butcher, indicated tenderness. Three scars crisscrossed along the ends of the two fingers that held the meat down viselike, but Angela Rosa had never seen any signs of the knife slipping—only the deep thrust and sweep and satisfying slash of the fat blue blade across the block cutting board. She admired the fluid efficiency of those hands, how they could instantly calibrate the force needed to split bone or shave fat or just wrap a square of waxy white paper around a meaty steak in four sharp tucks that came away so clean you could almost slip the package in your purse. She'd felt that precision in her own hands.

Standing in her kitchen on a Saturday morning after a late night at the feast, staring at the cut flowers on her table, she decided on sirloin for dinner. Eight steaks. Medium thickness. Fried. She could already see the glint of the butcher's knife, feel the weight of the white package in her hands as she strolled home. The olive oil, the garlic wedges sprinkled along the top of the steaks. Dicing Benito's portion in tiny pieces. She hoped he'd be hungry by then since he barely touched his breakfast and wanted only to return to sleep. Both her husband and Benito sleeping soundly at eleven o'clock on a Saturday. Agostino must have returned home from the store later than usual last night because of the feast. She wished he would go back to his tailoring and keep normal hours. He'd be up already and out of the apartment for his morning walk. Her boys were already loose in the neighborhood. She couldn't keep track anymore. How could anyone expect her to keep track?

She pounded twice on the bathroom door with the bottom of her fist, a cue for Victoria to turn off the shower already. The shower was new and everyone was fascinated by it. *"Vittoria? Alora?"* She didn't know if her nagging or her stories about the aqueducts back home did any good, but Angela

Rosa couldn't stop herself. Victoria had to learn. When Mama was a girl, she'd tell her, a small basin of water was all anyone could hope for.

"Where is everyone?" Victoria wanted to know when she finally made it out of the bathroom.

Angela Rosa had begun to dry a stack of breakfast dishes. "How much water you use?"

"The lake is drying up, Mama?" She pulled a cereal bowl out of the cupboard. "I know. The wells. But we don't have wells, Mama. We have Lake Michigan. That's why you came here, right?"

Anthony and Alfredo would whine some when she scolded them, but at least they'd show remorse, sincere or not. But this one. This one would be her end, she thought, one of Lupa's lines.

"Where's Papa?"

"Sleep."

"He's still sleeping?"

"He sleep."

"What time did he get home?"

And then that familiar shadowy glance that riled Angela Rosa, Victoria's eyes focusing just beyond her. A glint of concealment in those eyes. Her family, even Agostino, would keep things from her. They had the edge. They had the words. She cursed the years she spent isolated within her small circle of Italian-speaking neighbors. And the ten years of piecework for Zenith, where she became more or less proficient at Spanish, isolated her further. She found it ironic that lately she'd begun to think more and more in English. Her very thoughts seemed new to her.

"He come home when he come home. No you busyness."

Victoria slurped down a spoonful of Cheerios. "You can't even talk in this house," she muttered. "Cripes."

"No tell that."

"It's not a bad word, Mama. Relax."

"No, you relax."

"I'm eating. I'm sitting. I'm relaxed."

Maybe she was too rough on Victoria. For her own good. And maybe all mothers were treated this way in return. It was too late now to let up, though. Victoria would understand one day. Angela Rosa quickly pushed aside the idea that she'd not been much kinder to her own mother, which came through more in the things she'd failed to say or do than in any direct encounters. She turned inside herself then. She never had the nerve for the bitter tablets that Victoria's tongue spit out.

Victoria dropped her bowl in the sink. "What time did you get home? Did you see the Madonna pass?"

"No, no, I go before. Benito he cry."

Victoria's eyes swept the apartment. "Who's got my little guy anyway?"

"He sleep."

"He's down for his nap already?"

"He sleep."

Suddenly Angela Rosa gripped the counter near the sink, leaning into its coldness. She slapped down the ladle she'd been drying. Though she'd fully recovered from her labor with Benito, sometimes a thunderclap of pain laced its way around her pubic area and just seized her. Held her there for a pulsing moment or two.

"You okay, Mama? You gonna throw up?"

The thought of throwing up hadn't announced itself till then, and now it seemed like a real possibility.

"No, no. *Va bene.*"

She breathed slowly through her mouth and rocked on the balls of her feet. Everything would be okay, she repeated to herself.

Victoria had been looking for an opening, a moment of intimacy maybe—a moment was about all she could hope for with her mother—a pause where she could slip in a mention of her plans for the night. "I'm going to stop by Darlene's tonight," she'd say, without a trace of apprehension in her voice. Maybe drop the plans in her mother's lap as she passed at the sink. But now there was no lap and there'd be no easy way to broach the subject without seeming heartless. Lately her mother viewed Victoria's every move as an attack. Her mother had been poisoned by Lupa, of course. The reason Victoria wanted to visit Darlene, the logic went, was to insert a dagger in Angela Rosa's back. If that's what they believed, Victoria reasoned, then that's what they believed. Though she did little to dispel those ideas, maybe enjoying the power she held over them, she wished things were different. She was tired of struggling. There was a time not long ago when she looked to Santo for guidance. She studied him, watched him smile and kid his way out of the house, and imagined herself doing the same. But when she tried, she seemed outside herself and couldn't even muster a grin. She'd pace around the apartment as if she were inspecting cracks in the paint. And even if she'd been able to find a way out of the box she'd created for herself, it wouldn't have mattered. She understood that now. She understood it like none of her brothers ever could.

"Why don't you sit down, Mama?"

To Victoria's surprise, her mother put out her hand for assistance. *"Va bene."*

Victoria guided her to a chair. "What happened?"

"One day you understand."

"You having cramps, Mama? You know, your period?"

Angela Rosa glared at her. Menstruation was a private matter to be dealt with and not discussed.

"Forget," Angela Rosa said.

Victoria glanced through the screen to the gray porch. *By the way, I'm going by Darlene's tonight*, she thought. She tapped the table, then pulled back her hand. She thought about her mother scrubbing the screen. *You remember Darlene, right?* She stole a peek across from her. *I told you I'm going by Darlene's house tonight, right?* She could wait, let the sun come down, and when the last bite of dinner was swallowed she would rise from her chair, pat her full belly, and announce, "I'm going out," or "I'm going to the store," and maybe everyone would mistake her for Santo. Her damn brother. Who thought she needed him last night. Which is what she needed to talk to Darlene about. What happened last night.

She couldn't talk to Santo. He'd walked her home stone-faced the whole time. And she didn't think she wanted to talk to Eddie, not about her father. She needed Darlene, who would sit there with her elbow hooked along the back of the chair, cracking chewing gum, unfazed by anything Victoria could say. Yet she'd be there, nodding, taking in every pause and keeping every secret safe. The incident with the old woman raced through Victoria's mind like some old news footage that kept slipping off its sprocketed wheel. She saw Papa, then the old woman's hands, then Papa's shoulders, their movements disjointed and abrupt. She tried to convince herself that the man could have been someone else, not her father. She'd only seen the back of him, really, through all that smoke. And the woman could have been some lunatic, upset over the way he'd

walked by her. But it was Papa all right. Not his usual confident self maybe, but unmistakably him. She couldn't think of
any reasonable explanation for his being there with the old
woman, so she tried one preposterous theory after another.
The old lady's hem was crooked. Papa had sewn a crooked
hem. Victoria would be upset, too.

She had a fleeting impulse to bring up last night with
her mother to find out if she knew anything at least, but her
mother would erupt. "No you busyness," she'd say. If Papa
ever opened the restaurant he always talked about — Mama's
restaurant, next to the bar — that could be the name: No You
Busyness.

"You help today," Angela Rosa said.

It wasn't a question. It was never a question.

"You bring clothes down."

They studied the glare on the peach vase between them,
both thinking about simpler times, days when they took comfort filling that kitchen, two girls conspiring, not so much
against Papa and the boys, but to ward off the feeling of being
outnumbered.

"Okay, Mama," Victoria said. She turned the vase. "I'll
bring the clothes down."

A shimmer of light quivered through a crack in one of the
blinds, and Agostino knew by its intensity that he'd slept late.
He lay there bleary-eyed and still heavy from sleep, convincing himself that the Apennine hills dotted the morning sky just
outside his window. A stand of spruce trees undulating and
melting into the powdery-white horizon. Olive trees so close

he could touch their corkscrew branches. Fragrant cherry trees. A canopy of grapes.

Sew your dick to your pants, Vince had told him over and over again. Each time, his brother would grab his crotch and perform the procedure with mock precision, the imaginary sewing needle rising and falling in long, sweeping loops. Sew your dick to your pants. What did Vince know about it? He had his whores. Even if Vince found the wife he said he sought, would he give up the whores? Sew your dick to your pants. A reassuring thought at this point.

He'd tried. He'd really tried. Of all people, Vince should have understood. Women were like drink to Agostino. And like his brother, he was weak. Though no one would believe him, and maybe he didn't believe it himself, he wished sometimes that he looked more like Vince with his expansive forehead and jutting chin. And that ridiculous crookback lurch of a step. But Agostino had too much of his mother in him. A small dark face with thick brows and long lashes. Women were drawn to that face, a fact he'd never taken any particular pride in, but one he never denied either.

He heard himself starting to rehearse what he might one day need to say to his wife, and he kept returning to "I have weak." He knew how to say it correctly, and he knew what he'd say if he confessed in the language she best understood, but he suspected *I have weak* would inflict the least hurt.

He moved to the window and forced himself to peek through the glare at the rooftops and back porches. Though he still yearned for the mountains of his past, there was a beauty about the city, too, that he couldn't explain. He thought it might have to do with the sounds from the street. A lawn chair scraping against the sidewalk in front of Mio Fratello's that interrupted the slow drone of the neon arrow overhead. Tires gripping asphalt. Sounds he could never have heard back in his village. Sounds, he decided, were innocent.

From this view at the window, Agostino realized that the life he'd chosen for himself was all within sight. A twin-size bed with tousled sheets behind him. His store not six blocks away, though it seemed closer now. He knew which bulb needed replacing on the marquee that held the bent arrow. The uppermost portion of his brother's apartment window was even visible, something he hadn't noticed before. At night, one would be able to detect whether the living-room lamps were on or catch a glimpse of a silhouette or two behind the shade. He thought about Angela Rosa gazing out this window ten or eleven months ago on a clear, cool September night, and he shuddered. God, what had he done?

He pulled on his trousers and stumbled through the apartment ranting about a shirt he couldn't find. He had to find the shirt, he told his wife. He had to get to the store. Some important deliveries. No, no, Vince would sleep through it. He had to be there himself. No time for breakfast. He'd come back for lunch. Pulling a T-shirt from the folded pile on the dining-room radiator, he threw it on, bounced down the back porch stairs, and left without having looked his wife in the eye.

When he got to the store, both the front and back doors were wedged open, and Vince sat on the patio next to the bocce alley sipping coffee, scanning the newspaper. Alone, they always spoke the language of their *paese*. Broken English sounded ridiculous to them when no one else was around.

"Who died?" Vince wanted to know.

Agostino stepped back to catch a glimpse of himself in the window and shook his head. He patted down his hair and grumbled and sat across from his brother, who got up to retrieve another cup.

"Here. Drink," Vince ordered. "Leave the milk. Leave the sugar. Just the coffee." Vince sat down again and leaned back, his legs straight as crutches under the table. "What is it this time? Vittoria smoking? Santo and some girl? Lupa? Is she moving in?"

Though he hadn't added anything to the cup, Agostino stirred the coffee. His elbows rested on the table. "A long time ago, back in Italy, when we were kids, do you remember Papa sent us into town with his pantaloons? That little place next to the milk store? Capellini's? Capallano's? What was the damn name? He had beads hanging from the doorway that separated the front of the store from the back, where he did his sewing."

"I remember."

"I was twelve, I think. We dropped off the pants and as we were leaving this woman came into the shop. Breathtaking. Just exquisite. Tight legs . . . I held the door open and she swept by me — I can still smell her — and you walked on ahead. You didn't even notice. Capallano stepped out from behind the beads, and she seemed almost . . . happy to see him. He guided her to the back and I imagined all the measurements being taken. I could see those thick fingers pressing down the measuring tape along her thigh." He paused and shook his head at the vividness of this. "That was the day I decided I would be a tailor."

"That was the day we should have sewn your dick to your pants."

Agostino lit a cigarette and puffed hard on it. He nodded. "You should have. Then I wouldn't have my mess now."

"What mess is this?"

Agostino rubbed his forehead, feeling like the foolish younger brother. He focused on the farthest point ahead of him, a short row of red bricks that jutted out between the first- and second-floor picture windows of a neighbor's apartment, a ledge for flowerpots.

"Seems like another lifetime. She came walking—" He gestured toward the alley right behind them, a catch in his throat. "I'd never seen her before. It was last year . . . August, September maybe. I was sitting right here, behind the store, a slow afternoon. No bocce players yet. And inside, two old men playing cards. That's it. I was out here minding my own business. Are you the tailor? she wanted to know. Am I the tailor. What was I supposed to say?"

She had milky-white skin and papery hands that appeared older than her twenty-two years.

"She'd seen the painted sign in the front window one day. No one sees the sign. She saw the sign. Her godparents sent her money to get something nice for herself. She unfolded a picture. From a magazine." Agostino recalled his amusement over the faded creases. "Sophia Loren. Next to a fountain. Wearing this dress. She wanted a dress like the one in the picture. To wear with a sweater over her shoulder. I looked at the picture for a long time. A plain, black, sleeveless dress with buttons down the front. Something you might see in a movie with Sophia Loren next to a fountain. I didn't know if I wanted to spend three or four weeks. But—"

How could he explain to his brother the slide of the chalk across the coarse brown butcher paper as he laid out the design of the dress? Gripping the white leather tape measure taut across the pattern. Calculating and recalculating. All his movements streamlined. All his thought funneled through his fingers.

"So I brought her upstairs, took her measurements. Her left shoulder was a little higher than the right, and then—"

"Tell me."

"Then we came back down. We drank coffee. Right here. Behind my own store." And the two of them had talked. Just talked. He told her about the region in Italy where her godparents lived. She told him about her parents, how strict they were with her, their only child. Agostino could tell she'd never talked about her life in quite this way. But the words came easy to her. They spilled from her in a steady stream that would not be stemmed.

"And then?"

"We drank coffee." Agostino put down his cup. "That was all. I told her to come back in two weeks. To try on the pattern."

"And then?"

"And then she came back in two weeks."

"Where was I?"

"How should I know where you were?"

In fact, Agostino had told her to return on Wednesday, his brother's day to drive his Caddy downtown and visit Carmel.

"So the pattern."

"Yes, the pattern. I made a few adjustments. Minor. I showed her swatches of wool. Then we sat here again. A second time we sat."

She'd done something to her hair, brushed it differently, pulled it away from her forehead. She was eighteen and she was thirty. She spoke with more assurance. Agostino remembered thinking this one was off-limits. This one must not be had. In his mind, he'd been more or less faithful. Whatever straying he'd done had been just that. There had always been tacit agreements between him and the women. But this one he would have to forget.

Agostino picked up a whiff of whiskey from his brother's cup. "Your hip is hurting?"

Vince shrugged and nodded. "So where is the mess?"

Agostino sighed, his head sagging forward. "The next time. A week later maybe. The dress was finished. I didn't want to stitch the seams yet. So everything was pinned. She came in for a final fitting and—how can I say it? She wasn't right." She'd been crying and had braced herself to get through this. "She wanted to know if I could finish the dress right away. It was her father. He collapsed in the kitchen. Right there on the linoleum his heart stopped. And now she needed the dress for the funeral. My God, I thought. Her father's funeral." Somehow she'd broken away from the wails of her family to see about a dress that couldn't have meant less to her by then. No doubt she simply wanted to be with someone who had listened to her, maybe the only man who had ever listened to her, and Agostino didn't mind that it was him. He offered coffee, asked her to sit, but she wanted to see the dress. "She insisted on seeing the dress, so I brought her up . . ."

Vince rubbed his forehead and worked his hand down to his chin.

"Vincenz . . . No. No, it wasn't anything like that. It didn't start out that way. I was just going to show her the dress. I swear to my God." He stared down the alley. "Ah, damn," he said, and hurled his spoon.

Agostino led her upstairs to his old bedroom in the apartment, and with the dress draped over his arm he pushed it out to her. She slipped inside the bedroom then and eased the door shut. For the first time in that apartment, Agostino didn't know what to do with himself.

When she padded out a few minutes later, he could barely conceal his gasp. She was all liquid brown eyes and sleek black wool. He made an awkward motion with his fingers, directing her to turn. With her back to him, he moved toward her and pinched the dress at the waist and noted that he'd need to take it in two centimeters or so. But the shoulders were perfect. He asked her to turn around. To please turn.

She pointed to the bottom of the dress and tears welled up in her eyes again. "Can I wear this?" she wanted to know. With her palms, she brushed down the dress, taking it all in. "Can this be worn at a funeral?" The tears flowed freely now, and she wiped them with the back of her hand.

"Yes," he said, backing away. "You can wear. With a sweater over the shoulders."

One more step of retreat, just a modest step, a small turn, any slight movement would have ended it right there. But Agostino wasn't accustomed to stepping back. And standing there, he had another thought, a thought he knew now he'd never reveal to anyone, not even to Vincenzo. A thought that would bury him. He thought, *I deserve this*. He and his wife had barely touched in months. After Benito was born, a difficult labor, he waited on Angela Rosa, and it pleased him to do so. But it had been nearly five months now and he had needs. Undeniable needs. And needs were neither good nor bad. How could they be? *I deserve*, he thought. So he stood there on solid ground and asked if she was going to be okay. But— and this much was clear—he remained rooted there. Hands at his sides, he did not budge. He would not move forward, he would not move. As for his voice, he may have informed it with a softness that pushed her toward him. How could he say? He simply asked if she would be okay.

She stumbled toward him then and fell into his chest, Agostino's arms feeling weary as he raised them to embrace her. He knew even then that this holding would be the thing he'd miss most. The slow rocking and the warmth of her breath on his shoulder, too. As her sobs began to subside, he realized he'd held her too long, beyond the time two people use to comfort each other. She pulled away from him and reached across her body to the shoulder pin that held up that side of the dress and slipped it out. With the same hand she pulled at the other pin, and the shimmering wool cascaded to the checkered floor. Agostino felt the familiar tremble of that first glimpse at a woman's shoulders and cupped breasts that he knew he'd soon touch. She took his hand and walked him back to the bedroom.

"So what does she want from you?" Vince asked.

"It's what she has." He told his brother about the feast, how the woman's mother had threatened him. The old woman wanted justice. Old-world justice. "How can I even be sure it's mine?"

"It wasn't her first time?"

"I would say not."

"And that was the only time? Upstairs?"

Agostino looked away and tried to locate the spoon against the glint of loose rocks in the alley. He didn't want to answer. "She came back a few times after that."

"Ah, shit. What is her name?"

"Her name?"

His shoulders slumped, Agostino leaned back, reluctant

to utter the name. Once he said it, the matter would become public knowledge, part of the official record of his life, a sordid matter. The story would no longer be his.

"Gabriella Paolone," he said evenly. "Ella."

"We must find this Ella," he said.

Santo liked this view from inside, liked the idea of being seen by people passing on the sidewalk. Ribbons of sunlight streamed through the open doorway, yet the rest of the club remained washed in shades of pale ruby brown that spoke faintly of privacy. A couple of painted fans spun listlessly below the gray spackled ceiling. Two guys Santo didn't know shot pool. In the corner, Pooch flipped cards for solitaire. A bent toothpick dangled from the right side of his mouth.

"So what time did your old man get home last night?" Eddie said.

Santo shook his head. He reached for a Chesterfield from Eddie's pack on the table.

"Help yourself," Eddie told him.

"Right."

Eddie produced a book of matches from his shirt and flipped it across. Those long fingers.

"About last night," Santo said.

Eddie scooted forward in his chair, his head cocked to one side, ready to listen. But Santo stopped.

"What the hell happened last night?" Eddie said. "Me and Vicky was taking this nice walk—"

"Shut the fuck up about your walking already."

"Then you creep up all pissed off about, what, I don't know."

Santo began to feel the fury from the night before, but he couldn't sustain it, almost as if he could house only one concern at a time. Which was why he was here.

"Forget about me pissed off, would ya?"

"And then your old man getting into it with that nutcake."

Maybe Santo had given Eddie too much credit. If the old woman was just a nutcake to him, Santo could walk out into that light right now and forget he ever set foot in their club. But Eddie was hard to read. He kept shifting in his chair, cocking his head to one side then the other, his ears a flaming red.

"What a nutcake, huh, Sant?"

"Yeah, a real nutjob."

"And you and Vicky didn't need to take off like youse did."

Santo flicked his ash and nodded. There was no rush here. He'd paced Erie Street up and down for an hour before bumping into Eddie and acted convincingly reluctant about stopping by the club, shooting some stick maybe, so there was no need to push his hand now. As far as Eddie knew, Santo just wanted to warn him away from Victoria. A brother looking after his sister. They could both understand that. He wasn't quite ready to concede any of that, but maybe they could arrive at some sort of agreement. A simple understanding. Two guys talking. Santo wouldn't pounce on Eddie's face over talking with Victoria. He'd still keep an eye on her, nothing wrong with that. But she could take care of herself. In turn—they both knew how rumors spread—Eddie wouldn't say anything about last night.

"Hey, Pooch," Eddie called. "How 'bout a couple of bottles over here."

Pooch turned over a card. "What do I look like?"

"You look like a pooch, you big jamoch. A couple of beers, huh."

"Yeah, yeah." Pooch pushed himself away from the table and shuffled to the fridge in the back.

When the beers arrived, Santo took a deep slug and set the bottle between them. That was about all he ever drank. Working at the store and seeing his uncle's staggering took away most of the allure for him. He wiped at the wet label with his thumb.

"A little early for me," Santo said.

Eddie nodded. "I agree." He took another swallow. "One hundred percent."

Pooch glanced over every now and then, that same pouty glare weighing heavy on him, as if he'd just been coldcocked.

"So what's the word on tonight? You and your sister gonna be feastin' again?"

Santo glanced out at the leafy branches and dragged on his cigarette. What would Eddie say here?

"You gonna be there?" Santo said.

"Gotta pass through. Make an appearance, you know what I mean?"

"I don't know. I figure one night might be enough." He tilted the bottle and tapped it back down. Then he did something with his eyes, a slow hard blink meant to remind Eddie of what they'd seen last night. "More than enough," Santo said.

Eddie let out a sudden snort through his nose, the beginning of a laugh. "More than enough for your old man," he said. "That's for sure."

Eddie sank to meet Santo's eyes, the left side of his face tightening into a smirk. He was laying down his hand. He knew what Santo knew. The whole dirty mess. From what he could surmise anyway. They could come to an understanding.

"You know," Santo said. He imagined returning to the club one day and shooting some stick. No one thinking twice about him being there. "I'm probably working tonight," he said.

Victoria could take care of herself. Better than Santo ever could. Or knew how to.

"I don't know about Vicky, though," Santo offered, knowing that Eddie would take this as an offer. "She might be there."

Not a day went by that Angela Rosa didn't think about dying. Flat white thoughts that blinded her with their suddenness. The physical act of dying didn't faze her. She could endure the jolts of blaring pain, any duration of suffering. Pain, in fact, made her more alive, every nerve ending screaming for attention. It was the afterward that staggered her. How could she one day not *be*? How could everyone she knew not *be* in a hundred years? These paralyzing thoughts rarely intruded on her thinking during the day when she could busy herself with dishes and meals and more dishes. But in the middle of the night, feeling her way toward the bathroom, her body heavy and her breathing deep and labored, dying struck her as a maddeningly silent force that choked her. She'd have to turn on a light and fix her gaze on a towel or a shirt strewn across the floor, anything to root her in the ticking of the moment. *Caro, Dio*, she'd think. *Damme un'altro giorno.* Give me one more day.

Now that she was forty, every tightening in her chest or racing of her heart was accompanied by a surge of panic, which only served to clamp her chest tighter. Benito wouldn't have a single memory of her. He wouldn't be able to place her voice or recall the softness of her cheek. Any photos would only make her seem more distant to him. Anthony and Alfredo were still young enough to believe they needed a mother. But who could say if they'd ever fully recover? The rest of them, even Vittoria, would get along all right. Whenever this dawned on her, a revelation each time, a thread of self-pity laced its way around her like a wispy cocoon. But mostly she was grateful.

Angela Rosa was forty, but she blamed her back-porch neighbor, Louise, too, for the smoldering cloud that blackened her thoughts. Louise was the first American to make any real attempt at deciphering Angela Rosa's tortured English. She had thin hair, tinted straw brown and set at the beauty shop each week. Even under the slatted back-porch shadows, her rose-red lipstick gleamed in the night. Though she was made up, ready to venture out, she sat on her porch most summer nights while her garment-worker husband perched himself in front of the ghostly light of the television inside, recovering from the day's work.

If Angela Rosa reached out from her porch to Louise's outstretched fingers, they could almost touch. They'd throw brown bags to each other filled with bleached flour or anise seed or even eggs to complete a recipe.

"Hey, lady," Louise would shout. "Come out." She had a warm, scratchy voice that cut through the clatter of any kitchen noises.

When Louise found out Angela Rosa was pregnant, she

began calling her *Mama*, as if this were her first time. Anthony was already ten, so Angela Rosa, more nervous than ever, did feel like she was starting over.

"Hey, Mama," Louise called. "Come out and play."

She recalled one early evening in late September, just weeks before Louise would succumb finally to her lymphoma. Angela Rosa was eleven or twelve weeks along, just starting to show, and they talked about their own mothers. Louise had married, raised two boys, and now at fifty-six still harbored resentment or regret—she couldn't say which—over not ever knowing her mother, who died when Louise was a girl. The only memories she retained were images of the hospital. Peering up a long stairwell into bright light. Her mother waving and blowing kisses from the top landing, her other hand holding back the limp gown. Just a harsh silhouette against marble walls. With her cancer, they wouldn't let her own children near. Modern medicine. She couldn't touch her own children. How could anyone be so ignorant? So Louise had nothing to hold on to then. Only the green medicinal smells that permeated even the car during the long rides home.

Louise never got to see Benito either. Those bony arms never got to hold him. Once, just after Benito's birth, Angela Rosa walked out to the porch with Benito in her arms, and out of habit, nearly called out Louise's name. When she remembered, she whispered *Louise* and told Benito about his old neighbor. She wanted to believe that each death brought birth, or renewal at least, but she wasn't sure why this idea should comfort her.

Holding Benito now could still remind Angela Rosa of Louise's last days, the stench of death everywhere in her neighbor's apartment. She remembered bringing over a small bowl of shell pasta without sauce, something light. What else could she do? The cancer had spread quickly, taking away everything but Louise's faint smile. Angela Rosa recalled the shame she felt each time she went over there, thinking about Louise's mother at the top of the stairs, thinking, What if cancers *were* contagious? She fought back those fears and took Louise's hand and stroked her hair, brushed it lightly, but she couldn't erase that lump of doubt at the base of her stomach. Pregnant with her fifth child, and at her age, she had reason to doubt.

So, two days after the feast, when she went to check on Benito and found him dripping with fever, her poor baby still puffy-eyed and dizzy with sleep, Angela Rosa assumed the worst. His hair was matted, stamped down by the damp pillow. His diaper was bone-dry. When she lifted the shade a quarter, he turned away from the light and gazed blankly at the wall.

She placed a cool rag on his forehead, handed him to Victoria, and went downstairs to use old man Dominick's phone to call the Tuscan doctor on Ashland Avenue. She cursed the busy signal she got the first five minutes, then composed herself when he finally answered. A doctor who answered his own phone, that's why she went to him. He offered a few simple remedies she could try, but she insisted on seeing him, a steel urgency creeping into her voice. He agreed to stop by as soon as he could, in an hour or two perhaps. She torched up the stairs, taking in the reassuring slap of her slippers on each step, telling herself everything would be all right.

"He's burning up," Victoria said. She sat on the living-room carpet with Benito on her lap, rocking him.

"Bring towel—no, no, wait. Make wet."

They took off his clothes and wrapped him in the cold towel, which produced barely a shiver. He coughed once and blinked slowly, pushing out the tip of his tongue for a moment, then pursed his dry lips. The towel quickly became warm.

"Bring milk, eh. Go."

Victoria returned with his bottle. Angela Rosa raised his head and pushed the nipple into Benito's mouth. He sucked twice and stopped.

"You want to try a cup, Mama?"

"Yeah yeah."

Her American neighbors had told her Benito was getting too old for a bottle. And don't let him suck his thumb, they told her. And you shouldn't hold him so much. She was sorry she'd learned their English. Too much to listen to. And why was she thinking about their crazy worries now? She called for another towel, and for the next ten minutes they exchanged one warm towel for a chilled one, both of them glad to be busy doing something. Benito seemed content either way and looked as if he could fall asleep again.

"He feels a little cooler," Victoria said.

"Maybe."

Together they pinned a new diaper on him and slipped a cool, fresh undershirt over his head, working his arms through the sleeves one by one. They sat there on the floor listening to the refrigerator hum, the rhythm of a heartbeat. Sounds from the street drifted through the open window. The tapping of a horn, an engine's sputter rising and fading, something deeply reassuring in that sound. The languor of children's voices floated in the summer heat.

They waited. Benito fell asleep and they waited. Whenever a car door slammed Angela Rosa leaned toward the window and peered down. After a while, amid the silence, she could almost make out Louise's scratchy voice calling faintly from the farthest reaches of the apartment. *Hey, lady,* she called. Angela Rosa gazed at the fibers in the carpet and shook her head. It would be two years next month. She imagined Louise standing outside the kitchen door now, her nose to the screen, her hands cupping her eyes like visors so she could see inside. "Go away," Angela Rosa would kid. "Nobody home . . . go away." *Hey, Mama.* What she wouldn't give to hear that voice again.

Go away, she thought, a stippling coldness crawling up her arms. *Go away. Not now.* She glanced down at the street, a glimmer of awful light growing inside her head. *It's not time to meet my son.*

A Saturday-afternoon wedding party sailed by on Grand Avenue, their tin cans strung along polished chrome fenders, their horns pounding out a wail of urgent honks. That sound never failed to draw Agostino to the street, sometimes with a bottle of Chianti in hand to wave in salute. Every now and then an eastbound procession would slow down enough to grab the wine. But this time Agostino didn't move.

He sat in a corner booth and flicked ashes from his Lucky Strike into the mint-green glass tray. He liked how the scent from his laundered shirt slipped through the aroma of his cigarette, as if the shirt had its own smoky trail. The last taps of the horns faded down Grand, almost in time to the Sinatra ballad blowing out from the shelf speakers.

Three cigarettes later Agostino saw him. A young man with a tweed shirt who paced past the store, shielding his eyes from the sun. The man doubled back and retrieved a slip of paper from his shirt pocket and checked the number on the door. He glanced again at the slip, stepped back to take in the arc of letters on the window, then shuffled inside. He had short, sandy hair parted sensibly down the side. His eyes darted around in nervous alertness, a deep earnestness carved into the corners. He spotted Agostino and placed his hands in his pockets and hunched his shoulders.

Agostino suddenly recognized him, the young priest from St. Columbkille. "Father?" he said. "Come in come in. I don't see your . . ." He put his hand to his neck to indicate a priest's collar.

"Mr. Peccatori?" This was a voice unaccustomed to loudness.

"Yes. Sit please." He got up and waved the priest into the booth.

"I'm Father Ernie." He put out his hand.

"Yes. Yes. I am Agostino."

Father Ernie settled into the booth, and Agostino raced off for a carafe of Burgundy and two glasses. He half filled each glass and sat down with a sigh.

Studying him, Agostino recalled the expression, *a man of the cloth*, because this one wore no collar. Nothing to distinguish him, except maybe the diocese-issued black oxfords and the measured reserve in his voice. And maybe the hands, the slow priest hands that gestured in colossal sweeps. Priests invariably had a calming effect on Agostino. He could spot the corrupt ones and immediately find common ground, a wink here or there, a veiled smirk. And the ones who thought themselves more pure reminded him of what he once was. Either way he could think aloud.

Agostino pointed outside. "The wedding. You hear?"

"Sure," Father Ernie said. He had a high forehead, the hair already thinning along the top.

"You marry? You make wedding?"

"Sometimes."

"When you make, what do you say?" He pointed to his temple. "In here."

"What do I think?" He sipped his Burgundy and glanced out to the street, his eyes clear brown pools. "I think of the thousands of other weddings that came before in that church. And the tons of rice thrown. All the vows exchanged. One wedding dress after another. How they're all the same. But they're not. I feel renewed. Like I'm doing something worthwhile. I feel the same at funerals."

"Ha. I feel, too. All the time, automobile they pass." He pulled out his pack of Lucky Strikes. "Cigarette?"

"No."

Agostino grinned. He'd put off Father Ernie's business a little longer. "I want to ask. Do you wish, sometime, do you wish you make marry?"

Agostino finally got him to smile.

"I have this feeling you're talking about more than marriage. You're talking about carnal knowledge. The relations between a man and a woman. Is that it?"

Agostino shrugged. He thought, *You are a man of the cloth, I am a man of the flesh*.

"Even Christ was tempted," Father Ernie said.

"For him, easy, no?" Agostino looked skyward and with his whole hand pointed there. "He know."

"Know what?"

"Up there. They save spot for him."

"And there's no spot for you?"

"Maybe I don't deserve."

"We all deserve."

"You never answer. Sometime you wish?"

He spoke slowly, as if Agostino would miss something otherwise. "You become accustomed to a way of life, Mr. Peccatori. You don't imagine a choice beyond your own walls."

Agostino saw a shadow cross the priest's face.

"A man who asks about regrets," Father Ernie said, "has a few of his own maybe."

Agostino shut his eyes for a second and the image of sun-blasted olive trees appeared. He wanted their fragrance to engulf him, but all he smelled was the stale liquor that had penetrated the red vinyl seats.

"A young woman came to me the other day and spoke of you and your store."

"Spoke?"

"She stopped by the rectory. She needed help, she said."

"And you give help?"

"I tried. But I wanted to talk with you."

"A woman, she come to priest, and priest come to me. Ha."

"She mentioned a dress. She showed me a picture from a magazine. She'd been going through a difficult time, she said, and you helped her."

"And now she want help more?"

"Maybe."

Agostino spoke slowly. "How do I know—how do I know what you say is no my, how they say, obligation?"

"I think you know."

"Now I know everything. Maybe I put collar. Why you come here?" And who was this priest who wouldn't look you in the eye?

"The mother is upset. She wants what's right."

Agostino put out his hand and rubbed his thumb and fingers. "*Salda*. Money. That's what she wants. I have store, little business, and people, they make jealous. They don't know what I do to make business."

"Maybe I should ask the woman to come in."

"I don't think she come here anymore."

"Meet with her, then. If not for her, then . . ."

Agostino still could not gauge this young priest. Was he looking for his own share. Were those clear eyes full of deceit? Or did he simply want to wash his hands of the mess that Gabriella had dropped in his lap? Maybe there lurked a veiled threat in his urging. *If not for her, then* . . . Then what? For Agostino's family? To protect *them*?

Sitting there across from the young priest during an early afternoon in the middle of June 1957, Agostino finally understood why his father was shot during the war. Fifteen years ago now. The old images came back. German soldiers had marched into his father's village and settled in. In the middle of the night, a few families had decided to flee, including Agostino's father and mother, but his father, his father went back. Agostino and Vince were thousands of miles away at the time, probably sitting in this same booth reading a paper about the war, so they'd only heard stories. Letters were written, of course, speculating over and over on why his father went back, most everyone agreeing he was simply trying to protect what was his. Agostino couldn't dispute that, but he felt sure now that his father, having lost all he had worked for, went back because he wanted to die.

Vince ambled out from the back and stood at the bar with his hands on his hips. He'd been humming along to Sinatra, a soulful hum that didn't remotely match the tune. He looked toward his brother's booth.

"Che successo?" he asked.

"Wileyo. Come here." Agostino pointed to Father Ernie and explained he was the young priest from St. Columbkille.

Vince wouldn't look at the man. In Italian he asked, "Why do you bring a priest here?"

"Vincenzo, come here."

"I'm going upstairs."

"He come to bless the store."

Vince crossed himself and tread slowly toward the booth. "I know one day you come. Father Ernie, hey?"

The priest looked to Agostino for explanation and put out his hand.

"Who tell you?" Vince said.

"Tell?"

"You bless store, no?"

"Sure, I can bless the store."

"Who tell you to come?"

"Nobod—"

"I tell," Agostino interrupted. "I tell."

Agostino sent his brother for a bowl of water and explained Vince's obsession to Father Ernie. Before the Depression, Mio Fratello had been a funeral parlor, one of the first in the neighborhood. When the owner died, he became the last one waked in the building, and the place remained empty for years. So by the time Vince stumbled upon the "For Sale" sign, the price was next to nothing. He scraped the letters off the front window and scrubbed the floors but still worried that maybe he damned himself for pouring whiskey after the dead. Profit and hell are bed partners, he always lamented in his Neapolitano tongue, which explained the inconsistent price list with Vince at the register. He knew cost and rarely dipped below that, but prices varied depending on the condition of his conscience. Around priests he became especially jittery.

Vince returned with the water, and Ernie prepared to bless the store.

Benediction. Absolution. These were words Agostino had seen somewhere, but he'd never heard them spoken. He wanted to say the words himself now, but the syllables would sound foreign on his tongue. He preferred to let the words swim around in his head, hear them ring against the Latin incantations spilling from Father Ernie's lips as he dipped the tips of his fingers in the water. Benediction. Absolution. He wondered if there was time. He wondered if his own father had prayed just before he was struck down.

Vince hurriedly crossed himself as Father Ernie flicked beads of water toward the middle of the store. Agostino watched the spray turn into a fine mist and vanish. It bothered Agostino that he didn't know the name of the brass wand that priests ordinarily used to sprinkle holy water. If he knew the name he might have asked about it. Then Father Ernie could return another time with the proper wand and his collar in place and his whispered Latin filling even the darkest corners of the store, and then he could set things right.

When Agostino arrived home after four that afternoon, Angela Rosa was wiping the Formica countertop next to the sink with a damp rag. She saw herself through his eyes at that first glimpse as he crossed the kitchen, and she felt something like relief. Seeing the rag in her hand, her husband couldn't know about the fever and the doctor, and she could savor his innocence for a few moments.

"Something happened," Agostino said. It was a question. When they were alone they spoke their native language, interrupted increasingly over the years with clipped English.

"Benito. He has a fever."

"How high?"

"Too high."

"He's sleeping?"

"That's all he wants to do."

He ran a hand through his hair. He needed to tell her. Vince would advise against such a hasty confession, but he couldn't contain this. The whole business demanded a degree of deception beyond his capacity for deception. He'd always believed that life, in the end, was just. You got what you deserved. Having scoffed at America's preoccupation with infidelity, he knew this embroilment now was his due. There was no side-stepping that. Idiot Americans. They couldn't understand that infidelity meant nothing. It was the covering up that sent husbands and wives into separate bedrooms.

Until now, Agostino felt he had little to hide. Americans might have called his short-lived entanglements affairs, but that word carried far too much weight. He preferred *divertimente*. Diversion. Not something to discuss over dinner, but easily tucked away into a tidy compartment in his head that no one asked about and that caused harm to no one. But this.

He could hear Vince now—what if Angela Rosa needed a diversion, hey? He couldn't answer that one. He preferred not to think about it. He felt fairly certain that he and his wife had different needs and felt absolutely certain that had Angela Rosa strayed, the straying would *mean* something to her. And that made all the difference.

He tried to recall his wedding vows and could remember only one. The one about never parting. The one that had caused an itchy dryness in his throat and a hoarse whisper. But one he knew he'd honor. The only sacred one. Did he also agree to be faithful? He couldn't remember. Those three weeks back in his homeland—and it had felt like home, like he should stay—those weeks had raced by so rapidly that even his wedding lodged itself in his memory as a blur. *Festina tarde*, his new family urged. Make haste slowly. Three weeks suffused with celebration—sterling china cups clinking gilt-rimmed saucers, wine corks strewn along never-ending walnut tables. He had sewn mother-of-pearl buttons to the back of Angela Rosa's gown. Chose wedding bands from the suitcase of a neighbor who specialized in soft karat golds.

He returned to America of course, his new home, where the concept of an arranged marriage baffled his children. Finding a wife as he did seemed like some bizarre shopping trip to them. But what other choice did he have back then? He worked at the store day and night. His English was marginal. Where would he meet a wife? A real wife. Not like that blonde of Vince's. Besides, an arranged marriage came with certain understandings, both partners acknowledging that whatever passion grew out of their union would flourish only in time. The partners gave each other ample space. They took their time with each other. Time was the one commodity they could count on. In some ways, then, his marriage was created not in haste as his children believed. What else should he expect from them—they were American children after all. And his was not a marriage of convenience, a phrase that made him laugh. There was nothing convenient about learning to love a woman he'd never met before.

What did he know about love then anyway? A long courtship wouldn't have revealed any deeper truths to him. Love was a matter of will, a matter of agreement and duty. His was a marriage of making things work. Putting food on the table. Protecting the family.

And what did he know now about love? Only that he loved his wife, another certainty, a realization that hit him at once the day she told him she was pregnant. He recalled thinking, *I now share a life with the mother of my children. Our children.* Love became a natural outgrowth of that.

"I called Dr. Giannini," she said.

"The doctor was here?"

She nodded and placed a pan on the stove, poured olive oil to cover the bottom, and dropped in a handful of garlic wedges.

"Why didn't you come for me?"

"What would you do?"

"Do? *Do?* I want to know."

"Now you know."

He could never predict her anger or know whether it was directed at him or if it was simple worry disguised as anger. He felt dull during these exchanges, a spongy numbness settling in around his temples and blurring the edges of his vision. He'd slept late, left abruptly, hadn't returned for lunch. That was the cause, he decided. And she was worried. She worried all the time.

"What did the doctor say?"

"Stupid doctors. They don't know anything. He didn't know. I have to call him again tomorrow if Benito won't drink."

"Benito won't drink?"

"No."

"Maybe I can try."

She shot a look at him. If his own mother can't get him to drink . . .

"What can it hurt if I try?"

"Go. Try."

"I should wake him?"

"Yes, wake him."

Benito was sitting in his crib with his hands on his knees, staring at a shaft of light that fell on the hardwood floor.

"Piccolo, Benito," Agostino crooned. *"Piccolo."*

Benito turned his head toward his father but didn't break his gaze. Agostino picked him up. *"Bello bambino."* Benito rubbed at his nose with the palm of his hand.

Whenever Angela Rosa asked Agostino about one of the children looking pale, he could never tell. Pale was not a thing he could detect on his own. But Benito was pasty white, his skin nearly translucent. He radiated heat. Agostino took him back to the kitchen and asked Angela Rosa if they should call the doctor again.

"Give him to me," she said.

"Let me try a cup."

Agostino set him on the table, then sat down before him. "Benito, time to drink," he said.

Benito sighed and gazed blankly over his father's shoulder. Agostino tried to place the plastic mug in his son's hand, his favorite mug, the one with an orange sun and a smiling face with red cheeks on it, but Benito showed no signs that he intended to grasp it.

"Benito, drink."

Angela Rosa placed two fingers along Benito's neck to check his temperature. She touched his forehead. "Dear God," she said. "My God."

"What should we do?"

She turned to shut off the flame on the stove. "Bring him here."

He followed her to the bathroom, where she started a bath of cool water. Benito whimpered when they placed him in it but then sat there glassy-eyed as he'd done in his crib.

"He feels a little cooler," Agostino said after a while.

Angela Rosa explained that the same thing happened that morning. She and Victoria worked with wet towels to bring down his temperature, but the moment they stopped, his fever shot up again.

"What do we do?" he said.

She would prepare dinner, she told him. Maybe he would eat something now. Everyone would be home soon for supper. No sense that they should go without supper.

Yes. Supper, thought Agostino. No sense they shouldn't eat. They pulled Benito out of the tub, and Agostino whispered the beginning of a prayer. Later, when darkness descended on the house and the voices from the street spun out, replaced by night birds and crickets, he would confess what he could to his wife. He would tell her what she needed to know.

June 23, 1977

ALFREDO PECCATORI

❧

I f it weren't for our June meetings at the cemetery each
year, I probably would never talk to the cocksucker. My
big brother Anthony. Eleven months older than me and
still thinks he can pull rank. Lectures me on the soul. Tells
me I got to get back to the church. My brother Anthony who
dropped out of the seminary after a year telling me about
where I should stand on heaven and hell and all the rest of
that bullshit. Why the hell should I care? He says now that
Jinny is pregnant I have to think about someone other than
myself. I ought to do it for the baby. Maybe he's right. And
maybe I will. But not because he tells me.

One of these years, I think, we'll run into someone at the
cemetery. Maybe the old man or Vicky or some old neighbor.
But we never do. Or maybe they see Anthony and me milling
around and they wait until we're gone 'cause they don't want

to disturb us. I like that idea. The old man seeing Anthony and Freddy back together again, thinking about times past when no one could separate us. Anthony . . . Freddy. Like the two names belonged together. You called out one, and the other answered. Together we were anonymous, which made us tighter. We held our secrets to our chests and spoke in school-yard code. We even had secret-agent handshakes that I'm embarrassed to admit I still remember. For a while, about ten years ago, I could still get a laugh out of Anthony by putting out my twisted hand.

Even if Benito hadn't passed away, the two of us would have still drifted apart, I'm sure. No sense blaming our little brother for what's come between us. Fact is, Benito's death pushed us closer for a long while. Back then no one talked about a baby dying. They didn't have the words not to mention the balls to deal with the whole mess. So Anthony and me, we disappeared like they wanted us to. We became the plaster walls and the carpet and the kitchen table. We walked outside and became the street and the goddamn school and the softball game. What I wouldn't have given for someone to sit on the edge of my bed and explain to me that I wasn't going to get a fever myself. You think someone would have figured out that there was no way me and Anthony could have been doing as well as we looked like we were doing. We were thirteen fucking years old.

When we got back to school in September, the nuns they got in my face and offered their rosaries and scapulars. Sister Rosaline on the very first day began to talk about what it means to lose a brother. Finally someone could answer the thousand questions I had. I leaned forward in my little wooden seat, waxed new over the summer, a smell I'd looked forward to for weeks, and then slowly began to shrink and squirm as

Sister Rosaline reminded us of how special Benito was. He was in a special place now and God loved him more than we could ever know and we should be so lucky to be in that place. I wanted to kick something, rip the habit off her skull. I could feel the eyes of my classmates boring in on me. It was because of me that they had to listen to all this crap. *And we're not special?* I wanted to shout. Fuck special. Tell me about fevers. Tell me about death and cemeteries. Tell me about when the hell I could stop tiptoeing around the house. Tell me how I can get Mama to stop crying. Instead, we prayed every hour on the hour so that by the end of the day Sister Rosaline had traveled up and down her rosary about a trillion times.

I could tell by the tight look on his face as he walked out of school that first day that Anthony was hearing the same bullshit from his teacher. And I knew that the next day would be different. The next day and every day after would be like home. Everyone turning quiet around us. And no one would mention Benito ever again. As if nothing ever happened. Even our classmates would steer clear of us for a while, the two lepers.

So today we meet at the cemetery and my big brother says I should get back to the church. I look at him and hope that the look is enough to remind him about what the church ever did for us, but I'm wasting my time. It's twenty years today, he says. I say, No, I didn't know that, and wonder what the hell difference that makes. Nineteen, twenty. Dead is dead. Like he knows what I'm thinking, he says, Two decades. It's a milestone. Maybe it's a reminder. To get back to what's important. The Church has changed, he tells me.

You're right, I tell him. Absolutely right. With Anthony you agree with everything he says. He's always looking for a tiny crack of light he can crawl into. And I guess I admire that.

Once a year I admire that. But mostly I'm reminded of how brick-wall dense he is if he thinks I'm going to paw my rosary like a sixth grader at Wednesday-morning mass. I know what he thinks. He thinks, if I come back to the Church I'll come around more often. I'll get back to my roots. I'll march in the Columbus Day parade and wave the flag. I'll make red gravy on Sundays. Like old times. Well, I've got news for you, brother. All that Catholic bullshit is tied in with all that Italian-American bullshit and I don't want a thing to do with either one. It's all bullshit propaganda to me.

There are no old times. There's only now. There's this warm stone in the sun with Benito's name scratched into it. And there's this grass trying to grow tall around it. Benito's gone and he'll be two years old forever, less than two. And I'm here and you're there and that's all there is.

How's Jinny feel? he says.

Good. She's big as a house, I tell him.

You worried?

I wish I could tell you I wasn't, Anthony.

And he knows exactly what I mean. We're quiet for a while, the kind of quiet that seems right for a graveyard. We're reading the names on all the stones, all young kids, and he says, You ever feel like our family is cursed?

I used to think that, I tell him. I used to buy into that. But what good would that do? Look what it did for the old man. And Mama. Hell, the rest of them, too.

Anthony smiles.

What?

I was just thinking, he says, what Uncle Vince would say. *Americano*, he'd call you. *Americano, hey.*

He kind of spit whenever he said it. Remember?

We both laugh. A small cemetery laugh.

So why do you come here, he says?

Why do *I* come here? Don't tell me you come here to remove the family curse?

I just want to know, he says, why you come here. I didn't say anything about a curse.

Sure you did.

Forget the curse, he says.

I don't know why I come here. Not to be with you. That's for sure. You're a royal pain in the ass, you know that.

Anthony doesn't come back quick enough and there's this silence between us that's unnerving, like we both sense some truth in what I said and now I'm sorry for saying it.

I come here, I tell him, because I have to. Because he was my little brother. The reasons don't go much deeper, I don't think.

Anthony seems satisfied with that.

What I don't tell him is that when they laid out Benito at the store, moved all the tables to the side and covered all the mirrors along the walls, and I walked in and weaved my way through the crowd and saw him for the first time all drained of color except for that grayish-pink powder all over his face, I about fell back. That's me, I thought. That's my nose, and my hair all slicked down. And they even put him in the pint-size royal-blue suit I wore one time when I was four. My suit. Too big for Benito but they'd folded up the sleeves and cuffs to fit him. He was all ready to be buried. And sometime during that night between the wailing and the people shuffling in and out, I made a promise to the little guy that I wouldn't forget him. A promise between brothers. It seemed the right thing to do. I didn't know then the shape the promise would take.

Anthony gets in his car and I get in mine behind him. He takes off and I sit there awhile longer. Why rush? To get back to work so I can throw one more goddamn piece of luggage onto the airport conveyor? I close my eyes and go back twenty years. I try to remember what I was doing that day, what could have been so important to keep me away from my little brother on his last day, but everything that came before is hazy. I don't think about those days enough. That's the problem. I always thought they'd be there for me, like an old friend. Maybe that's another reason I come here each year. To hold on to the little that's left of before.

3

SEPTEMBER 5, 1957

❧

The front page of the *Chicago Daily News* had a photograph of the Arkansas National Guard standing at attention at the head of the stone stairs of Central High
School in Little Rock. They stand there without expression,
bayonets resting across their shoulders. Walking up the stairs
is a Negro girl who clutches a folder to her chest. She's wearing a plain white top and long plaid skirt, as if she's on her
way to a late summer picnic. The girl looks at no one through
her thick-rimmed glasses. There is no one to look at. Just beyond her a mob of women with twisted mouths stare after her.
And behind them a few blank-faced men with straw hats and
wide hatbands look on. Victoria Peccatori studied the girl's
fingers, the tight grip, as if the school folder were a precious
jewel. Victoria saw hope in the empty folder, work sheets to
be tucked into the pockets, an extra pen to be clipped onto

the sleeve, the folder growing thicker and more tattered as the days trudge by.

Before reading the caption, Victoria assumed the National Guard had been called to ensure the safe passage of the girl into the school. But soldiers were stationed there to keep her out. And Arkansas needed a small army of them. With bayonets. What did they expect from this girl? During the last couple of months, Victoria had been keeping a mental tally of stories like this one, stories that affirmed for her that the world was a nasty place and that her baby brother had been spared all the ugliness. Wars and bombs and bayonets. He'd been spared even death. Dying as young as he did, Benito couldn't have known anything about what was happening to him.

None of these thoughts had the effect of lifting Victoria's gloom, as she sometimes anticipated. Instead, they made her more bitter, made her more inclined to zero in on the corrosive details in even the most benign stories. And she'd become so comfortable in her gloom that even her closest friend failed to notice.

"What're you reading now?" Darlene asked. She'd gotten a page-boy haircut before the school year began and kept touching the edges with the back of her fingers. They sat in the school's makeshift cafeteria, a hall used for Christmas plays and Sunday-night bingo and potluck dinners. This would be the last year Victoria and Darlene would have to endure the canker-green walls and the hissing pipes.

"Just the newspaper," Victoria said.

"I can see that. Read me my horoscope." She cracked her gum at the side of her mouth.

"What do you want to know? I can tell you. You're going to marry Stick. And you're going to have twelve kids and they're all going to look like Stick but you're going to be this blimp this whale and you're going to sit in your house in the suburbs all day eating chocolate. Did I get it about right?"

"Jealous?"

"You bet." Victoria pushed the paper across the table.

Darlene eyed the headlines and asked, "Which lawn today?"

Victoria shrugged.

Darlene opened the paper to the horoscopes. "Says here there was a girl sent to jail for twenty years for swiping newspapers off lawns." She glanced over the top of the paper, her green eyes bright. "At least she'll have a lot of time to read."

"Does it have anything in there about the girl's friend who steals cigarettes from the A&P?"

"Yeah, they're cell mates, it says. Bad girls." Darlene put the paper down and touched her hair. She leaned over the table and sighed. In a low voice she said, "How are we going to make it through another year, Vick?"

Victoria glanced across the cafeteria at the clock. She'd been wondering the same thing. Everything about the day felt wrong, beginning with the picture in the newspaper. "Come on," she ordered.

"What?"

"Just shut up and follow me. Take the paper."

They walked out of the cafeteria, turned down the janitor's hallway, and slipped out the door that led to a ramp where deliveries arrived. They sauntered down the ramp, forcing themselves not to rush. They were in the stone courtyard now, the church towering over them on one side, the squat, two-story convent on the other. If they could get past the sacristy to the far end of the courtyard and through the tunnel without anyone springing out, they'd be free.

"I was thinking," Victoria said in the coolness of the tunnel.

She held her purse to her chest and thought of the Negro girl in Arkansas. She spoke louder than she needed to, wanting to hear her voice carom off the mortared walls. "This is our last year."

Darlene chewed her gum. "Yeah, our last year."

"What are they going to do to us? Kick us out?"

They came out of the tunnel and moved quickly down Paulina Street, then turned left on Ohio. "I figure I can handle three four days a week," Victoria said. "But that's about all."

Darlene's breaths were short. She reached into her purse for a couple of Lucky Strikes. "Slow down, will ya," she said.

Victoria heard the familiar exasperation in her friend's voice, and they both slowed and glanced at each other and rolled their eyes. It was a look between friends that said, *We've covered this ground before.* Something had changed between them lately, and they weren't quite sure what to make of it. Although Victoria had always been the more manic of the two in many ways, it should have been Darlene stealing newspapers and plotting to cut out of school. And Victoria should have been the one to worry and balk before finally agreeing to go along. They both counted on that. At least they used to.

Darlene tapped out a cigarette and held it out for Victoria. "Now what?" she said.

"We're out. That's what," Victoria said. "No mother-fricking shorthand drills today."

St. Columbkille offered the typical three-year high-school-equivalency program for girls that prepared them with typing and shorthand and taught them the necessary domestic skills they needed for their future as Catholic wives and mothers. In religion class, where they sat next to each other in the back, Victoria and Darlene had already begun the school year exchanging notes questioning the nuns' authority in such matters. "What does she know about husbands?" Darlene wrote about Sister Francine. "How does she please *her* man?" Victoria destroyed the note and returned a clean one that said, "Missionary style. Of course."

Victoria wasn't going to be stupid about the note passing, but who cared if Sister Francine found the note? They could kick her out and not let her graduate until next year and Mama would scream and Zia Lupa would join in. Or they wouldn't let her graduate at all and she'd go directly into the workforce without a diploma and Mama would scream and Zia Lupa would join in. Victoria might welcome the screams. Even Lupa's.

Darlene suggested they take the bus to the beach, but they both glanced at their school uniforms and decided against it. Victoria turned north at the next intersection, then turned east down Erie.

"Ah, I get it. Walk by the club maybe?" Darlene said.

"Maybe."

"I just don't get it."

"Get what?"

"You and Eddie."

"What's there to get?"

A car drove by, and Darlene cupped her cigarette inside her palm, away from the street. "He doesn't seem like the kind of guy you'd be interested in, that's all."

"He's cute."

"He's okay and everything." Darlene pushed out her gum into the silver wrapper she'd saved and tucked it in her purse. "You know that truck guy, the one with the tomatoes and strawberries and stuff? You know how he kind of looks at us, kind of creepy like?"

"Yeah."

"Well, he reminds me of Eddie."

"Get out."

"No, he does."

Victoria hadn't made the connection before, but Darlene was right. Pencil on a mustache and put a crushed red beret on Eddie, and they'd be blood relatives. Because of the way the truck driver looked at her, Victoria had imagined once climbing up on that truck and jostling through the crates of grapes and cherries to find a dark place at the back where the smell of dirt on the watermelon would mingle with the man's scent. She imagined those burned, leathery arms wrapped around her and the man's hot breaths and her gasping.

But that thought came *before*. The thoughts that came before, the vivid ones like this one that slammed into her present thoughts, caused a tight rippling in her chest. They took her back to a *before* when a little boy in a second-story apartment on Superior Street took up his own small space in this world and breathed his own pocket of air. She had to shake loose the icy shiver that ran up the small of her back.

"Maybe you're right," Victoria said.

"Maybe you and Eddie will get married and sell cucumbers off the back of a truck, huh?"

"Maybe." Victoria dragged on her cigarette. They walked awhile in silence. "Everything looks so . . ."

"So what?"

"Dingy."

"Dingy?"

"Yeah, you know." It was about as far as Victoria was willing to go to let Darlene know how she'd been feeling lately. And Darlene, who'd understood everything before, seemed unable to pick up on the subtle cues her friend provided. Darlene was under the mistaken impression that the two friends could simply return to the way things used to be.

"See that house over there?" Victoria said. "The one with the bicycle tire? Eddie says there's a family of Gypsies who live there. One of the Gypsy girls tried to pick up his great uncle. He's seventy-eight. Eddie says that's what they do. They find someone with dough and marry him. And then—" She lowered her voice as they neared the house, feeling the thrill of what she was going to say next. "Then they poison the guy, mix it in with his food. After a few weeks he can't even get out of bed."

Darlene stuck another stick of spearmint in her mouth. "No shit," she said. "Why didn't we think of that?"

"You're sick," Victoria said, and laughed, but felt disappointed that Darlene had missed the gravity of the story.

They smoked and drank 7-Ups the rest of the morning. In the afternoon they walked along Chicago Avenue and strolled the aisles of Goldblatt's and Woolworth's. The next day they cut school again but wore cutoffs under their skirts so they could stroll along the beach at Olive Park and sit on the stones at the pier.

"We should probably visit Sister Francine tomorrow, don't you think?" Darlene said. She looked out to where Lake Michigan seemed to touch the sky.

"Did they call your house yesterday?"

"No."

"They'll call today."

"You think?"

Victoria shot her an annoyed glance. "Do you think, do you think? Yeah, I think." Victoria took in the sweeping sky and the breaks in the tide and thought about the Arkansas girl who was probably not in school today either. There wasn't a single story about her in today's paper. In a couple of weeks everyone would forget about her.

"What'll you tell your mom?" Darlene asked. She held out a cigarette for Victoria.

"It's a mistake. That's all. One big mistake."

"What are they gonna do to us, right?" Darlene asked.

"Right. What're they gonna do?"

Victoria leaned over with her cigarette to get a light. At the end of the cigarette she saw the lighter's spark and the small flame, the plume of smoke rising, and beyond that, her friend's worried eyes. Victoria drew in a deep, searing drag on the cigarette and realized with a clarity that sent a pang of grief through her that Darlene understood everything. The worry in her eyes wasn't about her own punishment from Sister Francine. And she wasn't at the beach because she needed to be there. Darlene was there for Victoria. Because Victoria needed her there. There was even a note of apology in those eyes. They were saying, *I wish I could do more.* They were saying, *I don't know what else to do.*

"Thanks," Victoria said. "Thanks for the light." She leaned back against the rocks. "You think Sister Francine smokes?" she asked.

No one used the word *curse*, not even Zia Lupa, but that's what they all believed had befallen them. That's what the older ones believed at least. Angela Rosa and Agostino, Vince and Zia Lupa. Santo didn't know what to believe. A curse seemed to him about as plausible an explanation as any. Someone fucked up, maybe they all fucked up, and now God was having His turn. Santo was willing to admit his part in the grand scheme. He wasn't exactly living the saint's life. But if that's the way things worked in this world, if life was going to be a sonuvabitch, then he was going to be a sonuvabitch back. He didn't know what this would mean for him—the line was a version of one of Uncle Vince's—but it lifted Santo's spirits to make the sentiment his own.

Santo did feel like a sonuvabitch for allowing Eddie Milano to see his sister and for borrowing his copper-colored '52 DeSoto with the white top, Eddie's aunt's really, and for driving to the corner of Grand and Halsted to find the trolley bus that picked up a woman ten years too old for him, a married woman at that. He knew that Illinois Bell was on South Halsted, eight or nine miles down, but Sylvia Gomez would never believe he just happened to be driving by the very place she worked at precisely three o'clock as the day workers spilled into the streets. Instead, he would park southbound on Halsted until he saw a bus approaching, circle around to Grand, and by the time he returned to the corner, pulling up to her stop, she would be waiting there with a punched transfer crimped in her hand. She wasn't on the first bus, so he turned on Halsted again, sat back, and waited.

Summer hadn't materialized the way he'd hoped, of course. He spent most of his time working at Mio Fratello. After the funeral, his father sat him down in one of the booths that had held mourners just days before and slapped down four twenties, fanned out on the table. He gazed at his son, as if this would be a pivotal moment in both their lives. "You make eighteen soon," he said. "You need pay." He slid the money toward Santo. Then with a suddenness that startled Santo, he pushed himself from the booth. He looked at the floor and scratched the back of his head. *"Ogni venerdì. Va bene?"* Santo wondered if this salary was a new idea or brought on by what had happened to their family. "Every Friday's fine, Papa. Are you sure . . ." But his father walked away. Santo was never told what he'd need to do to earn his salary. He was never even given a schedule of hours. Though he saw some advantage in this, he felt he needed something more definite in his life. He sat in the booth, staring at the twenties, wondering what his father had planned to say to him.

Uncle Vince began treating him like a partner, showing him the three books he kept for the business. One book was for the IRS, Vince told him with a wink, another was for a potential buyer, and the third included the actual take and expenses of each day. The two doctored books were cheap, ringed notebooks from Goldblatt's. But the one with the real numbers had gold embroidery embossed on its rigid black cover, brought over from the old country no doubt, and the edges were dyed a pale crimson with gold stipples. Inside, the gridded pages were tinted mint green, and Santo knew the paper was soft by the way it absorbed the ink. That first day Santo was about to suggest using a pencil, but he liked the sound of the pen scratching along the paper and kept quiet. Soon Santo began to enjoy the afternoon ritual of retrieving the three books from three far corners of Vince's apartment and standing over his uncle's shoulder as he recorded and juggled and converted his numbers with a single-mindedness that was inspiring. Uncle Vince always complained that America had no history, that everything was new in America, and Santo assumed this handing down of the books was Vince's meager attempt at preservation. His ancestors across the ocean had the Colosseum; Santo would have this black book.

Regardless, Santo appreciated the small attentions his uncle paid. Uncles were good for that. They didn't carry the baggage of fathers, who had to keep their distance for reasons unknown to Santo. Uncles were allowed to wink and push a cigarette at you now and then, and they taught you to drive and lent you their car and winked again as they pointed to the backseat. They didn't tell you to be careful, they didn't warn you about taking care of the leather seats, they just handed over the keys. Santo decided he'd be more like an uncle than a father to his own son one day.

Another bus approached, and Santo was remarkably calm. He waited for the Halsted bus to pass him this time before he drove around. It would be better if she waited a few minutes. He circled around and spotted her from a block away and slowed down to catch the light. He'd planned on staring straight ahead for a while at the light before casually glancing over at the stop, nodding, then waving her toward the car. But this seemed to him like something his father would do, so he pulled up, leaned over, and pushed open the passenger door. There were two other women and a whiskered man at the stop, and they all shifted their gaze to the car. They stooped forward to peer inside, hope in some of their eyes, wariness in others. A wave of recognition hit Sylvia, and she took a step forward.

"I'm going your way," Santo said, which sounded to him like the dumbest thing anyone could say. But she got in. One bare leg after another. She pulled on the hem of her citrine-green dress until it covered her knees. They pulled away from the curb, and the would-be passengers looked on with envy.

"What a nice surprise. How are you, Santo? How's your family?"

"About as good as anyone can expect, I guess."

She touched his arm and told him how sorry she was about his brother and expressed a string of condolences. They talked about the car and her work and then settled into a strained silence.

After a while she turned to him. "Hula Hoops," she said, smiling.

Santo knew exactly what she meant but feigned confusion.

"Hula Hoops," she said again. "That's what I couldn't remember the name of. At the feast."

"Hula Hoops."

"It's a stupid name. That's why I couldn't remember it."

Santo wondered if others had these moments when your head suddenly swims at the recollection of an instant. Your thoughts reel and you're there for a second or two, in that *other* life, the sensory trace so palpable you can smell it, a whiff as potent as a sharpened pencil. And then the feeling passes and gives way to a kind of sadness that you can never adequately explain. For an instant Santo was there. At the feast. When life was *bigger*. He glanced out his window and sighed.

"My brother, Alfredo, has one," Santo told her. "But it got smashed in one spot and it doesn't really go around good anymore."

"You'll have to buy him another. Now that you're working."

"How did you know I was working?"

She'd been clutching her purse and now dropped it to her feet. She covered her mouth as she cleared her throat. No lipstick. Little if any makeup. A hint of weariness in her work-shift eyes. "Oh, I don't know. School's over. I just assumed, I guess. Your father said you could run the place."

"My father? When?"

"Out back. When we used to sit and have wine." She pushed her dark hair behind one shoulder. "I don't see him out there anymore."

Santo wanted to ask if that disappointed her. Not seeing the bastard out there. He wanted to tell her about the other bastard, his half brother. If he were alone in the car he'd start thinking about poor Mama and get crazy with rage, a rage targeted mainly at his father, but he'd been directing it toward his mother lately, too. For being so naive. For overlooking, as even Santo had, all the chances Papa had to cheat. During his morning walks, when he didn't come home for lunch, when Vince left him alone all day on Wednesdays, when he had to meet with the accountant from Abruzzi who ran a travel agency and did their taxes. Papa's cheating had never bothered Santo much before because he'd never considered the particulars. But now that was all he could think about.

He shot her a sidelong glance. "I *wasn't* just driving by," he said.

"Oh?" She reached around with her right hand, kneading the cold flesh at the back of her elbow. Until then, she'd never betrayed any signs of awkwardness, and Santo didn't know what to make of it. He should have never borrowed the car, he thought. Uncle Vince should have never taken him for his license. He tapped the steering wheel and reached to his pocket for a cigarette but recalled he had none. He hoped maybe she hadn't heard him or misunderstood.

"I was trying to think," she said. "I was trying to think what I was doing when I was eighteen. I can't remember. Eighteen was just like seventeen and just like sixteen. The only thing that sticks in my head is my cousin's wedding and how I wanted to get married myself. And then a little later my wish came true. But it wasn't how I expected. Not better or worse. Just different. I never had your eighteen, though, driving around in a car with the window open. I wouldn't mind trying it again, being eighteen again. But not in Cuba. Where I had to help my aunt most days. It seemed like we were always setting the table. Clearing the china. But you can't go back, I guess. I can't be eighteen."

She sidled over next to him and put her hand above his knee. He glanced at the speedometer, trying to keep it steady.

Leaning into him, she said softly, "I can't be eighteen again. I can be a lot of things but not eighteen." She sank back in the seat, gazing out the windshield, still close to him. She placed her hands back in her lap. After a while she reached over to rub the back of his neck. She turned to him. "Not for long anyway."

After they drove down her alley and Santo let her out at her gate and parked on a side street and walked back to her cellar door, after they collapsed on the twin mattress in the darkened laundry room of Sylvia Gomez's apartment, after, Santo cried. A single tear at first crawling down his face in jagged spurts that he wiped away with a finger. And then the other eye, the tear Sylvia Gomez would notice and brush away herself. It's okay, she told him, and pulled him into her. It's okay. And then the real tears, tears that this woman seemed to understand better than he did. She stroked his hair, and he ran a hand along the small of her back, soothed by her reassurances, mildly aroused again even in the midst of his tears.

These tears were for his baby brother, who filled his dreams at night. And for his mother, who sat on her bed for hours at a time gazing at the creases of light behind the window shade.

And for Papa, too, who looked lost lately in his pacing. He didn't want to admit that the tears were for himself, too. *I can be a lot of things but not eighteen. Not for long anyway.* He knew all this sweetness wouldn't last beyond the afternoon. He knew already that he would one day come to view this episode as an act of pity. *Poor Santo. He lost his brother and needs something, some loving.* He wasn't sure whether he really believed this, but the thought got him to stop crying finally. And then he felt something like remorse over what he'd led her to. This was nothing more than a onetime favor he'd silently begged out of her. A cheap afternoon lay. So he'd cried for her, too. For the whole fucking messed-up world he lived in.

He pushed himself away from her so he could cup one of her small round breasts. She kissed his forehead, and they made love a second time, the first time having ended nearly before it began. He would accept this one last gift from her. Then he would slip into the alley and walk to Huron Street, where he'd parked Eddie's car. He would return the car and work a few hours at the store, filling glasses, making change. Planning what he knew he had to do.

Victoria found him waiting at the end of her block, one foot propped on the length of black pipe that outlined one side of the dirt parkway, the rest of him leaning over his raised knee. She'd never met a priest before who seemed so normal. Except for the sturdy black priest shoes he wore, oxfords she thought they called them, he seemed like a regular person. Outside of church he never wore a cassock or a collar, so he may have felt some tug of obligation to wear the shoes at least. But he'd constantly poke a finger inside to stretch the leather or retie the laces, as if the shoes defined him and he was going to get the better of them.

"If I weren't a priest," he said as she walked over to him.

She smiled at their old joke. "What are you doing here?" she asked.

"No 'Hi, Father'? 'How are you, Father?' No 'Good to see you, Father.' What are you *doing* here? That's the best you can do?"

"Give me a break."

Those first few weeks after Benito died, Father Ernie came to check on Mama nearly every day, praying the rosary aloud while Angela Rosa followed along with her fingers, Victoria waiting alone on the back porch, her own fingers marking time, the very tips lightly touching the ghostlike beads that passed between them. After, she would walk him down, not wanting him to leave, not wanting to face Mama alone.

Father Ernie pointed to the knee-high black pipe surrounding the parkway. "What is this? This pipe. What's it for?"

Victoria stepped on one of the bars, walked across a segment of it like a tightrope artist, and jumped off. "That's what they're for," she said. "We used to do that all day when I was a kid. We'd have contests, who could stay on the longest."

"But what are they for? What's their purpose?"

"Everything has to have a purpose?"

He looked away from her. "Ah, this."

"You said, 'What's their purpose?' We all have a purpose, remember?"

"I wasn't trying to suggest the pipe has a soul, if that's what you mean. I just wanted to know their . . . function."

"To tell you the truth, Father, I never thought about it."

"When you grow up with something, I guess you don't notice it," he said. He placed a foot on the pipe, as if to walk on it himself, but he just looked at it. Victoria caught his bemused grin. He seemed lost in thought for a moment, probably contemplating his own kid games somewhere back in Pennsylvania. The branches of the catalpa tree canopied over his head, framing him, Victoria thought.

She imagined herself under the tree as a kid, how she must have looked to her father as he walked home and saw her and Penny and Darlene gathering the cigarlike appendages that dropped from the branches, for no good reason other than to collect them. As the image came back to her, a hot ache pulsed at the back of her throat.

She was about to ask him a question, which she promptly forgot when she saw Crazy Willie crossing the street one block over, his windmill arms sweeping the air in rhythmic slashes, his head bobbing in time to each step.

"Look," she said.

Father Ernie glanced over to where she pointed, but Willie was gone. "Crazy Willie," she said. "Do you know him?"

"I know who you mean."

"That's all he does. All day. He walks."

"He walks?"

"That's all he does."

"Definitely crazy. They should lock up all those walkers."

"You know what I mean. He's not all there. When I was a kid everybody would play tricks on him. The boys mostly. Get him to swear. Or give him gross stuff to eat. Leaves . . . ants. Worse things. But after a while everyone left him alone. Like they got bored with him."

"What about you? Did you participate?"

"I don't know. I laughed sometimes. Sometimes it was funny."

Father Ernie looked off to where Crazy Willie had crossed and scratched at his chin with one finger.

"I couldn't help it," she said. "When he said, 'That's BS,' I wanted to die. He had this round round face, all red and purply, like a baby. And the swearing coming out of that face . . . it was, you know, hilarious. And he didn't seem to mind. He'd laugh, too. His face would get . . . all red and—"

Father Ernie nodded and stuck a finger in his shoe, pulled hard on the leather tongue. Victoria kicked at the bar around the parkway and finally sat down on it. She hadn't seen her block from this angle since she was a girl, and the burden of the here and now, her seventeen years, seemed like a heavy weight on her.

"Sometimes when I see him now," she said, "I'm jealous. Isn't that terrible? I'm jealous. Of Crazy Willie." Her throat ached again. She seemed always to be on the verge of tears lately, and she was surprised at the sorts of things that could make her cry. But she swallowed and fought back the wavering that had crept into her voice. "Explain that to me," she said. "Tell me why I'm jealous."

"I think you know."

"You're going to pull that on me, are you?"

He sat down next to her, trying to tuck his legs under the bar as she had them, but they wouldn't fit. Resigned, he folded his arms and straightened his legs, and they sat there and stared at his shoes. "So tell me," he said.

"I don't know. I just think he's lucky in some ways. Like when we used to tease him, he didn't know what was going on. A few minutes later he'd be walking up and down the neighborhood, swinging his arms, talking to himself. He didn't care what anyone thought."

"So you don't think any of the teasing registered?"

She thought about it for a while. "No. I don't think it did. I really don't. He didn't have a clue. Sometimes he'd say—I guess it's okay to say it . . . I'm just telling you what he said— he'd say, 'Kiss my ass.' But we taught him to say that. And then we'd fall all over ourselves and he'd be snorting and slapping his leg, laughing harder than any of us. He had this over-bite thing and you could see all his teeth. 'Kiss my ass. Kiss my ass,' he'd say. He'd be talking to the ground. The only thing that registered, I think, is that he made us laugh. He liked to make us laugh."

She leaned over to pick up a catalpa leaf and began ripping it down the middle, small precise tears. She imagined the two halves to be identical.

"That's what I'm jealous of, I guess. That laugh. That crazy laugh. That laugh of not knowing any better. I mean, some-times it's better not to know. Like that Negro girl in Arkansas who's trying to get into that school. What kind of day must she be having, knowing that all these people just hate her. If she had stayed home . . . Gone to her old school."

Father Ernie cleared his throat.

"And don't be giving me that two-steps-forward-one-step-back crap. Those people would have pushed her down the stairs if they could've gotten away with it. Those Christians down there. Where's God when you need Him? He's never there when you need Him."

If Father Ernie had tugged at his shoe then to remind her she was talking to a priest, she wouldn't have said what she said next. But he didn't and she got caught up in her anger at the white Christians in Arkansas and God and blurted out suddenly, "He can kiss my ass." Father Ernie did tug at his shoe then, first the left and then the right, and she felt all at once the full impact of what she'd said and she didn't regret it. She didn't regret a word. *Kiss my ass, God,* she thought.

She turned to him. "You're pretty quiet today, Father. Seminary didn't teach you to deal with cases like me, did they?"

He rubbed his eyes and shook his head and wiped away a slow grin. "You're a case, all right. I guess there's nothing to say to you. You're one step ahead of me."

"Oh, swell, I get the priest who gives up. Tell me what to do. Should I apologize? Say three Hail Marys? What?"

"Is that remorse I hear? Or just words?"

She let the leaf float out of her hand. "Words, I guess."

"That's what I thought," he said. He folded his arms high across his chest, pushed up his shoulders, and rocked.

"What?"

"My father. He used to . . ." He seemed to be deciding whether to go on. "He would lift his hands sometimes to my mother. He'd have the perfect words for her later. He knew ten thousand ways to kingdom come to say sorry. And she'd fall for it every time. But I knew. The words fell around me like pocketknives." He was talking more to himself now. "She'd slap him away and between crying she'd tell him to leave, and I'd fall for it, too. Her words. This time she really meant it, I'd think. But then he'd whimper, on and on, and my mother would take him finally in her arms, and I'd go in my room. It was probably the only time they were really intimate. After she was bruised." He crossed his legs. "So don't think you're the first one to cuss out God."

Down the street old man Dominick was picking up scraps of paper that had blown onto his patch of lawn. It took all his effort to bend down like that.

Victoria's face felt hot. "So what happened? What changed?"

"Oh, I don't know. No one thing. When I turned sixteen I started stepping between them. And then he left for a while. When he came back he had a new job selling life insurance. He'd been working steel his whole life, pounding and flattening these rumbling sheets of it — his fingers looked like steel — and then he left it. Just like that. And he never hit my mother again. Not that I saw. They had a couple of happy years together before he died."

She could smell the rectory on him, a dark, musk scent that made her think of stained wood. "I would have never forgiven him," she said. "I would have never taken him back."

"That's what I used to think. Every day. And now that's my job, to take people back. The irony of that always hits me hard." He turned the ring on his wedding finger, as if he were gently twisting it on. She'd seen men play with their wedding rings before and always wondered if the gesture held deeper meaning, whether they felt lucky or trapped.

"So there's still hope for me?" she said.

"There's always hope."

He looked away when he said it. He wouldn't let his eyes bore into you, demanding answers. Only when he joked did he fix his gaze outward, as if this were the only time he really felt like himself. That's what she liked about Father Ernie. Anyone else talking to her about hope would have seemed solemn as sin, but this man threw out hope almost in apology, with a shrug. She wondered for the first time if he'd ever done it, if he'd ever been with anyone before entering the seminary. Something to talk about with Darlene. She started anticipating the conversation already, how both of them would get caught up in the wild possibilities. Father Ernie at sixteen in the back of his father's car. Father Ernie with Sister Francine . . . with Sister Margaret Mary. Sister Rosaline's name would come up, of course. She'd been their eighth-grade teacher, and every lecture she ever began always ended with sex. She'd warn the girls against bumping into boys in the halls because that's how it started . . . the itch. Don't dare scratch the itch until matrimony. She picked up another leaf, trying to wipe away the cartoon images in her mind.

"I didn't mean to swear, Father. Sorry."

"No, you're not."

"I mean in front of you. Sorry about swearing in front of you."

"To tell you the truth, I'm a little tired of people becoming all hushed around me. Like they're going to corrupt me. So I don't mind. I'd rather hear a little swearing, I think. It's more . . . human."

She glanced at his ring again. "Can I ask you something?"

He grinned and nodded.

"Why did you—I mean, I can see why maybe you didn't want to get married. But why, you know, a priest?" She felt instant regret for asking.

"Well, the circus wasn't accepting applications, so . . ."

"I'm sorry, I didn't mean to make it sound that way. I didn't—"

"It's okay. It's not you. I get asked that all the time. I must have this face that doesn't fit what people think of when they think *priest*. I'll have to learn to use that to my advantage."

"So why did you?"

"Which answer do you want? The one I gave when I entered the seminary? And you'd be surprised how seldom they asked after I was in. Young men weren't exactly beating a path to their door. Or do you want the answer I give to parishioners who don't really want to know, who just want to find a way to feel comfortable around me, a question to get out of the way. Which is okay. Or do you want the real answer, something I've only recently discovered?"

"Real."

"I'd like to tell you the skies opened, that holy light warmed my forehead, but I think, I really believe that I am a priest today"—he lowered his voice, as if he'd never spoken this aloud, and raised a fist—"because of this, because my father beat my mother. I don't know if I'd have seen her strength otherwise. I'd follow her to church most mornings—I'd have to set my alarm since she didn't have the heart to wake me—because I wanted to please her, to show her that someone would stand by her. But she didn't go to church for herself. She went to pray for my father, to save his soul. She saw goodness in him that I still don't fully recognize. And that's what I want, that peace, that capacity for forgiveness. It's what I work on every day. Maybe that's what all of us strive for, some kind of lasting peace."

Talking with Father Ernie pacified her, made her forget her anger for a while. She knew her calm would pass, though, so she clung to it, taking in the sided houses and the afternoon shade and the smell of the sticky catalpa leaf on her fingers. She thought she could will herself to smell Benito, but she couldn't. She couldn't even make out his face, which frightened her. She could only recall the softness of his skin and how she would lightly pinch the dumpling flesh of his arm with the back of her fingers. She'd give anything, she thought, for one last touch, that peace. Strangely, her eyes stayed dry. All she felt was a dull searing deep in her chest with each intake of air.

"Listen," he said. "Take care of Victoria. Crazy Willie and the girl in Arkansas, they can take care of themselves."

She waited for him to add Benito to the list. Benito could take care of himself, she wanted to hear. *Benito could take care of himself*. He didn't say it because it wasn't true. It couldn't be true. Even the people charged to take care of him couldn't do anything. They'd all been helpless as babies themselves.

Father Ernie stood and stretched his back, his signal to leave. "Do me a favor, will you," he said. "Tomorrow at school, sit in the front. Sister Francine, you know—" He leaned toward her. "She's getting up there in age, and you know how it goes, she must have missed you when she took attendance today. I can see how that could happen. All those uniforms in a row. Just wave to her or something, let her know you're there."

He gazed right at her, trying his best to appear earnest.

"Sure," she said. "Will do."

He squeezed her shoulder and turned. "We'll see you tomorrow at school, then. Okay?" He stepped away with a wave and turned back and said, "If I weren't a priest . . ."

"Can I ask you a question, Anthony?" Victoria asked.

She'd found him sitting on a folding chair on the back porch and joined him. Startled, he quickly palmed his rosary and jammed it in his back pocket.

"What?"

"Do you—where's Alfredo?"

"That's your big question? Where's Alfredo?"

"Well, you guys are always together, and—"

"I don't know where he is." He seemed startled still. Or angry. Even angry, he appeared kind. He'd inherited Papa's good looks, the angular cheeks and thick brows, and Mama's doleful eyes.

"Are you two fighting?"

He shook his head unconvincingly, and she understood his reluctance. Big sister might try to make things right. Though this wasn't her intention. In fact, she hadn't wanted to ask about Alfredo at all. She wanted to ask how he could still believe so strongly in God.

"Okay, forget Alfredo. Another question?"

"I don't know where Mama is either."

Victoria shook back her hair to hide a smile. She wasn't used to sarcasm from Anthony. "Forget Mama, too. I want to know . . ."

"What?" He squirmed but turned toward her. "What is it?"

She didn't care that he was fourteen, a child in many ways. More mature than many of her friends, Anthony possessed a calm resolve she'd always admired, a demeanor infused with innocence that she may have confused with wisdom. Though she wasn't embarrassed asking him about God and other such weighty matters, she didn't want him worrying about her aimless lot. And she didn't want him too aware of who he was—not yet. It was enough that he possessed goodness; he didn't need the burden of living up to that. She needed to strike the right tone.

"Do you think Benito—do you think he looks after us up there?"

A slow rocking, barely perceptible, took root in him. He shrugged. "What do you mean 'looks after us'?"

"I'm not sure what I mean."

Still rocking, he brought the front of his sneakers together, the heels apart.

"Do you think about him a lot?"

"Uh-hum." All anger was drained from him.

"Me, too." She took in a deep breath so she could go on. "And does praying help?"

"I guess."

"When you pray, do you, you know — how do you pray?"

"I just pray."

"For his soul?"

"For everyone's."

She felt small and full at the same time.

"Sometimes," she said, taking in the other porches, "I wish I was God." She let this idea settle. "And when you prayed, Anthony, for everyone's souls, I'd let you know I was listening. I'd give you a little sign. I don't think that's too much to ask for."

He leaned and rested his chin on his palm, his eyes downcast. "That would be nice," he said.

"I'd let you know somehow that sad things aren't going to last forever, that you and your family are not cursed. I'd make sure that kind words get delivered to you, to help you along."

She heard Mama's steps approaching the kitchen, so she lowered her voice, knowing their talk would be cut short, part of her relieved because she wasn't sure she could conceal her doubts about God.

"I wouldn't give anyone too much sadness," she added. "Just enough so they appreciate all the good things they have.

And I'd be forgiving, even if people didn't believe in me." She nudged him. "Do you think I'd be a good God, Anthony?"

He smiled shyly, maybe embarrassed by her blasphemy.

"Tonino," Mama called. "Alfredo."

"Coming, Ma."

He stood and reached into his back pocket. He faced Victoria and placed his rosary in her palm. "You know all those things you said, about what you would do?"

Her gaze swept from the midnight-blue beads balled in her hand to his steady brown eyes.

Without rancor or irony, he said, plainly, "I think He already does all those things, Vicki."

He didn't know how to think about it.

He hadn't expected to feel such relief, but that's what overpowered him. He was eighteen and no longer a virgin. He wanted to tell his father to sew a patch on his sleeve. *Look, Papa. I'm a man*, he could say. *From here on I'm a man.* Although he'd always seen himself as apart from the guys who hung around the steps of the school talking about nailing this broad or that babe, he felt he'd joined their ranks; he felt an odd sense of accomplishment—not for what he'd done with Sylvia Gomez but for what she'd irreversibly done for him. At the same time, he knew he wouldn't tell anyone, not until the episode had become just another story in his life, as if he were talking about another person. And when he told the story, he'd forget Sylvia's last name and bridge the gap of their ages some, maybe make it her car they rode in so that the listener—some girl, he imagined—wouldn't judge him too harshly for chasing a married woman just months after his little brother died. And he'd leave out the tears. If he told about the crying, he'd have to mention Benito and be reminded of what a prick he was for breathing and working and drifting away from the knowing that should have paralyzed him still. For weeks after the funeral he couldn't finish a piss without the cold truth buckling him. And now there were chunks of time when he'd lose himself in mindless thoughts about a car he yearned for or the feast back in June or a new method for stocking the bar or just a fall breeze. His mother and father and even his sister hadn't for a moment forgotten. He saw in the blankness of their stares what he should have felt.

He'd cried, sure. But he couldn't sustain that pure ache of memory that gripped him at first. When the pain left for good, Santo feared, so would Benito. So when the tides of grief swept through him, he welcomed the pain. He welcomed the bright images of Benito at the kitchen table spooning down a lump of mashed potatoes and smearing a handful across his ear. The brightness was always fused with the shadowy fever images, sometimes choking Santo, but he welcomed that, too.

At the bar now, he paced from one end to the other, wiping a table along the way, nodding to the two leathery-faced men playing *scopa* in the booth. Out front, a few regulars milled around chomping on toothpicks, watching traffic whiz by. The days were getting shorter and they wouldn't be out front much longer. Santo ducked in and out of the back to rinse his rag, exaggerating every movement so that Uncle Vince on his hard-backed chair just outside the screen door might be distracted from his smoking. Vince sat with legs crossed, his hands cupped on his knee, a trail of smoke curling from his fingers. When he drew the cigarette to his mouth, he pulled in quick, short drags, just enough to let out a single ring of smoke each time. He seemed absorbed and absent at the same time, clumps of ash falling to his black canvas shoes and the crease in his trousers.

Santo knew what he wanted but didn't know how to form the questions. And he needed to act quickly before his father returned. Agostino spent most of his time at the store these days, but he'd disappear without notice for stretches at a time, sometimes fifteen minutes, sometimes an hour. Hands in his pockets, he'd walk the streets. Birdwalking, Vince called it.

"*Mio Santo*. How many?" Vince called from outside.

"Two at a booth. And Carlo and a few others out front."

"When more come, you call, hey."

"I call."

Santo twisted and squeezed the rag and watched the water pool up around the drain, then swirl down, a satisfying sound. The scent of rat poison and the disinfectant meant to hide that caught in his throat. Rag in hand, he took a step toward the screen. "Did you call in the order?"

Vince turned in his chair and shook his head. He blew out a smoke ring and watched it rise. He'd get to it, his eyes said. Anyone other than Santo would have remained doubtful, and a small part of Santo always was, but his uncle came through each time, never annoyed by Santo's reminders.

"You Papá. He birdwalk, hey?"

"I guess." Santo put his face to the screen and looked out through the mesh of wire squares. "Did you catch the rat?"

"Ha." Vince leaned over the table and stubbed out his cigarette in one of the silver ashtrays Santo emptied each night. "No worry. I get," he said. As he leaned back he winced in pain and touched his hip. "Acchhhh."

Santo played with the hook on the screen, latching and un-latching it to the eyelet.

"Where does he go?" Santo asked. "When he walks, where does he go?"

Vince brushed the ash off his pants with the back of his hand. "No place," he said. "Joosta jaywalk. Ha."

"It's 'just,' not 'joost,'" Santo said.

"Che?"

"Nothing. Forget about it. I was joosta making fun."

Vince shrugged and tilted back in his chair, his hands folded behind his head. "You tell me forget, I forget."

Santo stepped outside and wiped Vince's table. "So he doesn't stop anywhere? Maybe visit someone along the way? Stop for coffee maybe? A cup of coffee?"

Vince's brow tightened, his amused grin slowly fading. His gaze swept from the rag to Santo's eyes. He straightened his back. "Coff, you say? We have coff. Every day I make coff."

"I don't know. Maybe someone else, you know, makes coffee better." Santo wanted to wink like he'd seen Eddie do, but winking didn't come naturally to him. But Vince understood.

"Mio Santo. You talk crazy. Why you talk crazy, hey?"

His hands were moving wildly now, and he broke off into Italian, damning America and the boat that brought him.

Santo sank into the chair across from his uncle, certain now that Vince knew all about the girl at the feast and the baby. The baby was a boy. Some detail about that night told him the baby was a boy, but he couldn't recall what it was. He fixed his gaze on his uncle, took in his long face and day-old whiskers. Vince knew. Santo's father and Vince had talked about the girl, at this table maybe, and she had caused shouting and table tremors. Uncle Vince wouldn't have been able to grin and shrug this away. Not this. Not then, not now.

But would Vince help him find this girl and her baby?

Santo brushed off a leaf with his rag, anticipating his uncle's myriad denials and questions. *Why you need to find?* his uncle would say. *Is no you busyness. This girl, è una putana. She make baby with someone else. Mio Santo. Santo, mio Santo. After you find, wadda you gonna do? Make one big famiglia?*

Until now, Santo hadn't thought that far ahead. He knew only this much. He had a baby brother out there, a half brother or whatever they called him, and he wanted to look in his eyes to see those wide brown orbs gazing back, the baby in some primal way sensing the tie between them. And Santo would lift the boy high with both hands to let him know he hadn't been abandoned, that his veins ran wide with Peccatori blood, that his lineage was composed of proud people who worked without complaint, who savored bread and wine and who danced and swore, who faltered and fell, too, but endured and loved without condition.

He had the other thoughts, too, of course, the thoughts that rose swiftly in a flash of white and seized his heart, hope bursting out of him. Maybe, just maybe, he'd see a part of Benito in this baby. And then he'd get another chance. He'd be a brother to this one. Maybe Papa's mistake wasn't a mistake after all. Maybe there were no mistakes. Soon enough, these surging thoughts gave way to despair, though, because he knew, he knew with a certainty that doubled him over, that this baby couldn't replace Benito, that nothing could. Even in the midst of his despair, however, or maybe because of it, Santo could never talk himself out of finding the poor kid who might otherwise grow up without a big brother. *Sweet obligation*, Santo thought. He couldn't recall where he'd heard the term, school or church probably, but the words surfaced whenever he thought about his June-feast brother. That boy out there was his sweet obligation.

"Remember that night we were looking out at the Ferris wheel? The chairs seemed to come out of the trees. You remember that?"

"Upstairs."

Santo leaned forward, his chin almost touching the white tabletop. He could still push himself away from the table, he thought, sweep up the front. The front could always use sweeping. Instead, he imagined he was Eddie Milano, with the same assured voice and the cagey eyes that wouldn't be averted. "Something strange happened that night," Santo said. "The old ladies were carrying the Madonna, collecting money the way they do, and everything was so loud, you couldn't think. I was holding my damn ears it was so loud. I turned around, I don't know why, but I turned around and behind me, down the street, this crazy old lady, an old bag . . . she wanted to—I don't know how to say it—she wanted to strangle Papa."

"You Papá?" Vince tried to look surprised and then baffled, but he had an awful time hiding what he knew, his bushy brows curling and uncurling with each new thought.

"She kept poking her finger at him. Like this. If her fingers were a gun . . . *pfff*." He reached for a cigarette from the table. "Did Papa ever mention anything about that night? What the old lady wanted, anything like that?"

"The feast, hey?"

"Yeah. Right on the sidewalk. In the middle of everything."

"Joosta you Papá and old lady, hey?"

Santo nodded. "Do you remember Papa telling you anything about that, Zio? What she wanted with him?"

"Hmm . . . old lady." He glanced at his thumbnail and then

used it as a toothpick between his two front teeth. "I no rememb."

"You no rememb, huh?"

"What. Why you laugh?"

"I don't know. You have such a good memory, that's all."

"If I no rememb, I no rememb. What I gotta do?"

"Help me."

"Help?"

"Just tell me her name."

Vince sprang from his chair and began pacing from the table to the screen door, lamenting in two languages to every saint he knew and some he didn't about the *capo tosto* young people today. They didn't know when to leave things alone. They opened everything, they had to peek inside, they had to know the secrets that were better left buried. Some matters were private and should remain private forever. But not today. Not in the year one thousand nine hundred and fifty-seven. *Televisione*, that's what ruined everything. He stopped pacing and bore down on his nephew. "Santo," he pleaded. "You tell before, old lady she crazy. No? That's all. She crazy. Now you forget, hey."

He looked like he might say more, but he turned abruptly and left.

Santo watched the screen door slap shut behind him as he disappeared to the front. His uncle wouldn't give him the chance to protest or explain or push further, and Santo didn't blame him. His uncle would wonder for the rest of the night whether Santo had seen the girl and the baby, too. But he wouldn't ask.

When the lull came at ten as it usually did, Santo crept up to Vince's apartment to retrieve the store books. Every time he gathered them he wanted to laugh, as if keeping them separate would foil some surprise investigation by the IRS. Now that he knew his uncle's elaborate accounting system, he was the only one to ever touch the books, jotting down the day's receipts in one, and inflating and deflating the figures in the others. He enjoyed every part of the process—separating and stacking the dollar bills, totaling each pile, writing the numbers in the gridded ledgers. Seeing the day's inky numbers dry on the page gave him the sense that his life was moving forward. The numbers mattered. The numbers he could control.

The figuring wouldn't begin until midnight, after the doors were locked, but tonight Santo wanted a look around. He placed the first book from Vince's pajama drawer on the kitchen table and began searching the apartment. If he heard someone coming up the stairs, he would race to the bedroom closet for the second book and claim he was getting ready for the counting. Vince was so inept at hiding things, mainly because he worried he'd forget where he hid them, that Santo felt certain he'd find something, some clue about where he could find his half brother. Thinking about him that way, as his *brother*, seemed reassuring and jarring at the same time, like trying on one of his father's tailored patterns just before he stitched the seams.

He moved quickly from room to room, stopping at the kitchen each time to listen for footsteps. The lights around the neon arrow outside the front window blinked lazily, washing the apartment in a haze of pink with each pulse. After searching both bedrooms, he'd found two clumps of dollar bills stuffed into a single sock, a handful of envelopes shoved inside a bigger envelope, a small stack of magazines featuring women partially clothed, and a box of old photographs, nothing he hadn't seen before.

He couldn't tell whether he'd been searching for five minutes or twenty-five, so he slipped back down to the store and refilled drink after drink. Two rounds later, as a trolley bus clanked past Grand Avenue, an image took hold of him. He'd been mulling over where else he could search and remembered the envelopes. He hadn't been sure what he was searching for—an address book, some personal belonging of the baby that his father had stole away—but not an envelope. This one, letter size, thrown in among the stack of correspondence from beverage distributors and utility companies, must have caused Santo to pause because in his mind's eye now he could see the brown letters emblazoned across the return: Saint Somebody Savings & Loan. His uncle didn't trust banks—*number one crook Americano*, he called them—which is why Santo had paused upstairs. Whenever they passed a bank, his uncle scoffed and talked about how money was handled in the old country. The time he bought his Cadillac, he took out a fistful of cash from his pocket. He might as well have been buying a loaf of bread.

Santo bounded up the stairs and, short of breath, stared at the envelope with the brown block letters that would lead him to his brother. He gently pushed back the seal and reached inside. A waxy yellow money-order receipt. The numbers stamped by a machine: 10,000 United States Dollars. And typed below that: Ten Thousand and Zero/Hundred Dollars. Santo's hand shook. He studied the name imprinted in the carbon. He tucked the receipt back in the bank envelope and that one into the larger envelope and whispered the name. He wanted to hear it. He wanted to remember.

4

❧

When she was nine Victoria came home talking about the bomb drills they'd practiced at
school with their desks, great big desks with
florid iron legs that would protect them from all dangers, and
Agostino couldn't find it in himself to reassure her that their
house would never be bombed. After some delay, he told her
everything would be okay, of course, but he knew his words
came too late and that each reassurance fell hollow on both
their ears. It seemed to him that the older his children got,
the more distant he got from them. He once believed that the
American education he paid for had split him apart from his
children. But now he understood the silence between them.
He couldn't stop the bombs or halt the disease or lower the
fever. He couldn't do a goddamn thing. And as his children
grew older, this revelation slowly dawned on them, too.

The moment he lay down in his bed and reached to his
wife to satisfy his cursed urges, the moment he planted his

wetness, he'd brought sure death to all his children. That was his gift to them, the one burden he could never lift. Having children, Agostino decided, was the most selfish of all acts.

These ideas had crossed his mind before in brief snatches, but now they became his obsession. In the middle of pouring a drink or counting change, he could think of nothing else. If a customer asked how he was doing, he'd fight off the twitch at the corner of his mouth by tightening his lips, creating an inward sort of smile, and spout off about Russia or Sputnik or whatever else was in the news that day. But the whole time he'd be thinking about his gift to his children.

The other thoughts, the more recent thoughts that coiled around and through him and stabbed him with their precision, he could usually keep at bay. All he had to do was organize the register or stack the tumblers at the bar, the daily rituals that he yearned for in the middle of the blue-black night. But a wayward glance from his brother was all it took to remind him he'd brought misfortune to his family. Events didn't happen in isolation. He had sinned, and sin would follow him. This became his credo, the words he would live and die by. The only consolation that wasn't really a consolation at all was that his shame was private. He had to face only his brother, whose reprimand remained unspoken but constant. Agostino had spent a lifetime ridiculing Vince's ancient way of thinking, and now Agostino had *become* his brother.

Agostino had never confessed a single deed to Angela Rosa as he'd intended. He didn't want to hurt her further. But he hated the idea that he'd gotten away with something. The gravestone he had picked out, a task he insisted on doing alone, was a constant reminder that he'd gotten away with nothing.

Walking helped. He usually took a circuitous route past the church, sometimes stopping to light a candle, and then ambled toward Chicago Avenue to the Hub movie theater and watched whatever played on the screen. Sometimes he'd walk in on a cartoon and leave a few minutes later. Or he'd catch the last few minutes of a musical or leave in the middle of a love story he knew would end tragically.

The girl in the ticket window called him Mr. Agostino and tried to point out the times the shows began. She told him what was coming next week, told him to have a nice day. Agostino nodded and thanked her but couldn't say much more. An odd feeling would pass over him then, the feeling that he missed his old self. He'd walk past her, past the candy counter and the first pungent wave of popcorn, and ease himself down into one of the front rows, bathing in the cinemascopic images flashing before him.

Over a period of three days he saw most of *The Pride and the Passion* with Frank Sinatra and Sophia Loren. Sinatra tried to pass himself off as a Spaniard by combing his hair down, but Agostino couldn't get past the hair. Listening to Sinatra's music, Agostino often felt as if he knew the singer. He felt that, other than the voice, the two of them were alike in many ways, and at times he even wondered what his crooning friend would do in one situation or another. What would Frank do? But Sinatra on the screen as a Spaniard or a dancer or a leading man did little for Agostino. He was just another actor muddling his way through lines someone else had written. The only reason he watched as much of the movie as he did was that he imagined his own hair pushed down over his forehead and imagined himself playing across from Sophia Loren, the only illusion that made him feel like his old self again.

What else could he do? When he went home to try to bridge the widening gulf between Angela Rosa and him, she shut him out. She fixed his meals and washed his clothes, but she wanted him to know that her grief was superior to his. Her grief reached depths he could never know. Agostino would have been happy to grant her this edge, if only he had had the chance.

When he walked, he thought of words he could offer to soften her. He thought of rocking her as he'd done for days after the funeral. He pictured trips they could take to faraway places where they knew no one. He imagined bringing her home to her mother, the home they could have had in the old country. After they were married, they could have stayed. The possibility had been a faint one, but it had pressed into him. Had they stayed, maybe they could have avoided all this. He would have a small shop with a lead-sturdy sewing machine bolted to the floorboards and surround himself with spools of multicolored threads. Out back would be a vegetable garden bartered from some farmer whose furrowed fields never ended. That's what he missed. Fields that went on forever.

In the city everything came up on something else, choking him. One-way streets and dead-end roads. Boulevards and avenues jammed with automobiles and their blue exhaust. Only the sky went on, and he found himself gazing upon it often. This was the same sky that held him as a boy, the same sky that Benito once glimpsed and that had dwarfed Frank Sinatra and Sophia Loren when they filmed their movie about the real Spaniards who sweated under the very same expansive patch of blue. He found himself thinking more and more in circles like this, which made his own problems seem small.

The Pride and the Passion had been held over another week, and Agostino watched the last twenty minutes and a newsreel about Elvis Presley. Walking out of the theater, he enjoyed the assault of light, the painful squint of it. He meandered back to the bar, an hour of daylight left.

Vince was on the phone with his woman friend, Carmel, but cut short his conversation when Agostino walked in. Vince seemed especially jittery lately, stumbling around as if he'd forgotten to do something, checking his pocket for lost change.

"How is the hip?" Agostino asked.

They sat at their booth and lapsed into Italian. Vince glanced down at the invoices he'd been thumbing through earlier.

"The hip?" Vince repeated. "It is always there," he said.

"The pain?"

"The hip."

"And Santo? Where is Santo?" Agostino asked.

"I told him to take the night off. There is nothing to do here."

Agostino got up and walked to the front window, peeked out, paced behind the bar to make sure they were ready for the night, then sat at the booth again. He could never sit still lately. When he sat, he felt as if someone were holding him underwater. Even in the theater he would take frequent breaks to the men's room or stand in the lobby to catch his breath. The feel of the lobby's soft carpet under his feet pacified him, a sea of wine-colored crushed velvet, the dim light hiding the syrupy black spots stamped throughout the rug.

"I talked with old man Dominick," Agostino said. "He does not want his children to have the building. They never visit, he says. Why should they get anything? So he wants to sell. He asked me."

"Do you want to stay?"

"Eh—Angela Rosa. I do not think she will ever leave."

"She stays inside still?"

"She goes to the store. That's all. She will not even sit on the porch."

"Give her time."

"Tomorrow morning, I was thinking. Maybe you can drive me to Polk Brothers. I want to buy a television."

"Agostino Peccatori with a television!"

"I thought Angela Rosa, she might watch."

"Maybe."

"Everyone has television now. I thought—"

"Well, sure. Tomorrow morning, then."

Restless, Agostino got up to flick on the lights out front. On the way back to the booth he pushed in the chairs around the tables. "And my daughter," he said. "She asks about a phone all the time. Maybe I will call tomorrow. Let them bring a phone."

"Ah, and maybe she stays home. She can watch television and talk on the phone."

"Eh. What else am I going to do? Why should I save my money? So I can grow old and have no one to give it to? Like old man Dominick?"

"And Santo? He will watch television?"

"What do you mean?"

"Nothing. I only said, maybe Santo will stay home, too. If you are going to have television, maybe he will watch. Stay home. Keep him out of trouble."

And there it was, Vince's jittery hands, the absent reach to his pockets. Mock surprise registered on his raised brows.

"Why do you talk this way?" Agostino demanded. "What do you mean?"

"Nothing," Vince said. "What do you mean what do I mean?"

"Santo is in trouble?"

Vince groped for a cigarette.

Santo was in trouble, thought Agostino. Of course. He'd sensed the uneasiness between his brother and his son for some time but hadn't really thought anything of it till now. Santo had gotten some girl in trouble. He was his father's son after all.

"Tell me," Agostino said.

Now Vince got up. He carried his ashtray to the bar and set it there, lit a cigarette, placed the ashtray back in his palm, and paced.

"Vincenzo," Agostino called. He rose from the booth and followed Vince, keeping several paces behind. "Tell me about Santo and the girl he got pregnant. There's nothing you can tell me that will . . . I am vaccinated against bad news. Answer me . . . Vincenzo. Tell me he stole a car, then. Tell me anything."

"So you are accustomed to bad news, are you?" Vince puffed furiously now, shuffling from one end of the floor to the other. "Bad news follows you, does it? Is that what you think? Well, maybe you are right." He stopped at the window and peered out at the trees that would shed their leaves soon. When he reached the end of his cigarette, he seemed suddenly calm.

"Remember Dante? Maybe this is Purgatorio," he said, still gazing out the window. "Do you ever think about that? That we are nowhere. That we are standing here, you and me, two brothers, in our own little place, but we are nowhere. We were not good enough or bad enough and now we are stuck here where we are not good enough or bad enough again. I look at everyone else and they are going somewhere. But you and I, we are stuck here. Nowhere."

"Thank you for including me in your hell," Agostino muttered.

"We are not there yet, my brother." He snubbed out what remained of his cigarette. "Santo knows," he said. "Your son knows. He knows who he is. And he will not be stuck here with us for long, I am afraid."

Agostino recalled hearing the expression *spell it out for me*— it had to be from radio or from one of his walk-in customers— and now said this to his brother, which caused Vince to laugh. Vince nodded and said he would spell it out. He told Agostino what Santo knew, slowly and evenly, without a trace of satisfaction or reprimand. He told him about Santo seeing the old woman and how he probably knew the rest, too. Santo was a smart boy. "He wanted to know the woman's name."

"My Santo," Agostino said. He held back a sigh. He reached into his pants and pulled out a pocket comb and considered running it across his hair but just fanned his thumb across the plastic teeth, listening to each plink. After a while he pushed through the swinging doors and slipped into the back to wash his hands. He leaned into the sink to hear the blast from the faucet. He dipped his face into his cupped hands and, for a moment, forgot himself in the cold hard splash.

She wanted to forget. She didn't think that was asking too much. She wanted to spread across her bed, shut her eyes to the world, and for five minutes stop the wind tunnel of thoughts that coursed through her. It wasn't that she needed to be alone. She could deal with the outside world all right. Her cold, hard stares caused everyone to cower, and they let her be, biding their time. Time would be on their side, they probably thought. Time would heal—though she couldn't begin to imagine this. No, all the mindless worldly concerns didn't concern her one way or another. It was the internal that plagued her night and day. When she closed her eyes she felt a slow, rootless spinning. The physicality of this would eventually become grounded in the flow of her blood or whatever it was that stopped the turning, but her thoughts still floated above her in treadmill persistence.

Benito stared out at her through flat, brown eyes, appearing always composed, his dark hair patted down in long, perfect swipes. Sometimes his little mouth would move, and she wanted to reach out to him and lift him, pull him away from all the hurt. She felt a power wash over her then, a power she hadn't felt since she was a girl, back when she believed with all her girl might that she could shape the world through her own pure wishing, that she could right any wrong. Now when she felt that power in her jangled bones, she clutched at it with a desperation that surprised her. Angela Rosa could rescue her son finally with pure will.

More often, though, she simply replayed the awful last day. She felt her son's cheek, warm against her own, the soft brush of it. She remembered his fingers running through her hair, the milky smell of his pink arms. She worked and worked to resist the other images, Benito fighting for air, coughing up blood, but those images always sucked her in, sinister and seductive in their pull. The apartment had been filled that last night with the deep breathing of sleep. Only she and Benito remained awake, an eerie, peaceful pall blanketing them. She was glad that everyone could slip away into their dreams for a while. They rested, assured they would rise in the morning to a better day, and this eased Angela Rosa's worries some.

She paced the long halls of the apartment with Benito in her arms. Every few minutes she tried to feed him and even offered her breast, which would no longer yield nourishment. She tried anything to break the cycle of the last twenty-four hours. A song returned to her, something her mother once sang. The words held no meaning for her, but she heard her mother's sweet pitch in her own voice. She rocked Benito, changed him, laid him in his crib, picked him up, pointed to lights outside the living-room window. Superior Street, she whispered. This was their life. Benito responded with the same plangent stare, the tugging at the ear, the pouting of the lips, dry and cracked. He brought his tiny fists to his eyes and rubbed them raw. His skin looked paper-thin, translucent pink.

Over and over she gave herself five more minutes. If Benito didn't drink something in five minutes she would wake Victoria and have her phone the doctor at his home above the office. Victoria would have to walk to the corner, though—she couldn't wake old man Dominick at this hour. Angela Rosa pictured the walk—two blocks down Superior to Ashland, cross the street to the phone booth, deposit the dime, wait for it to drop, listen for the dial tone and the ringing, the endless ringing, and demand help. Would Victoria be able to convince him to come? She was too American. To her family she could snarl for no good reason, but she became a lamb to everyone else. The doctor would simply give Victoria instructions and promise to visit in the morning.

So Angela Rosa waited. Sitting on the living-room carpet, bracing herself against the couch, she waited. Five more minutes. Then five more. She let Victoria sleep. She let them all dream. Until the coughing. A hacklike cough that wouldn't let go. She patted him on the back, lightly at first, then with a resounding slap. He coughed harder still, one racking cough after another, his little face inflamed. Wheezing finally, he caught his breath and heaved a sigh. And that's when she spotted it. A single drop of blood on his right shoulder where the sleeve began. Her baby was coughing up blood.

She couldn't recall the words she uttered then, but something hoarse erupted from her throat, a wail, a plea for help maybe. She needed to see. She needed more light. For a full second or more she had to think where the light switch was. She flicked it on finally, and the bare bulb washed the room in pale amber light. She gently pushed the end of a bath towel into Benito's mouth and the towel came out matted red. Again she screamed.

Victoria padded out first. When she saw the panic in her mother's eyes, she turned pale. She nearly buckled over when she saw the towel. Did he fall? she asked. Did the baby fall? She searched for signs of a cut, feverishly examining her brother's head, his arms.

Angela Rosa couldn't respond. She let out another wail. A light went on in the kitchen. Where is the doctor's number? Victoria wanted to know. Where is the number? Angela Rosa pointed to the kitchen, and Victoria raced off. I'll go downstairs, she said. I'll go downstairs and call right away.

Agostino stumbled in, his eyes swollen with sleep. He scratched at the back of his neck and stood there looking puzzled.

"Auito," she said. Help me.

Agostino took Benito in his arms. What is this blood? he asked, suddenly alert.

"Auito," she pleaded, sobbing now.

"Angela Rosa!"

"O mio Dio," she muttered over and over. *"Gesù Cristo."*

The blood, Agostino demanded. Where did it come from?

She couldn't move. She wanted to show her husband the blood, but her arms wouldn't move. *"Mio Dio."*

Santo suddenly appeared, then Anthony and Alfredo, all of them rooted at the far end of the room, waiting for permission to move.

I have to show him, Angela Rosa kept thinking. *I have to show him the blood*. She folded the towel in on itself and pushed a clean portion into Benito's mouth. The stench of blood filled her with new dread, but the towel came out less bloody this time.

There, she said. My baby's bleeding.

Agostino felt his son's forehead. He's not burning up like before, he said. He pried open Benito's small mouth and searched inside and shook his head. He glanced up at his sons, and Angela Rosa saw the question in all their eyes. *What do we do?* She knew they looked to her to nurse them. But this time she was immobile.

Victoria marched in and announced that the doctor would be there in fifteen minutes. She took Benito from her father and wiped Benito's face with a cool wet rag she'd brought with her. She dabbed his mouth, talking to him, telling him that everything would be all right. She put him over her shoulder and patted his back while she paced, gently rocking him with each step. Tears began to well up in her eyes. Your sister's here, she whispered. Victoria will take care of you.

Angela Rosa crawled to the window and looked for a car. She prayed silently but hung her hopes on the Tuscan doctor who smelled of stale chestnuts and spoke in reassuring tones. He'd glide through the door and in one fluid motion he'd loom over Benito, checking his eyes and his ears, pulling out his silver instruments one by one from his black bag.

Thank God for Victoria, she thought. She needed a few moments to gather herself. She had never felt so crippled. Her daughter's whispers covered her like a thick quilt.

Nobody said a word then, each of them alone in their thoughts. They gazed at the fibers in the rust-colored carpet, studied the chips in the enamel at the baseboard, glancing up at Benito now and then, hoping he would remain calm. His head snug against his sister's shoulder, Benito closed his eyes and breathed evenly.

Angela Rosa prayed to her old neighbor Louise. In death, Louise had become her guardian, a palpable force in Angela Rosa's private life. Her placid smile would press itself into Angela Rosa's thoughts throughout the day. She asked Louise now to ask God to take *her* instead. This would be the only way the world would make sense. If God took her son, He would be taking her as well. There was no reason for both of them to die.

In the midst of her praying, a glimmer of hope began to rise in her. She thought suddenly of cupping her breast to Benito's lips and could almost feel his warm mouth pulsating, greedily sucking in her milk. She thought of his brown eyes peering over the top of a bottle as he swallowed and swallowed, one satisfying gulp after another. She hadn't tried hard enough. That was all. She would force-feed him. Whatever it took. She was his mother. He would eat for his mother. *When you eat, you never die*, her father used to tell her. Those words had always kept her safe.

The towel. The towel had been less bloody the second time. The hard cough had caused the blood. Nothing else. Something had ruptured while he coughed. But the coughing had stopped now and the healing had already begun. Children were resilient. If mothers paralyzed themselves with worry over every ailment— The doctor should have arrived by now. She leaned into the window well and touched the screen with the ends of her fingers. If she pushed hard enough the wooden-framed screen would fall to the bushes below. She couldn't count the number of times Anthony and Alfredo had pushed out the screen as they jockeyed for a better view of the street. A lifetime ago. She'd have to scold them each time. You'll fall out, she told them. You'll fall.

Distant street noises filtered in through the window. Middle-of-the-night noises. The beginning of birdsong. A bus clanking along somewhere. Where did people go at three in the morning?

Angela Rosa pushed herself up and marched to the kitchen for a bottle, warming it in a pot of water. Something like ela-tion filled her. Everything would be all right, she kept repeat-ing, thinking of feeding her son. She tilted the bottle and let a drop fall to her wrist and licked it clean. The doctor would arrive in minutes, and when he saw Benito sucking at his bot-tle, he'd wonder why he was called in the middle of the night. Crazy woman, he'd think. She didn't care. He could think what he pleased.

She marched back to the living room and found Victoria sobbing. A torrent of shrill, muffled cries shook out from her. She clutched onto Benito, her body heaving with each sigh.

Angela Rosa gently pried her baby from her daughter's arms and placed him over her shoulder. The bottle fell and rolled to the crease between two cushions. Victoria picked up the bottle and, with both hands, brought it to her own cheek, sobbing uncontrollably now, curling into herself.

Angela Rosa turned away. She held tightly to her son and walked the length of the apartment, an audible ache rumbling from her chest. She strained to feel the warmth of her baby's breath on her neck, she strained to feel his breath, but felt only her own arms go cold and a trembling in her legs. She thought she might collapse. If she could breathe she would wail. She would wail until the entire block awoke. But no, not yet. She wouldn't allow that quite yet. She held on. Hoping now that the firm taps on the door would never come.

What could he possibly say to his son? What lessons could he impart? Sew your dick to your pants? That was something. A lesson Agostino himself had never heeded. Not until it was well past too late. Besides, why should Santo listen to him now? Here he was approaching fifty, still groundless, still making seventeen-year-old blunders. At seventeen, Agostino thought, a young man had the energy to correct his mistakes. A young man had the advantage of inexperience. He could call himself a stupid, reckless prick. At one time Agostino had even taken a measure of pride in acting recklessly. But a reckless middle-aged man was pathetic.

If he only knew why Santo needed to dig into his private affairs, then he might know what to say to his son. He could probably make up a story about the old woman at the feast and hope Santo wouldn't ask about the rest. If Santo persisted, well . . . *Her name is unimportant, my son. What's important is she came to me. She was needy. And I have weakness. What I did was foolish, but the old woman's claims of blood ties . . . the old woman is even more foolish.*

Agostino recalled the first time he suspected his own father of straying. He was about Santo's age and couldn't imagine his father being intimate even with his mother, let alone another woman. While sitting in Capallano's tailor shop one day, Agostino spotted his father stepping out from Elena's bakery without so much as a loaf of bread in his hands. His father glanced up and down the cobblestoned street and gave his shirt one last tuck before stepping from the entryway. Son of a bitch, Agostino thought. What stuck with Agostino was his father's skittish gaze, his dark face that otherwise rarely revealed any emotion.

She came to me, Santo. Do you understand? How many other men did she go to? Son of a bitch, she came to me. Santo wouldn't listen. Maybe he simply wanted to meet the bastard boy. Little Benito was gone, and Santo wanted to embrace this boy who could or could not be his brother. Agostino had considered seeking out the boy himself. How could he not? There were moments when he shut his eyes and tried to recall the boy in the stroller at the feast, but no images came to him. Which was just as well. If he had a clear picture of the boy's thick hair or round Peccatori face, he probably couldn't keep himself away as he intended. The boy would be just as much a child of his as the others. Agostino worked instead on convincing himself that the boy was not his. Another child out there was an unthinkable burden.

Just after one o'clock on a Wednesday afternoon,

Agostino decided he wanted to touch his wife. They had gone too long, barely brushing up against each other as they passed in the apartment's narrow spaces. When he brought home the television last week, he had squeezed her shoulder as she sat dazed in front of the shadowy images flickering on the screen. With his thumb and finger he lightly massaged the soft curves at the back of her neck. But that was all. She hadn't taken his hand and pressed it into her shoulder as she could have. She hadn't turned or leaned into him. She just sat there at the end of the couch, her back straight, her hands folded in her lap as if she were waiting for the bus. And now Agostino ached for more.

He found her sitting on their bed, folding laundry, the volume on the radio turned low to a station that played instrumental versions of popular tunes. Supermarket music, Agostino called it. Never Sinatra. As he moved toward her, he longed to hear her mock reprimand—*Did the store burn down? What's wrong with you? Get to work*. When she saw him, she glanced up and offered a trace of a smile and went on with her folding. She wore one of her black blouses and the dark wool skirt he'd made for her years ago. She'd lost weight and the skirt was a sheet on her.

"Where is everyone?" he asked, knowing this was a foolish question.

She gave him a tired look. "School. They are all at school."

"Of course. School," Agostino muttered.

"And Santo?" she said.

"He's working. Santo's . . . He's a good boy." Agostino eyed the basket at Angela Rosa's feet. "What can I do?" he said.

"I don't know."

He moved to the window and peered down to the alley.

The garbage men had been by, and all the trash-can lids were strewn along the ground. "I need to help you," he said. His voice sounded thin against the glass.

"You need?"

"Yes, I need."

She tossed a pair of his socks toward the dresser. "And I am the one who will help you, then?"

"Don't turn my words around. We are both alone in this house."

She stopped and glanced out the doorway. "This apartment is too big," she said, more to herself than to Agostino. "Maybe we should rent a small house."

"You want to move?"

She let out a deep sigh. "I do not know what I want."

He eased down next to her on the bed and touched her shoulder, as if to balance himself, then pulled back his hand. "Maybe," he said, "we will buy the building from old man Dominick. He wants to sell."

"I can't think about that. I can't think."

He put his hand on the bed, close to her, close enough to feel her warmth. The corner of her eye began to redden and a slow tear fell down the side of her face. She hadn't let him see her cry in some time. "I should have never stopped," she said.

"Stopped?"

"I should have never stopped feeding him. If we had been back home in . . . I would have never stopped with my milk."

Agostino felt an odd mix of relief and remorse. She didn't blame *him*. She didn't see *him* as the source of their pain. But they would remain apart. That much was clear. There would be no touching. She brushed away the tear with the inside of her wrist. If they had been back home, in their own country—

that's what she had wanted to say—none of this would have happened.

"It was no one's fault," he said, hoping to convince himself. "We could not have known."

A long silence engulfed them. He took his hand from the bed and rubbed his forehead, resigning himself to not touching her. She didn't want to be touched. She continued to fold. She folded with an efficiency that frightened him. He could see that there would be no more tears either.

"I keep dreaming," she said.

Agostino glanced at her, then turned his gaze back to his hands. What she said, the way she said it, reminded him of confession. He wasn't sure he wanted to hear.

"It is always nighttime in the dream. The lights from the automobiles are going by. And Benito, he is sitting in the middle of the dirty street. Hungry. But he does not cry. He just wants to eat. And I cannot reach him." She told him how her legs wouldn't move, how she saw him then in his crib, the bars like steaming radiators, the steam burning her eyes. And still she couldn't reach him to feed him. Her own baby.

She looked out the window. "If I had never stopped . . . I can't stop thinking. And now the women around here, they avoid me. Their tongues become like cardboard around me. They think I bring trouble. Well, I know what to say to them. Go to hell. That's what I say to them. I do not need them."

Agostino marked her rage as a good sign. *Continue to rant*, he thought. *Keep breathing fire*. Though rage had always been more or less foreign to Agostino, he understood its usefulness. He saw its power in his wife and in his daughter, and he would welcome it now in his own life. Even as a boy, Agostino would retreat during scuffles, just enough to defuse any attack—one step back and a quarter turn away, slightly out of reach, harmless. With each passing year he became more and more deft at sidetracking whatever anger sprang up in him. He'd been stepping back his entire life.

He stood up and moved to the window again. He decided to stoke Angela Rosa's rage. Anything to drive her out of her stupor. "Maybe you and Lupa should take a trip. Go home for a while. Visit your mother."

She snapped one of Santo's shirts and folded it in two sharp tucks. "Go to work. You can talk foolishness with your brother. You and he can talk foolishness all day."

"A short trip. That's all."

"I cannot take a vacation from my dreams. Do you think—"

"No, but—"

"It is the idea of a . . . a buffoon idea." She pointed to the jumble of unfolded laundry. "And who will do this? A maid will come when I am gone?"

"Victoria can—"

"Ha!"

"Victoria would do it."

Her hands moved nimbly, tucking and folding. She wouldn't look at him. "And the money?"

"The money will always—"

"You buy television, you order a telephone. You want to buy from Dominick. Buy buy buy. I don't—" Her voice broke. Her hands collapsed to her lap. She had to breathe through her mouth. "I want my son."

The dull burn began in his throat and radiated through his chest. He'd felt dead for so long that he welcomed the heat that brimmed his eyes. *I want my son.* He thought his wounds had begun to heal, but he had only covered them over. He wanted

Angela Rosa to see him cry. He wanted her to embrace him, to cradle his head. He wanted to fall into her and sob.

But the hot tears were slow in coming. He stood by the window and didn't make a sound. *Look at me, Angela Rosa. I feel. I hurt.* When she stood up and set the basket on her hip, he reluctantly choked back all that had welled up in him. *Maybe another time. There would be another time to show her his pain. Another day.*

She slipped out the door. *Another day*, he told himself. After a while, he heard the muffled sound of dresser drawers opening and closing. The sound seemed unusually distant, reaching him in thin screeches. And that's when he stumbled to the bed, collapsing in a heap, letting the tears come now. His hand brushed against a rosary beneath the cold pillow, and he swept it to the floor. What had always served him well—living only in the moment—mocked him. He didn't know what to do with *now*, how to get through it.

He listened to Angela Rosa's footsteps. Each bedroom had its own pattern of creaks, and he knew exactly where she was treading. He followed the creaks from dresser to closet to window, where she pulled down a paper shade. He recalled more peaceful times, lying there with his face in the pillow, listening to her familiar stride. He could always tell when she had the baby in her arms. Her steps would be lighter, more deliberate. Late mornings, she would sometimes bring Benito to him, deposit him on Agostino's chest, and the two of them, father and son, would lie there together until the smells of breakfast billowed toward them. Then he'd take Benito's fingers one by one and pretend to eat them. He recalled this now with such clarity that he could taste the milky sweetness of those fingers and hear his son's gurgling laugh. That laugh would fill both of them. Benito's brown eyes would hold him. Just before Angela Rosa called them to the table, Agostino would gaze at whatever light poured in through the window and listen to his son's shallow breaths, taking inventory of his life, always struck by his good fortune. A father and his son getting ready for the day.

He heard Angela Rosa slip out the kitchen now, the screen door slapping shut behind her. She'd be back with a fresh load of laundry, her steps plodding and heavy. It was hard not to feel pity for himself, for Angela Rosa, too, and he let that wash over him for a while.

He recalled the newspaper Vince had left out for him that morning. People building bomb shelters in their cellars, stocking them with cans and dry goods and jugs of water. All you had to do was hide under a school desk, he had told Vince, and they laughed. *If this were a real emergency.* But there was nowhere to go, nothing a man could do, no one to tell him how to walk through his own house.

June 23, 1977

ANTHONY PECCATORI

❦

Freddy calls me the almost priest. I like that.

This is what he does as he says it. With his right hand he slashes a slow cross before his eyes in solemn benediction and shifts his gaze just beyond me, adopting an air of ceremonial awe that doesn't suit him well. Those hands are better suited for lifting and moving than blessing, though the lifting and moving possess their own grace and substance. Anyone can see we're not close anymore, but when he calls me that, we're twelve again, back when we could say anything to each other across the flinty darkness between our beds.

It was twenty years ago to the day. That's what I tried to tell him at the cemetery. But I'm sure he didn't hear. After Benito passed on, Freddy was the baby for a while, and the loss may have hit him hardest. He was the solid, stocky brother, broad like Mama, with two feet on bedrock. Any kind of abstractions bored him, and he didn't know what to do with Benito's death. Half the time he walked up and down the apartment looking like he wanted to throw something, and sometimes I wished he would.

One time he caught me praying the rosary on the back porch and started calling me Saint Anthony after that. I didn't mind. It was the closest I'd ever felt to a calling. Sometimes he'd pass me and offer up a mock prayer. *Lord, let my brother, Saint Anthony, help me find my little cobra-eyed marble that I don't know where the hell it could of gone except maybe in the bottom of his drawer where he keeps all the other stuff he steals from me.* I usually chased and tackled him, pretending to be angry, labeling him on the shoulder a few times to sting him. After a while, though, when I started spending more and more time looking past him, distracted, wanting to be alone, he became genuinely annoyed. I didn't mean to get under his skin and I wasn't fully aware at the time that I was acting any differently. I needed to pray. That was all. To be by myself and pray.

It seemed at the time that I was the only one to sense Benito's presence in the apartment. If he had died somewhere else, in the car on the way to the hospital or at the hospital or anywhere other than the apartment, maybe that would have changed things. But he was in Mama's arms. She cradled him, carried him from room to room. For weeks afterward, death filled that apartment like a scream. I'd sit on the living-room floor and sweep my hand along a spot on the carpet where Benito had lain that last night. I tried to picture the slight indentation his head would have made and imagined how that spot must have felt warm to the touch, and for just a moment or two, my fingers felt a quiver of heat. I sought all the other places he touched, and those places shimmered.

For months the door to his room remained half-open, but I was the only one to pause before the doorway and peek in at the empty crib. Everyone else quickened their pace and averted their gaze, as if Benito never was. So I prayed. I asked God to keep me poised for other signs of my brother's presence, increasingly embarrassed by the shrine my father was erecting in Benito's room. I wouldn't interfere with Papa's obsession with some starlet—perhaps this provided solace, I reasoned—but I wouldn't stop praying either. Then He sent us Nicholas.

I couldn't stop feeling guilty at first, thinking that Nicholas was a replacement. God's give-and-take. Which seemed silly even then, but there seemed to be something right about the idea. Nicholas was sent to save us. That's how it felt sometimes. That Nicholas was no ordinary baby.

For starters, he was the only Peccatori child to be born in Italy. Papa had urged Mama for months to take a trip back. Stay a month, two months. And that's what she did. She stayed three, maybe more. No one bothered to tell me that Mama was pregnant when she left. Maybe no one knew. But I remember the flurry of phone calls between Papa and her. They had to decide whether he should go back or she should come home. She didn't want to fly while she was pregnant, she insisted, so she stayed. She wanted plenty of bed rest. She wanted to do everything she could to ensure a safe birth. And she was in good hands. Everyone else should stay put. There was no need to disrupt everyone's life. She'd have the baby and bring it home as soon as arrangements could be made.

She had Lupa to watch over her. And they had dragged Victoria with them as well. They wanted to uproot her. They didn't like the changes they'd seen in her, smoking right in front of them, arriving home at all hours of the night. They would drag her back to dirt roads and sheds for toilets and make her tend to the fields and prepare dinners and knock out all that American nonsense that filled her head.

Uncle Vince and I picked them up at the airport. I sat at the arrival gate fingering the rosary in my pocket. I felt like one of the old churchwomen. Vince paced before me puffing away at his cigarette. I imagined holy incense curling out of the caked ash at the tip. Walking through the jetway soon would be Mama, Lupa, Victoria, and the answer to my prayers. A living, breathing package.

They stepped out of the tunnel, one after the other, looking weary-eyed and heavy, their bodies weighed down by eight hours of jet stream and months of sharing the same small space. Aunt Lupa held the baby to her chest, shielding his eyes from the bright lights. Mama smiled and pulled on my face. I couldn't recall the last time I'd seen her smile and touch me like that. Victoria's eyes were swollen, and she looked sleepy and startled at the same time. She gave me a quick hug, then barely looked at me.

I pushed past Uncle Vince and tugged on Lupa's arms so that she'd release her grip some. I think I may have held my breath. But the moment I laid eyes on him, my new brother, I felt betrayed. I had envisioned a replica of Benito, and until that moment, hadn't been fully aware of the impossible expectations I'd set up in my head. He had the same sad mouth and wary eyes, like Mama's, but his skin was lighter than Benito's. I could tell even then that his nose was too straight, nothing at all like Benito's. My face grew hot with shame, but no one seemed to notice. They were already clutching shoulder bags and pushing their way toward the stream of concourse traffic. They didn't want to be singled out and delayed at customs.

They wanted a fresh start. They were eager to show Nicholas his new home.

So I followed, the proud big brother trailing behind, listening to the clicks of their heels. Nicholas began to cry, and Aunt Lupa pulled a bottle from a zippered pocket in her flight bag and fed him as she walked. I'd never seen a baby sucking so ravenously. A few gates down, as she was about to shift him to her shoulder for a burp, Aunt Lupa glanced back at me, to check whether I was still behind them, it seemed. But there was something else I read in that look. An iron sternness. A resolute calm that made me feel small. She wanted to make it clear that things would be different now, that this baby would be in able hands.

5

For weeks Santo did his own birdwalking—down Grand past Ashland up Hubbard—slowing down near a dirt lot across from 1515 West where he hoped to catch a glimpse of the stroller. There were twenty-seven Paolones in the phone book but only two within walking distance, and he was able to rule out the other almost immediately—an old man with two poodles and a German shepherd. The dirt lot was a twenty-minute walk from Mio Fratello, so he brought along a Clincher softball to bounce on the sidewalk along the way. At the lot he hoped to find a pickup game so he could mill around and watch the house at the same time. Twice he saw a few kids playing 500 with a dusty softball, but otherwise the field remained deserted.

He'd been tempted to ask Eddie Milano to ask his cop cousin about the Paolone house on Hubbard, but he was never sure when to trust Eddie, who had a complex code of loyalty that Santo could never understand. Sometimes an offhand comment by Pooch about Eddie's mother would turn him cold. A few minutes later, Eddie would be cursing his mom himself.

The house on Hubbard had a picture window with avocado-green curtains roped off toward the middle with thick braided cords. From across the street Santo could see the table lamp that filled the small space behind the window, its watery pink porcelain base with glass chandelier knives encircling the bulb. He couldn't see the table, but he imagined a mahogany tabletop with precise beveled edges and a lace doily tucked beneath the lamp. Atop the front entrance of the house hung a new awning, a yellow-lime piece of ridged plastic that made the house an eyesore amid all the other weather-beaten bungalows. He wondered whether his father's and uncle's $10,000 helped pay for the lamp and awning.

Santo had abandoned the idea of being big brother to this baby. What could he possibly say to the boy when the questions began? Santo would be content to meet the boy and whisper a few words to him, transmit the entire Peccatori history with the gravity of his voice and the lightness of his touch. He might simply tell the boy that Benito would watch over him. Santo needed to tell him that much. He needed to believe that Benito's brief stay on this planet had served some purpose.

One Wednesday morning in late October he finally saw someone emerge from the side entrance. An old woman wearing a gray fall jacket and a silky babushka. She rushed down the sidewalk with her head down, a cloth grocery bag hanging from the crook of her arm. He followed her for a few blocks, trying to imagine her poking a finger into his father's chest, but he couldn't be sure.

The next day he saw the girl. He hadn't really looked at her that night at the feast, but he remembered her deliberate stride, the way she gripped the handle on the buggy. She bent over the buggy and bundled up the baby inside, then wrapped a tan scarf around her head. She walked briskly, glancing down at the infant, oblivious to everything else.

Santo followed on the other side of the street, allowing himself to get within a few hundred feet. He'd settle for a glimpse now. He would cross the street and lengthen his stride, and as he came up on her, there would be a brief exchange of smiles, a few words, two people on the street admiring a baby, and ultimately she would feel compelled to slow down and show him and maybe even let Santo hold the baby. And that would be the end of it. One day he'd tell Uncle Vince about the exchange, provide just enough details to hook him, and before long Vince would tell Santo the story of the $10,000, how Vince had been forced to do business with the crooks at the bank.

Just a glimpse, he had to keep telling himself. Otherwise, he would have turned back. He crossed over finally and moved nearer, and when he got to within a few feet he felt emboldened by the sweet scent of baby oils. Benito's scent rising from this other infant. His tiny half brother. For a moment he imagined that Benito himself lay in the cradle of the buggy, that his death had been all a mistake.

The girl slowed and finally stopped to speak to the baby. Santo could have passed her had he kept moving, but he stopped and tried to peer around the girl's long wool coat, hoping not to startle her.

She turned and spotted him. Two sidewalk squares behind her, he remained frozen, not a single graceful escape open to him. He glanced at the flats of her shoes and scratched his head, no words coming to him. He thought he might turn and run.

"I didn't mean to—" he said. "I thought you were some-one."

She nodded, showed a trace of a wary smile, and walked away.

Wait, he wanted to scream. *I'm not what you think.* But she kept walking, faster than before, glancing over her shoulder. She had no way of knowing that the three of them were bound together in some odd familial way. *Wait, wait. Your baby is my brother.* And what did that make her, this woman child with the ample cheeks and fair skin?

Just a glimpse. And then she could think what she wanted. She could tell her family about the pervert she met just outside her house. She could tell them he chased her, any damn thing she pleased, as long as she allowed a brief glance and didn't holler for the police. He'd been thinking about this moment for so long, confiding in no one, play-ing out what he'd say to this child, and now it was falling apart. He'd never factored in the girl, never pictured her. His dream image contained only himself and this child, two Peccatoris huddled together against the outstretched fingers of the world.

He began to follow her again, hoping she'd turn onto Ashland and slip into a storefront where he could bump into her again, and they'd laugh about the awkwardness on the sidewalk. She did turn, and he lost sight of her for a while, and when he got to Ashland she was gone. There was an apartment, the gangway to the apartment, a shoe repair, and a currency exchange all near the corner. He peered into each of these places as he passed, but there was no trace of her. He made his way back to the corner, and when he reached the apartment, he saw her emerge from the gangway. Her shoulders slumped when she saw him.

She stopped and glared at him, her grip tight on the handle of the buggy. Santo looked toward the baby. "I'll scream," she said.

"No no no, do I look . . . no." He sounded like Anthony or Freddy with their high-pitched squeals. "I'm not that or anything like that. Oh, brother. My name is Santo and—"

And what? I want to hold your baby?

She angled the buggy toward the corner as if she were bracing herself to run, but she didn't move.

"I didn't mean to scare you. Really, I didn't."

"What do you want?" Her voice was scratchy and hoarse.

"I just wanted to apologize for startling you before. I didn't want you to think . . ."

"I won't. I won't think. And now I have to go."

She waited. She wanted his assent, his assurance that he wouldn't follow her. She rocked on the balls of her feet, readjusted her grip on the handle of the buggy. Just a nod from him and she'd be gone. In a moment he'd never see her again.

"Let me ask you one question."

She shifted her weight and stared at the sidewalk. She would let him ask his question.

"Do you know Agostino Peccatori?"

She looked at him then, studied his face, disbelief giving way to worry.

"I'm his son."

She turned away from him and covered her mouth with trembling fingers. Santo could see what had drawn his father to this woman. The pear-shaped face, a soft rustic look to it, the kind of placid face that filled old photo albums. The long dark lashes that might have ordinarily disguised her worry and offered refuge, but not here. Her gaze shifted slowly, never landing upon anything higher than the sidewalk. There was no darting about the eyes typical of the girls Santo knew.

Santo inched a step closer. "I'm his son," he said again.

She drew in a deep breath to settle herself. There was something crooked now in her expression, a tilted mouth, a narrowing of one eye.

"I didn't mean to upset you," he said. "I just wanted to meet you."

They stood there for a while in silence. Light traffic streamed by on Ashland. He'd give her time to take in what he'd told her.

"Four months ago . . . my baby brother, Benito . . . he passed on."

She clutched the frayed end of her scarf. "My God," she said. "I can't imagine—" She began to reach out, as if to touch his arm, but held back.

Santo hadn't muttered his brother's name aloud since his death and felt his throat constrict and a hammering in his chest. But talking about Benito made his brother's death seem ordinary, too, another physical event, Santo's thin voice unable to match the resonance of his thoughts. "He was almost two, always smiling. He'd go to anyone. He had these short, chubby legs." He let himself picture Benito clomping around the apartment, barely sidestepping chairs and other obstacles in his path. "When you picked him up he never tried to wiggle out of your arms. Not that anyone could hold him for long, the big—"

He didn't care anymore whether she was listening. He was talking now for himself. And he couldn't stop. He told her about the last night and the funeral, how the whole neighborhood filled Mio Fratello. All the while the girl rocked her baby, pushing and pulling the buggy in short tugs.

"I'm not sure why I'm telling you all this," he told her, hoping that the child in the buggy was taking in his voice, the only Peccatori voice he would ever hear. "I'm not sure . . ."

But he was sure. Uncle Vince always complained there was no history in America. But he was wrong. This was Santo's history. Right here on the sidewalk. And he wouldn't let that pass. He told her about his other brothers and sister, wanting her to assemble the pieces into a brilliant kaleidoscope, to discover how all their lives intersected. She couldn't fully understand her baby's place in the world otherwise. This child had to know his past.

"Thanks for not running away," he said. His eyes followed the path of a trolley bus heading southbound. "I didn't mean to, you know . . ."

She turned to him. "What has your father told you?" Her eyes had softened, but the muscles around her jaw remained rigid. Santo had seen the same defiance in his sister.

"My father didn't tell me anything."

"Then how—"

"I don't even know your name." *Only Paolone*, he thought. "My father doesn't know I'm here. He doesn't know anything."

Her eyes downcast, she muttered, "Ella . . . it's short for Gabriella." She looked at him again, her eyes brown pools, and Santo saw regret there. She walked around to the front of the buggy, reached inside, and pulled her baby to her chest.

She turned the child around to face Santo. "This is Joseph," she said.

"My God." Santo sighed. He pushed his finger into the child's tiny fist. "He's beautiful. He looks just like you." And nothing like a Peccatori. He tugged on the boy's doughy arm and imagined he'd feel an onslaught of joy upon touching this child, but more than anything he felt bewilderment. Here was a brother of his who had none of Angela Rosa in him, who would never have a brother or sister of the same flesh.

"Can I hold him?"

She leaned into Santo and allowed the boy to slip from the cradle of her embrace into his waiting arms.

Santo let him settle there, whispering to him in Italian broken phrases from the few words he knew. *Caro bambino. Giuseppe piccolo. Dio benedetto.* The baby's big eyes locked on Santo for a long while before he began searching for his mother.

"How old is he?"

"Twenty-four weeks."

Santo quickly calculated. Joseph had been only a week or two old at the feast. His father may have first learned of the baby that very night. And this Ella. She had to chase down her mother to stop her from strangling Agostino. But why then? Why that night? Ella must have just told her. Santo imagined the exchange between them, her mother's persistence. *Who is this strange man?* her mother probably screamed. *The baby needs a father, for Christ's sake.* Her mother's persistence had worn down her resolve, and after returning from the hospital, Ella must have caved in finally to unburden herself of her shame. Ella had been mistaken, though. Her mother would not sit quietly with this information. She would either destroy

Agostino or use the information for her own gain. And Ella's shame festered when she realized her mother's intent.

All this occurred to Santo in a matter of an instant. And he could see in Ella's eyes something passing there as well, a flash of insight maybe into who they were, Santo and Ella.

"How did you find me?" she asked.

His first impulse was to lie, to create an elaborate story about chance meetings and shared destinies.

"I saw the check," he said, without thinking.

"The check?"

He searched her eyes for signs of coyness or teasing, and when he saw none he felt something drop in his chest. Santo knew then that Gabriella Paolone was her mother's daughter. Whatever defiance she harbored never surfaced around the old woman. And this bastard child only enhanced her submission, gave Ella's mother reason to tighten her steely, old-world grip. *Look what happens to these girls in America.*

Joseph began to grunt and squirm, and Santo was glad for the distraction. He held the child out toward his mother and wanted nothing more than to bolt back to Mio Fratello, where Uncle Vince would be hobbling around the bar, cussing every technological breakthrough of the twentieth century. At times like this, Santo took great comfort in his uncle's slant on the world.

"You said you saw the check. What check?"

"I don't know anything about the check," he said.

She placed Joseph in the buggy, as if to shield him from whatever was about to erupt in her. She turned to Santo.

"Tell me about the check, Santoro."

"Santo."

She shot him an impatient look, and Santo cowered. He

tucked his hands in his back pockets and hoped she'd take pity on his sorry self.

"I really don't know anything about the check," he said.

But after what his father had done, he felt he had no other choice. A simple bank draft wasn't going to erase all obligation to this girl. He owed her an answer. He told her about the receipt he'd found one night among Vince's papers. He told her the name on the check. And the amount stamped on the pink sheet. He hoped that would be enough. He didn't want to tell her he'd seen her before, that smoky June night almost dreamlike in his memory now, those images rising up before him when he prayed from his pew on Sundays.

She began to sob, tranquil sobs that sealed her off from him. Some time between the moment Joseph was discovered and the moment Agostino was identified as the father, Ella had become a commodity in her mother's eyes. No reassurances from Santo were going to soften that.

"I have to leave," she said. Her voice was thick with tears.

Santo nodded and retreated a step. He peered into the buggy for one last look. "Can I walk with you?"

"No, I better go."

She glanced at the baby, checking to see if he was safely strapped, and began to stumble away. After a few steps, she slowed down and called out over her shoulder, "I'm sorry about your brother."

Victoria had once relished the sound of her voice in the confessional, the way the words took on a velvet weightiness amid all the polished wood before they spilled across the tissue-thin curtain. In order to hear this, to feel the gravity of the words, she had to speak in a hush, in a near whisper, and then she'd forget that anyone was listening and recite the list of venial and mortal sins she'd committed in the days since her last confession, primarily sins against her family and friends, disobeying one and acting meanly toward the other. Until that Saturday afternoon she had never considered mentioning impure thoughts. Not that she had none. She simply took matters into her own hands in those cases and added a few Hail Marys to her penance, which is what the priest would have prescribed anyway. Besides, giving voice to those thoughts would have given them more substance.

But this time the impure thoughts were different. She was sixteen. Eddie's hands had traversed her body, his fingers slowly penetrating her as they pressed up against each other in the backseat of his car. Which is not the thing that bothered her. It was the yearning for what would come next that consumed her with guilt. She imagined the priest falling off his stool with a thud as she revealed her dark passions. And if she cloaked her desires in the pat phrases of the nuns at school, Father Ernie or one of the others would recognize her voice and write an entire sermon about the body as temple, and everyone in the parish would glare through her from their pews because they would know she was the one.

Her mother probably already knew. Angela Rosa's questions as Victoria tried to leave the house had become more insistent lately—*How long will you be? How can I find you? Will Darlene the* puttana *be there?* Then she'd lay into Victoria about finding new friends, corner her in the doorway before she left, and finally demand that Victoria honor her mother. Or she'd never leave the house. Her eyes would bore into Victoria and her voice would turn shrill, as if she could will obedience with her screeching.

Bless me, Father, for I have sinned. Bless me, Father for I have sinned. Bless me, Father, for — The window of the confessional slid open. "Bless me, Father," she whispered. "It has been five weeks since my last confession. I've been mean to my mother. I can't help myself, I guess. She doesn't understand. She doesn't understand anything."

Father Ernie's confessional voice scratched through the flimsy screen. "Go on," he said.

"I disobeyed her, you know. Went somewhere she told me not to." She heard the rustling of his cassock. "Also, impure thoughts. And I stole something. I took a cigarette from my dad's shirt pocket."

"Go back."

"I disobeyed my mother. I had to."

"The other one."

"I took one cigarette. It's okay that my dad smokes. He started when he was twelve. But I can't have one cigarette. That makes a lot of sense."

"Impure thoughts. Tell me about that one."

"I know that's a sin, Father. I'll say three hundred Hail Marys. Really I will. Anything you say." She tried to sound sorry but didn't feel it and wondered now why she'd come at all.

"Are they just thoughts?"

"Isn't that enough?"

Father Ernie let out his familiar exasperating sigh. She knew she could wait him out, but Darlene would be at the school steps in a few minutes. "I have to go, Father."

"Just awhile longer."

"I'm sorry," she said. "I don't . . . I can't—" She stepped from the kneeler, the creaking loud in that small space, and slipped out of the confessional. In a single motion, she dipped her fingers in the bowl of holy water, crossed herself, and then pushed through the mahogany doors without looking back.

At the church parking lot she saw that Darlene hadn't arrived yet and slowed her pace. Out of the corner of her eye, she caught a flurry of movement behind her. Father Ernie in his confessional vestments, his arms pumping wildly, glided toward her.

"You're a fast one," he called, slightly winded. "I guess the Jesuit sisters didn't fill you in on protocol. You confess, I give you penance, and *then* you leave." He leaned his head back toward the church. "Why don't we try again?" A trace of pleading hung at the edge of his short breaths.

She refused to meet his eyes. "I have to find Darlene. I don't have time. Really."

"Darlene will wait."

"And this is kind of strange," she said, pointing to his cassock flapping in the October breeze, "talking in the parking lot like this."

"Because this is still confession? Since you didn't finish. Is that what you mean?"

"I don't know. It's just strange."

"Forget confession," he said, catching his breath. "Let's just talk." He unzipped his cassock and draped it over his arm. "You could have said less. You wanted to talk. Now finish."

He was right, of course. She'd kept the depth of her desires hidden even from Darlene, which felt like a kind of betrayal, and now she needed to tell someone.

"I don't have time to get into it," she said.

"What's the boy's name?"

Her eyes followed a winding crack in the asphalt. A gust blew a few stiff leaves across the crack. "This is not exactly the kind of thing you talk about with a priest in the middle of a parking lot, if you know what I mean." She could use a cigarette, she thought.

His eyes swept from the rusting spire of the church back to her. "So forget I'm a priest. I'm just another person. Someone who doesn't want you to do something you don't really want."

"Everybody knows what I want all of a sudden?"

"What you want changes."

"Especially at my age? Is that what you mean?"

"I didn't—"

"Well, maybe I'm old enough to—to decide what I want. Why doesn't anybody ever think of that? My mother thinks I'm four and my dad listens to whatever she says, like he's afraid of her or something. Anthony and Freddy, they give me these looks, like, 'What's wrong with her?' Santo's the only one lately—but it's not like he . . ."

"What's the boy's name, Vicki?"

Victoria studied him, the way he stood there like a rake. If he got rid of the priest gown on his arm and someone handed him a cigarette, and if he combed a dab of Brylcreem into his regiment of hair, he'd look like one of the guys hanging on the corner.

"Why do you want to know?" she asked. "Are you going to check up on him? Check him out? Make sure he's safe for me? The last thing I need is another brother."

"If you'd step back for a minute, for a second even. Cut through to the honest to God truth and . . . how do I say this . . ." He moved his cassock to his other arm. "This is about your brother, isn't it? This is about Benito. This is your way of—"

"What are you talking about?"

"I think you're feeling—you have this heightened sense of fairness I've always admired. You're able to take the long view. But if something happens to throw off your"—he used his hands as scales—"your sense of right and wrong, then you want to lash back. It's stamped all over your face. After a while you walk around thinking, 'What's the difference?' Am I right?"

Her hands shook and she ached for the calm of a cigarette.

"Believe it or not," he said, "I know that recklessness. It weighs you down, pulls you away from yourself."

"Like I know who I am."

"That's a good one. Vicki Peccatori doesn't know who she is. If that's what you want to keep telling yourself, then maybe . . ."

"Then maybe you shouldn't have come out here?"

"I didn't come out here to be your conscience."

"Then why'd you come out here?"

"I don't know. Maybe because I like you. Because I know what it's like to walk around aimlessly, thinking that a certain thing is going to make everything all right."

"What's wrong with wanting a certain thing?" she said.

"Certainty nearly always disappoints us."

"What's that supposed to mean?"

He rubbed his tight forehead, examined the scuff marks on his oxfords.

"Listen," he said. "Running around is not going to change anything. It's not going to ease your grief. It's not going to get your mom off your back. It's probably not even going to bring you any closer to this boy you're thinking about. That's my guess at least." He tugged on the band of his wristwatch. "If you won't tell me who he is, will you at least tell me why you're interested in him?"

"He makes me laugh."

"Crazy Willie makes you laugh, too."

She thought about what Eddie would say. *Ballbuster,* he'd say. Though not to a priest. And never to her. He said things like that to others to perform for her, it seemed.

She grinned. "He takes care of me."

"Does he?"

"He does."

"Gives you cigarettes?"

"Maybe."

"Treats you right?"

"Sure."

"A good guy?"

"I guess."

"You're not sure?"

"I don't know. He's good enough."

"You want to run around with someone who's good enough? You're going to settle for good enough?"

"He's not a priest."

"He could do worse." Father Ernie scratched his chin, as if wondering how to proceed. "Does he stay out of trouble?"

She shrugged, hoping he'd take the shrug as a yes.

"So you're dating a hoodlum. Is that what you're telling me? A hoodlum who makes you laugh."

"I thought you weren't going to be my conscience."

"Someone has to do it."

"Yeah, and I get the priest."

"So you think you're going to reform this boy? Is that it? You're going to save him?"

She looked for Darlene. Where the hell was she?

"Tell me one thing," he said. "What's the rush?"

"You wouldn't understand."

"Because I'm a priest?"

"Yes, actually."

"Then explain it to me. Why is a sixteen-year-old running around with a—how old's this guy?"

"Nice try, Father."

"Ah, he's older, too. So why's a young girl like you running around with an older guy who's probably ready to move a lot faster than she is? Where is the rush?"

"I should've just confessed," she muttered.

"I'm glad you didn't."

"Why?"

"Nine times out of ten it's all rote in there anyway. People aren't contrite. They just want to feel better." He shook out his cassock, pulled it around his shoulders, and zipped it. "I can see you've made up your mind about this boy. I can have you say ten rosaries, but that's a temporary wash. And you know it. When you decide you want to talk, let me know. I'll pray for you."

He'd kept his head down, and his entire weight seemed to slump with each word. She wondered if there was something tactical in his resignation.

"Thanks, Father."

"You can take care of yourself. I'm fully aware of that. But . . ." He shook his head. "Let me know what I can do."

"Thanks."

He pointed to the school steps. "Your friend is waiting."

He walked away without his customary wink. She suddenly yearned for the wink. She yearned for the customary teasing that followed. *If I weren't a priest* . . .

On Thursdays, after putting in a four-hour shift at Mio Fratello, Santo would stroll down to the Erie Street social club to play a few hands of five-card draw in the burgundy-washed light of the old storefront. He loved squeezing the cards open one by one and taking in the shimmer of the red and black suits as they fanned out near the end of his cigarette. With each drawn card Santo's breaths became shallower and his worries dropped off like spent matchsticks. And it didn't matter what he caught. Missing an inside straight gripped him the same as finding three of a kind unfolding before him. He wondered whether the shimmering and the flashing he sensed when he gambled matched Uncle Vince's jittery rush for a drink, whether one obsession was the same as another. He'd been thinking lately that obsession ran in the blood — his uncle with his drinking, his father with his women. Even Mama with her kitchen life. All of them were plagued with the same narrow scope that blurred their own nagging worries for a while.

Even cards, though, couldn't stop Santo from thinking about Ella Paolone. He hadn't ventured toward Hubbard Street in over a week, not since talking with her, but her face was imprinted in his mind. Anyone vaguely resembling Ella would cause him to pause and do a double take. He thought he saw her pass Mio Fratello one time, which would have been remarkable, he felt. Another time he was sure she'd disappeared into the church, her dark hair lilting, shielding her eyes. When he followed her inside to steal a closer look, she turned out to be twenty years older and a few pounds fuller than Ella.

Sitting in the club now across from Pooch, he thought about Ella's last words to him, kind words about his brother. Pooch dealt him an ace, a jack, and a king. *Sorry*, she'd said. She'd meant it to sound tender, Santo knew, but the words had come out flat. Her eyes were full and sad, though, which was how he wanted to remember her. After she walked away he had stood there on the sidewalk for a long while before turning back toward Grand. His last two cards were fours. Eddie opened for a quarter and drew two. Johnny C wanted one card. Santo threw away the pair and looked to fill out his straight. He knew it was stupid to throw away a pair, but from the looks of it, catching another four wasn't going to help him anyway. On his left, Tony drew three cards. Tony was twenty but already soft in the middle.

"Asshole Pooch," Eddie said. "You deal like shit."

"You just better have openers," Pooch said. "You cuntlap." Playing cards was about the only time Pooch seemed comfortable with himself. The only time he stood up to Eddie.

"Yeah, you cuntlap," Tony said.

Tony had a habit of repeating the latest cut and then laughing freely, as if this were the most clever thing he'd ever heard. Johnny C didn't say a word. He studied his cards through hooded eyes, tugging nervously on the sleeves of his T-shirt.

The cop's wife from upstairs, Eddie's cousin, walked by outside with her hair made up, and Pooch said, "I wouldn't mind going to pork city with that thing."

"She'd hurt you."

"Not to mention her husband."

"Then hurt me," Pooch said.

Santo drew a ten and a seven but didn't fold immediately, thinking he might be able to bluff someone out. But when Eddie and Johnny C both stayed, he tossed his cards in the middle. He'd been playing for twenty minutes now and hadn't come close to a winning hand.

"Not my day," Santo said. "Might as well just throw another sawbuck in and you assholes can split it up."

"Make it a C-note," Pooch said. "The way you're going."

"Yeah, a C-note," Tony said, and snorted.

"Why don't you shut the fuck up, Tony?" Eddie told him.

Tony turned to Eddie, then back to Pooch. He wouldn't back down. "Yeah, shut the fuck up," he repeated.

"Who you talking to?" Eddie asked.

"All of youse. Every one of youse shut the fuck up."

Eddie shook his head and dragged on his cigarette and let the smoke blaze out through his nostrils. "You're so fucked up you don't know you're fucked up. You pissant."

"Pissant," Tony mumbled.

Santo pushed himself from the table and stepped outside. There was a chill in the air now, a marked change from when he'd walked in. He peered down Erie, thinking he might walk clear down to Hubbard Street and look for Ella Paolone. And then he saw them, his sister and Darlene leaning against a fence in the middle of the block. They'd been gazing at the club and when they saw Santo they huddled closer together, talking back and forth. It wasn't until Santo shrugged, asking them with the shrug what they were doing there, that they moved toward him. He stepped from the door and met them midway.

"Dinnertime?" he said.

"No. Just walking around," Victoria said.

They still had their white blouses on from school and they'd replaced their pleated skirts with jeans.

"How you doing, Darlene?"

She smiled at him, her red lipstick bright.

"So what are you two doing here?"

"Nothing."

"Nothing, huh?"

"We're looking for someone to play double Dutch with," Darlene said. She studied her chewed nails. "How's about a cigarette?"

Santo had a couple of puffs left on his and offered it to her. Darlene puffed twice and dashed the butt under her shoe. "Eddie in there?" she asked.

Victoria's brow tightened and she shot Darlene a stony look.

"Eddie who?"

"Eddie Eddie."

"What do you want with Eddie?"

"We need to ask him something. That's all."

Santo thought he'd given up protecting his sister, but here it was again, the old urge to shove someone. He felt his fist wadding up.

"He's playing cards. Taking everyone's money. He's not coming out of there." And there was no way any neighborhood girls were going in.

"It'll just take a second," Darlene said. "Can you get him?"

"Why don't you go home and watch TV or something. Red Skelton's coming on."

Behind him he heard Tony calling. "Hey, Santo. You in?"

Santo waved him away. "Deal me out," he shouted. "I'll be there in a minute."

Tony disappeared and Santo turned back to Darlene. "See you later, huh. I have to go win my money back."

"So you're a loser," Darlene suggested. "Is that what you're saying?"

"You got a mouth on you sometimes, you know that?"

"Yeah, and I can go for another cigarette. My own."

"You call me a loser and now I'm supposed to fork over a smoke?"

"Let's go, Darlene," his sister said.

"Hold on. Like he's gonna miss one freaking cigarette."

Darlene looked over his shoulder then, her eyes widening, and Santo turned to see. Eddie stood at the doorway of the club, running a comb through his slicked-back hair that didn't need combing. He remained rooted there, as if expecting the three of them to come to him, but no one moved. After a while he tucked the comb into his back pocket and swaggered toward them.

"Never mind," Darlene said. "Maybe Eddie can spare one damn cigarette."

Santo wanted to slap her. Just once. For the mouth on her. And because Vicki wouldn't have come around on her own, not here. They'd established an understanding, the three of them. Eddie could talk to Victoria when Santo wasn't around. But they all had to pretend that nothing was going on. When Santo and Eddie were together, Vicki's name never even came up. And when Santo was with his sister, Eddie didn't exist.

"What's the good word?" Eddie said.

"*Cigarette*'s a good word," Darlene said. "How 'bout a cigarette?"

Eddie pulled a pack of Chesterfields from his shirt pocket and handed a cigarette and a book of matches to Darlene.

"Want one, Vick?" Eddie asked.

"No, she don't want a smoke," Santo blurted.

"Oh, no?" Eddie said.

"No, they were just going," Santo said to no one. "So why don't you go already?"

"What's the hurry?" Eddie said.

Darlene leaned into Victoria and muttered, "The loser's gotta win his money back." Victoria looked at her and flashed a reluctant smile back.

Santo wanted to ignore it. She'd said it soft enough for him to ignore. But the way she'd said it, with the unlit cigarette poised at the corner of her mouth, and using his sister against him like that, tore into him. White heat radiated around his eyes and his temples throbbed. He took a half step toward Darlene and snatched the cigarette from her mouth and crumpled it and slapped the shredded tobacco to the ground. "And Darlene don't need no smoke neither."

"Hey—"

"What the fuck you do that for?" Eddie said.

Santo grabbed the Chesterfield pack from Eddie's curled fingers and crumpled those, too. He let the pack drop from his fingers and roll to the curbstone. "I told you they don't need no cigarettes. That's why, asshole."

Eddie took a step toward his cigarettes on the curb, then turned to Santo, standing chest to chest with him now. "What's your problem?"

Santo wanted his warm breath out of his face. He shoved him, his hands thudding against Eddie's chest, sounding more like a punch than a shove. Eddie had to shuffle back to avoid falling, and Santo marched toward him. "They don't need your fucking cigarettes, I said."

This would be the end of it, Santo thought. Eddie would make some smart remark to save face because that's what Eddie did. Always dodging. Sidestepping. Keeping the upper hand with his wide smirk. But this time Eddie glared back and poked Santo in the chest and said, "Don't you ever fucking push me again. You hear me?"

Santo reared back and drilled him, the punch landing on the fleshy part of Eddie's chest.

"What are you doing?" Victoria shouted.

Darlene stepped up behind Santo to pull him back by the shirt, and Eddie got a shot in to the stomach. Santo doubled over and pulled away from Darlene's grip and rushed Eddie and shoved him with both hands. "You prick," he blared. He reared back again and landed a right on Eddie's jaw. He felt movement there and a stinging in his knuckles. There was a flurry of wild jabs from both sides then and blood smearing the front of their shirts and Victoria and Darlene wailing for them to stop please stop and the guys from inside the club rushing out finally to break them apart.

"You guys gone fucking crazy?" Pooch said.

"Yeah, you fucking crazy?" Tony repeated.

Santo leaned over and caught his breath. "I told you they don't need your fucking cigarettes." He straightened up and said, "Let's go."

But his sister and Darlene were already up the block, two houses ahead of him, moving fast.

He thought about the jacket he'd left inside the club, a maroon windbreaker draped over a folding chair near the door. He'd leave it. Give them something to think about. They could burn it, the assholes.

None of Eddie's jabs had hurt much, but his arms burned and pulsated and he could barely lift them. He tried to shake off a dull ringing in his left ear.

Eddie spit on the ground, checked his jaw, and headed back toward the club. "Crazy fuck," he said.

Only then did Santo start walking in the direction of his sister and Darlene, wondering what he'd say to them when he caught up. He was fighting over a cigarette? Over a stupid smoke? Because Darlene had called him a loser? Because he *was* a loser? He couldn't explain, not so that anyone would understand. Even his sister who'd seen it all wouldn't get it.

He tasted blood on his tongue and spit out a dull red glob. *That prick Milano.* He glanced at the rawness of his knuckles. He'd never hit anyone in the face before. He thought he might feel regret, but smashing Eddie's jaw brought a kind of relief. He wouldn't have to pretend anymore. Eddie was a piece of shit and Santo didn't have to let his sister anywhere near him. Even if it took more raw knuckles.

Since June he'd assumed that Eddie had something on him, that Eddie could make trouble for his father. But now he understood. Santo finally understood. All along he'd been protecting his sister. Because on her own, Victoria wouldn't piece it all together. And this is what that bastard motherfucker Eddie had agreed to the first time they'd met at the club—to leave Victoria in the dark. But that would change now. Santo would talk to her himself, tell her everything. He needed someone else to know.

For three days she avoided him. Wouldn't pass him the bread at dinnertime. Wouldn't look at him when he spoke to her. On Sunday morning when her mother and Freddy were gone to church and her father was out walking and Anthony slept, Victoria charged into his room and turned on the light overhead and pulled the pillow out from under his head. She hoped he'd been having a pleasant dream, running through a field with Brigitte Bardot maybe or just beginning to embrace her.

Santo made a few guttural noises and shielded his eyes. "What," he grumbled, tucking the top of his head under a corner of the bedspread. This angered her more and she took hold of the corner and ripped the entire covering from the bed in one swipe. An instant of panic surged through her followed by relief when she saw he had on a pair of boxers.

"Get up," she said, surprised by the authority in her voice.

Santo moaned. "Whata . . . What time is it?"

"Time for you to get up, Santo Peccatori."

"You my mother all of a sudden?"

"Call me what you want. But I've got a few things to say to you. And I better not have to say it ever again. Are you listening?" She waited for him to lower his hands from his eyes and glance in her direction. "If you ever embarrass me like that again, I'll . . . you'll be sorry. I don't need you, I don't want you acting like I need you to protect me or something. Who the hell do you think you are?"

Santo scratched his head. "You're sixteen."

"I don't care if I'm twelve. You better butt out."

He rubbed his eyes and sat up and stared at his feet.

"I mean it, Santo."

He peered up at her, one brow arched. "Or what? You're gonna tell on me?"

"You're such a—"

"Go ahead, you got names for me? Fire away."

She had names, all right. But she'd imagined this exchange going differently. She'd expected Santo to fall over himself with apologies.

"Mark my words," he said slowly. One of Eddie's expressions.

Victoria ignored his wagging finger and tried to cut him off with an icy glare.

"You keep messing with Eddie," he said, "and you're gonna have your own names."

"And that's any of your business? What're you worried about, that people will start talking about Santo's sister? What they'll say about you? It's all about you, isn't it?"

"No, it's all about him. There's only one person that Eddie Milano's interested in. And that's himself."

"Is that right?"

"That's right."

"And you're any different?"

"I am."

She was surrounded by people who thought they saw more than she did, who knew her interests better than she did. Her mother, Lupa, her other brothers, Father Ernie, and now Santo, who'd been leaving her alone. What they didn't understand, every one of them, every day of her life, was that their warnings pushed her closer to the things they cautioned against. They were stupid not to see this.

"So tell me. How are you any different, big shot?"

"I'm not a piece of shit, for one."

"Yeah, you should know." She moved toward the doorway, wanting to be as far away from him now as she could. "You only see him when he's with the idiots at the club. That's why you think that. You all act like idiots when you're together."

"Trust me on this one. A royal piece of shit. That's all he is. He doesn't care about you."

"Santo the expert. Maybe you should go on *What's My Line?*"

"For this you wake me up?"

"So go back to sleep. I'll just rip your eyebrows out when you're sleeping. Would that be better?"

"What the heck do you want from me?"

"I want you to promise."

"What?"

"To butt out."

"To butt out."

"I mean it," she said.

"You mean it."

He got up and headed toward the hallway, scratching at his pelvis. She thought of crossing her arms and planting herself in the doorway, but she knew she already lost what little advantage she'd held. He hadn't cowered as she'd expected. As he neared her she stepped aside.

"Son of a bitch," she said.

He stopped. "What makes you think he even wants to go out with you anymore after what happened? You think he's going to want to be looking over his shoulder every time he's with you?" He waited and glared at her and shook his head. "That coward."

Whatever had first attracted her to Eddie welled up in her now. Eddie wasn't only forbidden fruit. Eddie was older and dangerous and took her away from her nooselike family and her dreary neighborhood and the routine of her life for a while, and he made her feel oddly safe at the same time. She didn't care that he wasn't perfect. She could change that. People changed.

She let her brother pass and called him a son of a bitch again and walked through the kitchen and down the porch stairs. The streets seemed more deserted than usual for a Sunday morning, people sleeping late or holed up in church. She wished it were night so she could wander off toward Erie and wait for Eddie to appear and they could take a long ride together in his aunt's boat of a car and she'd let him do whatever he pleased finally.

She reached the end of the block, worrying about running into Mama and Freddy returning from church, then spotted her father turning from their alley. When he saw her he ambled toward her.

"Good girl. You're going to church?"

"Yeah, Papa."

"That's nice. Santo and Anthony, they're still sleeping?"

"I think so."

Her father's hair had gone from a shimmering silver to a street-snow gray since June. He seemed more distracted, even forgetful lately. But he walked with confident strides and smiled easily, and she felt ashamed to admit that she didn't worry about him. He had his business, with Santo and Uncle Vince watching out for him; he had Mama, who cooked and cleaned for him, who never once objected to his strange devotion to a buxom film star. Victoria barely thought about him at all, her own father.

"That's good," Agostino said. "They need sleep."

For the first time she noticed the deep circles under her father's eyes, this man who'd lost a son five months ago. She wondered if he ever had the same thoughts she did, if he ever wished that God had taken him instead.

"I better go. Okay, Papa?"

He gazed just beyond her. "Yeah yeah. You go. You pray

for me." His voice seemed to be calling out from some other time.

He kissed her lightly on the cheek, reminding her of girlhood days when he'd pick her up and they'd dance together in the apartment, gliding from one far end to the other. When he got to the threshold of the dining room or the kitchen he'd leap into the room and swing her around and land with the most nimble of feet, and she felt she could stay in his arms like that forever, her fingers wrapped at the back of his neck, his shaving smells filling her. After a few dances he'd become winded and put her down and they'd waltz together for a few minutes more until the radio announcer broke in with a few words of station news. After that the spell would be broken, but he'd keep her hand and they'd walk through the neighborhood, father and daughter. He'd have her imagine they were walking through his village in Italy, and he'd describe the mountain ranges they'd see, the olive trees they'd pass. She'd stare up at the catalpas and the maples and imagine groves of them dwarfed by mountaintops, and the shingled houses before her would recede as she squeezed Papa's hand, her thumb pressing into the cleft of his warm palm.

As she grew older something happened between them. Something wedged them apart. In her memory, it happened overnight, though she knew this couldn't be. She started changing, and her father didn't know what to do with her, how to hold her, what to say to her. The pudgy hand he once reached for was no longer there. In its place was this new hand with delicate fingers. Overnight, their dancing days fell behind them like stiff pages in an ancient photo album.

She watched him walk away and wanted to return to the safety of his arms. She wanted to tell him everything so he would keep her at his side and protect her from all the imperfect men in the world. She wanted to glide in his arms again and feel the softness at the back of his neck, take in his barbershop smells. But as he turned into the gangway of their apartment building and disappeared, she knew that those desires would be muffled soon by other more pressing urges she could barely control.

December 1957. The first Christmas without Benito. No one had bothered to haul up the tree from storage in the basement, its silver spindles leaving the familiar trail in the narrow stairwell. Santo remembered the ornament Mama had picked up last year from one of the dime stores on Chicago Avenue, "Baby's First Christmas," his only Christmas. The spot in the living room where the tree would have gone, centered before the window, seemed gaping, another reminder to Santo that he had to leave, start anew. He had some money put aside, enough to last three or four months in an apartment of his own, and if he could find a job, a real job, he'd be fine beyond that. But he needed a safety net.

He got to the store early and found Uncle Vince seated at a table near the window. The bell above the door jingled, and Vince tossed the *Daily News* onto the table. He gazed at the darkening sky. "Reading newspaper," Vince said. "Is like . . . what they say . . . masturbate." He made a quick stroking motion with his left hand. "Like masturbate."

"That's the first thing I think of," Santo said.

"Every day I read. And every day nothing change." He pushed the paper away from him with the tips of his fingers, as if it were soiled. One of the headlines read SOVIET MISSILES READY TO FIRE AT U.S. BASES. Another story highlighted Eisenhower's recovery from a mild stroke, accompanied by a diagram of the exact spot the stroke began and its alleged progression. In a tiny photo next to the illustration, Nixon looked on perplexed.

Vince heaved a sigh. *"Ah, mio Santo. Como stai, eh?"*

He'd been at the bourbon. Santo sank down across from him, wondering if it was possible to smell bourbon oozing out of a man's pores. "I'm good, Uncle Vince. How's the hip?"

Vince shrugged and said, "Right now. No too bad. Before. Whew." He shook his right hand and mimicked a wince. "Why you come early? I no need?"

"Nothing to do, I guess."

"And *mio fratello?*"

"I don't know. He's probably out walking somewhere. Maybe he went to the show."

Santo had followed his father during a recent snowfall. He'd kept his distance, retreating at the slightest turn of Agostino's head. His father walked past the houses and the hot-dog stand on Ashland, and the A&P farther down, and stopped at the entrance of the Hub movie theater on Chicago Avenue. He reached into his trousers for a wad of bills and leaned toward the hole in the ticket window to say something to the girl and thumbed through his money to locate the right bill as Santo had seen him do a thousand times. Yet his father seemed like a stranger to him. Which wasn't an unusual reaction for Santo—seeing his father as a blur. But this was different. All the mystery was stripped from him. He became an ordinary man paying for a movie ticket on a weekday afternoon. Santo felt partly relieved but mostly disappointed by the ordinariness of the moment. His father had nowhere else to go.

When he saw his father swallowed by the darkened interior of the lobby, a thought suddenly occurred to him. He had tried to dismiss it as paranoia, a product of being a Peccatori. And he felt embarrassed by his suspicions. But he couldn't stop himself. He thought, *Maybe Ella Paolone will show up.*

The corner Woolworth's had a silver-rimmed clock that jutted out from the second-story sandstone, and Santo had waited a full ten minutes before heading back to work.

"Some a time . . . I worry about your Papá," Vince said. "He change. *Non è facile per perdide un figlio.*" It's not easy to lose a son.

"I know," Santo said. And before he could stop himself, he muttered, "He lost more than a son."

"And Mama today?"

"She won't stop cleaning. Yesterday she painted the kitchen. Took down all the wallpaper, the paper with all the strawberries on it. She painted the red legs of the table. Everything's white now."

"She stay busy, eh? That's good."

"I guess."

Vince leaned into the table. "Santo . . . you think about some a thing. *Si?*"

"I'm always thinking about *some* thing, *Zio.*"

Vince shook his head. "You want I give cigarette? Then no talk stupido."

"Sorry, *Zio.*" Santo hadn't noticed Vince's Pall Malls propped up against the ashtray. He reached over and grabbed one and lit it.

"So. You think about some a thing?"

How much did Vince need to know? How much did he know himself? "I was thinking about Christmas and New Year and after. What I was going to do after that." He glanced at his fingers. They seemed ridiculously small. After a while he felt a restlessness in his legs and he got up and walked to the radio near the bar and turned it on low. Italian radio, but he didn't bother to switch the station. He came back to the booth and sat down, looking for the nerve to go on.

Vince studied the traffic on Grand for a while, picked up the newspaper, and deposited it in front of Santo. "Here," he said with his half grin. "If you no wanta talk, play with your *cucuzzo* instead, eh." And he made the stroking motion again.

"Thanks, Zio. I'll keep that in mind."

Vince leaned back and folded his arms, waiting.

"I was just thinking . . . about where I want to be. You know . . . next year, the year after that." He held his cigarette as he puffed to see how far he could lengthen the ash. "How old were you, Zio? When you left? When you got off on your own?"

"Ha. *Dio mio.* Let me see. I come 1932." He glanced at the ceiling and calculated with his fingers. "Nineteen . . . twenty. I make twenty year when I come." He shrugged and said to himself, "Long time ago."

"And then what?"

Santo had heard the story before, but this time he wanted to listen for signs of apprehension or fear. He wanted to find out how a man could leave his native country with few skills and little English and still prosper on his own. Santo wasn't sure he had the same drive or fearlessness or whatever it was that pushed someone out into the world.

Vince told him about the small hotel room on Huron where he stayed the first few months. Just a bed and a common bathroom for everyone on his floor. He was working at a factory that manufactured rivets and washers, and one day on his way home, he saw a sign. A small black sign with red letters that said FOR RENT.

Vince touched the window where they sat, where the sign had hung nearly twenty-five years ago, and explained why the rent was so cheap. The place had been a funeral parlor—rezoned or out of business, Vince didn't know which. He couldn't understand how a funeral parlor could ever go out of business, and each day as he walked by, he wondered what else could fill that space that people would need every day. Anyway, no one wanted to have anything to do with the place. So he moved in, walking from one room to the other, imagining changes. The embalming room caused him to pause, he admitted, and he avoided the first floor entirely after dusk, but day by day the place started feeling like his own.

"Before, when they make funeral, they take liquid out from every one. Now I put a liquid back inside. So busyness is same, eh?"

"I never looked at it that way, Zio. You should teach college."

Vince laughed. "College, eh. I go to six grade."

"Where else are people going to learn about running a business and liquids going in and out. You could do a whole semester on the three *C*s. And don't forget the newspaper. How to Read a Newspaper 101."

"Oh, yeh. You stay by me and I teach every thing. I teach to drink and lose wife. I teach to pee in big pot because the hips they make a pain. *Dottore Vincenzo. Professore primo.*" He talked slowly now, punching each word. "Vincenzo teach you to live upstairs by you busyness so you no go no place for twenty year."

"That's just it," Santo said. "I don't mean disrespect or anything. But I don't want to get stuck here at the bar for the rest of my life. I need to get out."

"Out, eh?" Vince seemed to consider this. "When?" he asked.

The ash on Santo's cigarette threatened to collapse, and he twirled it around one last time before flicking the caked ash into the glass tray. "I don't know," he said. "Soon, I guess. Maybe in the summer."

Santo could be ready next week, but *summer* sounded far enough away that Vince would view his leaving as just talk.

"Summer, eh? And who pay apart-a-ment?"

"I've been saving."

"You save, eh."

"Yeah. I mean . . . I could leave now if I wanted."

Vince shot him a wary look. "You leave now?"

"I could."

"*Gesù Cristo.*" Vince slapped the edge of the table with both hands, rattling the ashtray. "*La famiglia* Peccatori, they lose two son in one year. Mama no cry 'nough? Ay yi yi. When she hear . . ." He made a hurried sign of the cross. "You make eighteen?"

Santo nodded. "Eighteen and a half."

"Why you no wait? Save money. I buy you car. And pretty soon you make three *C*s. You stay, you make happy. You see."

Santo hadn't considered happiness. He only knew he needed distance from his family and that he wanted to be nearer to other things—his half brother for one. He'd been walking by Ella's house again, recalling the sadness in her eyes. If he could talk to her. She'd warm up to him.

"I guess I'm tired of waiting," Santo told him.

"You tired. Ha."

"Well, yeah. I've waited long enough. This is my time. I think." His fingers drummed silently on the table. "I was thinking of my own business maybe."

"Busyness. Ha."

"I thought, you came here from another country and you did it."

Vince shrugged and nodded to concede the point but threw up his hands at the same time. He pointed at Santo and spoke with slow precision. "But now. Is different. Today, busyness they close every day. What kind of busyness you make?"

Santo mashed his cigarette into the ashtray. "You remember Russo's cousin? Petey I think his name was. He used to have that hot-dog stand with the cart. He'd be so busy he didn't have to move the cart all night. He just sat on the same corner all summer. The last time I was at Russo's, getting a haircut, I saw the whole cart thing behind the shop—the cart, the big wheels with the wooden spokes, the awning. The awning was a little ripped. But the whole thing was just laying there. I could fix it up. Paint it. Buy a new awning. Something with red and white stripes maybe. I'm telling you, people would line up." Just talking about the cart and thinking about the steam from the silver box and the warm smells from the hot dogs and the mustard made Santo's mouth water. "I think it would work. I could sell hot tamales, too, maybe."

"And when winter come? You take wheels off? Make big sled."

"Yeah, I'll slide around on skis. Look, I haven't figured out winter yet. Maybe I'll make so much money I won't have to work in the winter."

"Yeah. Like me. Every winter I close."

"C'mon, Zio. I'm serious. I was looking for a little encouragement. What if someone had come up to you when you were buying the store and said, 'How're you going to sell drinks in an old funeral home?' Nobody gave you that, did they?"

"Back before. Nobody say good. Nobody say bad. I joost do."

Santo waited and listened to the silence build between them. He looked at his uncle and said, "There was no one around to ask then. Was there?"

Vince grinned, and Santo watched the slow change in his eyes. His uncle realized at last why Santo had come to him. Sitting there in his own bar, thousands of miles of ocean separating him from the places he'd left so many years ago, Vince couldn't resist laughing. "So, what a you need?" he said, his face flushed.

Santo wasn't sure. Now that his uncle had offered to help, that seemed almost enough. He asked about permits and vendors and what to charge, and after a while Vince started offering his own ideas—this corner versus that one, special condiments, possible emblems Santo could paint on the cart.

Vince glanced at the clock and pushed his chair from the table. "*Mio Santo.* Listen to me." He gripped the edge of the table. "Why you no try like this? You sell hot dog. *Si?* You make money. But you stay home. And save. *Abiti nella tua casa.*"

Santo nodded, willing to consider this.

He could get himself established on some corner, venture farther and farther from the neighborhood each day until no one even realized he was gone. The one thing his parents understood was work, so when they saw him making money, they wouldn't object.

"Okay, Zio. I'll think about it. But do me a favor. When Russo comes in, ask him about the cart. If you talk to him, he'll probably give it to you for nothing. That's what I'm thinking. It's just sitting there."

"Sure, I do anything for *mio nipoto*." He stood up. "Ahh. But now . . . I pee."

Victoria was in no hurry to get home. School had let out for Christmas vacation. Darlene was gone, picked up by her mom from school and taken to Michigan, where she'd be spending the next two weeks with cousins. Eddie had been cool to her lately, and she couldn't understand what she'd done wrong, only that she was sixteen and couldn't get out of the house to see him whenever he wanted and that Eddie seemed to be tiring of that. She'd try again to stop thinking about him. And so she walked.

She strolled up and down the east-west streets near school — Huron, Ohio, Ontario — avoiding Erie, until she came upon Crazy Willie at North Paulina. She turned to follow him, to find out where he went each day. He trooped down the sidewalk, so Victoria had to adjust her pace to keep up with him. His arms traveled too far in their upward swing, and his stride was nearly a lunge, but there was a solid rhythm in his movements, his head bobbing deep with each step. Even the slight hitch as he pushed off his left leg was fluid. He was tall and lumbering and slightly bloated, and his swiftness created the effect of treading water, that if he slowed up he might sink.

Usually Willie was a blur that flew past her at one corner or another, but following him produced a calmness in Victoria that surprised her. Neither of them had anyplace to be. Halfway down the second block on Paulina, Willie suddenly stopped, turned, put his open palms on his hips, and stared directly at Victoria with his crooked glare. With two fingers he pushed aside a strand of hair that had fallen over his right eye. When he straightened his neck the hair fell right back over the eye. He wore the same dumbfounded smile he always wore. As she neared him she thought she might veer away toward the other side of the street, but she'd established her own rhythm and kept moving toward him. He began to chew on his palm.

"Crazy Willie," she called. She said it brightly, knowing that the invitation in her voice would set him off laughing. His laugh was a low rumble that came directly from his throat. "How are you, Willie?"

She didn't slow down, knowing he'd start up again when she passed. She heard him chuckle slightly behind her, then next to her.

"Walking, Willie?"

"Yeah. Walking," he said. He talked out of the corner of his mouth. "I like to walk."

"Where do you walk?"

"I like to walk."

"You're lucky, Willie. You get to walk all day. Anywhere you want to go. It's when you stop that they bother you sometimes, isn't it. They don't mean anything. But sometimes they go too far. I know. Don't let them bother you."

Victoria had been dragging when school let out, but the brisk walk slapped her awake. A ring of moist warmth began forming along the back of her neck, dampening the collar of her blouse.

"You don't even know how lucky you are, Willie. Do you ever read the newspaper or listen to the radio?"

"Yeah yeah yeah, the radio. I like the radio."

"I mean the news. Do you ever listen to the news? People doing all kinds of awful things to each other. Things I don't even want to think about. You're lucky. You don't follow any of that, do you?"

She turned east and he stayed with her, his meaty hands cutting the air. She hoped that no one she knew would spot her walking with Willie, her new boyfriend.

"What about a girlfriend? Ever had a girlfriend, Willie? Not that you're missing anything. My boyfriend, he's been, you know, impatient lately, like he can't wait for me to leave or something when I'm with him. Ever since we, you know. And I don't think it's just my imagination." Under her breath she added, "If I'd of known he was going to act this way, we would've never ended up where we did."

Twice, in the backseat of his aunt's car, she had let Eddie go all the way. He was tender and careful each time, whispering reassurances, but it ended too abruptly, her every movement clumsy and deliberate. She could only remember her legs and arms, how her feet pushed into the car door to ease away from him, causing a tightening in her thighs, and how her one hand clenched that backseat while the other reached and fell loosely along the front. The rest of her was vaguely numb. And though she wanted to be with him, she found herself waiting for him to finish so they could just hold each other like they used to. Holding him would have been enough. And touching would have satisfied her, taking in the contours of his chest and the shadow of an arm across the seat. All those intimate glimpses that were burned in her memory would have been enough.

But she knew there was no going back. She would turn seventeen soon and she was no longer a virgin, an idea that stopped her cold sometimes but also amazed her, how quickly she'd become used to this new self, easier than breaking in a new pair of shoes.

She walked faster, taking Willie out of his rhythm now. He nearly stumbled.

"Let me ask you a question, Willie. Are all guy pigs? Once they get what they want, do they all turn into big fat pigs?"

Willie snorted, looking more amused than usual.

"And if my boyfriend is a pig, where does that leave me?"

Willie snorted some more. "That's funny. A pig," he said. "Eddie the pig."

Victoria suddenly stopped and looked over to where Willie would have been had he stopped, too. But he kept moving. She ran to him, shuffling and sliding to keep slightly ahead of him so she could look him full in the face. "Jesus Mary Joseph," she said. "You son of a—how'd you know Eddie was my boyfriend. How'd you know about Eddie and me?"

"Ha ha. Eddie the pig. I like that."

"Yeah, real funny. A riot. How did you know Eddie was my boyfriend?"

He wiped his nose with the back of his hand and wiped the hand on his pants.

"Will—ee."

Willie snorted.

"For cripe's sake, Willie. Talk to me. Do you ever talk to Eddie? Is that how you know?"

Willie seemed content with the image of Eddie as pig and snorted again.

Victoria stopped pressing. She looked ahead down the block and fell in step with her new friend. The shadows from the trees had become longer, their leaves less distinct. The sky was lead gray. "So what else do you know? Are you some kind of genius or something who knows everything but can't get it out? Are they going to write a book about you someday? Call it *Walking Willie*?"

"Ha. Yeah. I like to walk."

Or *Crazy Willie Walking*, she thought. Or not so crazy.

They walked awhile longer, Victoria feeling the pull of home. Her mother would be pacing already. Willie, though, had all the time in the world. And no worries. None that he could carry with him at least. Willie, she decided, was someone she could dump all her worries on and who wouldn't be weighed down by what she saw as the enormity of those worries. She told him about the fight between Eddie and Santo and storming into her brother's room one Sunday and how Santo leaped at any chance to lecture her.

"After the fight, three, four days later, Santo went on and on about seeing Papa at the feast. I'd mostly forgotten about that. Too many other things to think about with all that happened. But Santo . . . He told me Eddie would try to tell me some crazy story about why the old lady was yelling at Papa that night. Like Eddie's going to know anything about Papa. Or care. Here's the crazy thing—Santo is all bothered by Eddie and some story, and Eddie has never said a word. Not a single word. I think what it is, is that my brother likes to think he knows things that no one else knows. He walks around with this look, you know, like he's hiding something. Well, I know a few things, too, Willie. You know what I know? I know shit from shinola. That's right. And I know the backseat of a car even though I regret it mostly. And I know what it's goddamn like to lose a little brother in my arms and I know I don't need another goddamn person telling me what to think."

Willie had stopped smiling and was gnawing at his palm.

Victoria touched his elbow to slow him down. "Sorry, Willie. I didn't mean to upset you. I won't talk like that anymore. I promise. How does a pig go, Willie? That's right. Eddie the pig. Everything's going to be all right. We'll walk some more. Then I need to get home. I need to get home, Willie."

Part 2

August 1977

NICHOLAS PECCATORI

Mama's boy they used to call me at home. What did they expect? I came into this world on the heels of a brother who'd become a saint by dying. What else could I be? Anthony or Freddy would have been shamed to earn such a label. But I didn't mind. If it wasn't Mama getting meals for me or washing my face, it was Victoria patting down my hair and getting me ready for school. I didn't feel any weaker for giving in, for allowing my sandwiches to be cut or my shoes to be tied. Even early on I knew I was giving Mama and Vicki what they needed, what we all needed, despite the teasing the others doled out.

The teasing will end for good soon, I suppose, once I leave for college in the fall, not such a monumental move since I'll be staying close, but I wonder sometimes how such changes begin. I try to trace them back to their source, and when I think about my role in the family, I always come back to that first touch. Mama and Papa had lost a son. They no doubt slogged through the apartment for months afterward—I've seen such periods of isolation, slow winters and even slower summers. They ate, they worked, they slept when they could. Then one day in the fall of 1958, when everyone was at school maybe or in the middle of the night, in the darkness of their bedroom, one of them reached out to the other and with the barest of touches said, *Enough*. I never imagine beyond this, of course, but that first contact is so visceral to me, the reaching, the craving. I am the result of that throbbing ache which has since faded to the dimmest of memories.

Nine months later I came along, the only Peccatori child to be born in Italy, an irony which is not lost on me. Without me they might have all turned on each other, aimless and bewildered. But more likely, I was not their savior. They would have plodded along and found distraction or more elsewhere, I'm sure. All except for Papa, who may have suffered the most since his distractions were either hopeless or juvenile. His love for me, though real, seemed always reserved, as if he were trying to protect one of us, though I'm not sure whom. I often felt as I grew up that I had two mothers and no father.

Having played out my role in the family, I'll be leaving soon. I may have been a painful reminder at times of what they'd lost, especially early on, but I'm fairly certain I did some good on Superior Street. I provided a target for their love when they needed it most.

I had hoped to do more. There was a brief span before high school when I'd hide amid the stacks at the library on Chicago Avenue, searching through records of all the children who'd died in Illinois around the same time as Benito, trying to discern a pattern. Something they'd all eaten or drunk. A toy they'd chewed on. Places they'd visited. Common medicines. Days of transferring names from the obituaries to my composition book made me feel important. When I showed the 213 names I'd collected to the librarian, she gazed at me warily over her mauve-rimmed glasses. I studied the rims, how they compressed her face and made it seem distant, and explained I needed more information for a school project. She considered this, her eyes shrinking further, then turned abruptly to the reference desk, where I followed. She showed me how to write a letter to the medical examiner's office and made several phone calls, excited by this unusual task that took her away from the stamping and sorting that filled her days. After weeks of culling through documents and charts, I learned about abrasions, contusions, shaken babies, apnea, malnutrition, poisoning, and other unsettling ways to die. The charts revealed patterns, of course, but the one category that most interested me—Unexplained Deaths—revealed little, and I felt no closer to understanding Benito's passing than when I'd begun. I had seen the death certificate at the bottom of Papa's strongbox, the word *Unknown* listed unobtrusively next to *Cause of Death*. I imagined a stiff-postured secretary scanning her notes, precisely tapping out the seven letters that meant nothing to her, and I had hoped to march into Mama's kitchen with raised pages that would shed light on everything. *Look, here's the cause. There's nothing you could have done. You're off the hook, for Christ's sake.*

Maybe I'll do some good, too, by leaving. Mama can take care of Papa, Vicki can get on with her life instead of dropping by the apartment every few days, Freddy won't need to feel guilty about not stopping over, Anthony can stop his praying for me, and Santo, I can't say that I've ever mattered much to Santo. He was off on his own before I learned to walk. After I leave, we can all get together, the seven of us, as unlikely as that may be, and enjoy one another's company on a Sunday afternoon, with the red gravy simmering and the spoons stirring espresso, and wonder why we don't gather more often.

But for now I'll settle for the usual Sunday dinners with Mama and Papa and Victoria and every so often Anthony. Papa will take his nap afterward, Mama will wash the dishes, and Vicki and I will play cards and talk about school. She'll ask me if I'm going to play baseball next year, and I'll say that no one has offered me any money, so probably not, and she'll say that's too bad, and the conversation will be easy and I'll feel like I belong, like I've always belonged, and I'll ask about her husband, who usually can't make Sunday dinners because he works a second job on weekends, and I'll wonder aloud whether they're going to have children, and Vicki will turn shy and shrug off my suggestion. Later we'll hug good-bye and she'll tell me to stop by the house anytime, I'm always welcome, and I'll tell her, I know I know, and we'll hug again. And I'll tell myself as I watch her descend the stairs and disappear from sight that I know what love is.

6

ぎち

After Santo had alphabetized the whiskey bottles along the bar—Ballantine's, Canadian Club, Chivas Regal, Early Times—all the while listening to Uncle Vince tell his father about the vacation that Angela Rosa and Agostino needed to take, he borrowed Vince's Cadillac and drove to the A&P, where Ella Paolone had gotten a job as cashier.

Gordon's, Grant's, Haig & Haig, Old Kentucky, Old Smuggler. Twenty-five labels and no one ever asked for any by name. But Vince liked the display. Whatever bottle Vince happened to grab would be the bottle he'd recommend to the customer. And if Uncle Vince liked the display, there was no sense arguing because his persistence always wore you down. So when Santo heard him insisting that Mama and Papa take a trip back to Italy, Santo knew the trip was inevitable. The passports would be stamped, the tickets would be bought, and Santo would be in charge of the apartment for three weeks or longer.

These were the things he hoped to talk to Ella Paolone about, the circumstances of his life, the ordinary daily concerns that two people enjoyed sharing with each other. He'd been to the A&P several times in the past month, sometimes just buying a bottle of 7-Up and a bag of Jay's, and she'd been cordial to him at least. She hadn't called the manager to boot him out, as he'd feared.

When he got to the store, Ella was ringing up a big order for a mother with three kids, one of them trying to wriggle out of the mother's arms. Santo swung around, picked up a quart of chocolate milk and a packaged sweet roll, and stood in line behind the mother. The other cashier, a young girl with too much lipstick, eyed her empty lane, glanced at Santo waiting in line, then drew her attention back to her nails and her chewing gum.

"You've got your hands full," Santo said to the mother.

Ella peeked up from the cash register to see whether Santo was talking to her. Assured, she turned back to the groceries.

The mother sighed and said to Santo, "You can't even imag—could you please push that jar here please?" The woman's cheeks were flushed.

"Sure," Santo said. "Would you like some help getting all this to your car?"

With a quarter turn of her head and a partial roll of her eyes, Ella let Santo know that she wasn't that easily impressed.

"That would be great," said the mother.

Once the woman paid and got her Green Stamps, Santo put aside his milk and pastry and turned to Ella. "Now don't go selling this to anyone. I'll be right back."

Ella shook her head. "Yeah, sure," she said. "Like there's going to be a big run on chocolate milk in the next five minutes."

When he returned, the other cashier was busy with a customer, and Ella was ringing up an order of flour, eggs, milk, and a package of Hydrox cookies. Santo was tempted to comment but decided to wait his turn. He noticed that Ella's hair had been set or arranged or whatever women called it when they went to the beauty shop. Which worried Santo. Whenever he thought of Ella, he thought of her sitting at home with her baby, not getting herself ready for a night out. Her hair did look pretty, he had to admit, short and wavy and fuller than he remembered, falling just over the edge of the collar of her A&P smock. The smock was an ordinary brown, sleeveless shirt worn over Ella's own blouse, a new name tag pinned to the orange-yellow plaid pocket, but Ella made the smock look shapely and stylish.

"How's the baby?" he asked after the customer ahead of him had left.

"Not such a baby. He'll be walking any day now."

"You don't say."

"I do say. That's why I said it. That'll be eighty-seven cents, I do say."

"It's just an expression."

"It's a stupid expression."

"I guess."

"You have anything smaller than a twenty?"

He searched in his pocket and found exact change.

"So you'll be taking him for walks soon."

She put the milk and roll in a brown paper sack and pushed it toward him. "Yeah, I guess . . . maybe," she said. She glanced behind her at the light pouring in from the glass doors. "Good weather for it," she added.

He leaned in toward her and said softly, "You know, we're not strangers, you and I."

She leaned forward, too, so that their heads nearly touched. "You're crazy if you think I'm going to get involved with you."

Out of the corner of his eye he noticed another customer approaching Ella's lane. "Involved?" he said. "What does *involved* mean?"

"It means have a nice day."

The customer behind him began unloading her groceries on the belt. A woman in her sixties, she'd put on jewelry to come shopping at the A&P.

"Look, I've got my uncle's car. Let me come back when you're through here and I'll give you a ride home."

The old woman offered them a polite smile, a trace of embarrassment in her smile over having overheard.

"You have to leave," Ella said. "I've got work here."

"A short ride. What's going to happen?"

"Please."

"I won't leave till you say okay."

The old woman smiled again, at Ella this time. She seemed to be encouraging Ella to say yes.

"Please," Ella said. "Please go."

Santo reached into the sack and pulled out the quart of milk and began tugging at the spout.

"Okay okay," she said. "I'm done at seven."

"Seven," Santo said. He liked the sound of that. "Seven . . . good. I'll see you at seven."

As he neared the door he heard the old woman. "He seems like such a nice boy, that one," she said.

"You got a haircut," Ella said as she scooted into the Cadillac.

"I like the smell of a haircut," Santo said.

"I don't smell anything."

"I should get my money back. What good's a haircut if you can't smell it?" He clicked on the radio and a rapid-fire voice announced an auto race coming Sunday Sunday Sunday. "Did I tell you your hair looks nice? That's what I was thinking at the A&P waiting in line, that your hair looks nice."

He could see she wasn't used to hearing this. He placed the car in gear and eased out of the parking lot. "I mean it," he said.

"I believe you," she said. She gazed out the window.

"Aren't you going to ask me about the car? I figured the first thing you'd mention would be the Caddy."

"I guess I don't care much about cars."

The Platters came on the radio and he tapped the steering wheel.

"Look, I'm just going to drive you home. A five-minute ride. I thought we could have a pleasant five-minute conversation."

"I've been standing for six straight hours."

"That's better."

"That's better?"

"Sure. Tell me about your day."

"You saw my day."

"C'mon. Tell me. Who did you want to slap? What was your biggest bill? Did anyone pay with pennies?" As he thought about it now, he really wanted to know. "How about your most obnoxious customer today?"

She crossed her arms. "I think you know that one. Turn left here."

Santo took in her sneer and her sarcasm but wasn't much bothered by either. She was in his car. And talking to him.

"You want a cigarette?"

"I don't smoke."

"I thought everyone smoked. Even my sister smokes."

"Well, not me."

"You want to stop by Battiste's a minute? Get an Italian lemonade?"

She smoothed her skirt and gripped her knees. "I have to get home."

"I understand."

"I'm not sure you do."

"So tell me."

She turned. "What are you, eighteen?"

"Nineteen soon."

"I'm twenty-two. I have a kid. Not just any kid. What do you want from me? And my mother, she would rip you apart. I think it would be a good idea all around if you left me alone. Turn right at the corner."

"Let's just suppose. For a minute. What if I were twenty-two and you didn't have a baby and your mother liked me?"

"My father used to tell his friends, 'You talk like a jack-ass.' You're not twenty-two, I do have a baby, and my mother wouldn't like you."

He wanted to unbutton her smock. "Just pretend," he said.

"What's the point?"

He placed his arm across the seat back. "For the sake of argument, that's all."

"The sake of argument? You call this an argument?"

"Another stupid expression. Forget about it." He took his arm back. He felt himself sliding away, saying things he imagined some other person would say. "I have to tell you. I'm getting a little discouraged here."

"A little discouraged? What did you think? That you'd pick me up in your big Caddy and tell me my hair looks nice and that I'd just spread my legs? Is that what you thought? The father comes in first and then the son . . ."

Her words this time cut into him. She'd had hours to decide why she should resent him, Santo thought, and this is what she'd concocted, a deranged conspiracy between father and son.

Santo felt himself slipping further away. He gripped the steering wheel with both hands and squinted hard out the windshield. He took control of his breathing. "I remember when I was a boy," he said, "and I'd be sitting in the kitchen with my father and his coffee. He'd take a sugar cube and put it in his mouth whole and then he'd take a long sip of coffee. He'd do that every time, swallow about six or seven cubes with each cup. I tried it with my milk one time, and my mother slapped me across the ear when she caught on. I still see my father with his sugar cubes and his coffee. But, you know, I haven't done that with my milk since I was a kid. I'm not going to apologize for my father or try to explain him. But I'm not him. I am not my father."

He turned onto Hubbard Street. "You're tired," he told her. "You've been standing for six hours. I know how that can get to you. I'll leave you alone. I promise." He stopped at the end of her block. "Here. I'll let you out here."

As Victoria made her way to the corner of Ohio Street and Marshfield Avenue, she thought about the tight grid of city streets and how they'd defined much of her life. She grew up on the 1700 block of Superior, and anyone living a mere block east or west on the same street didn't exist. And you could forget the other streets altogether. As she got older she made new friends at school, of course, but they existed only until the school bell sounded. When she was older still, her network of friends broadened, but only relatively so. Her life was still dictated by the chance turns within a narrow strip of neighborhood streets.

She'd been thinking about those chance turns almost obsessively lately, struck by their power. If Santo hadn't battled Eddie Milano, Eddie would not have turned away so quickly and Victoria wouldn't have been so despondent. And if Darlene hadn't gone to her cousin's house in Michigan last Christmas break, Victoria wouldn't have gone walking after school that day to overcome her despondency. And if Willie weren't crazy, he wouldn't have been out walking and she wouldn't have run into him. And if she hadn't done that, if she hadn't befriended him, if she hadn't ignored the taunts of Darlene and more than a few others over walking with Crazy Willie, she would have never met Willie's brother, Richard.

She'd seen him before, of course. Everyone knew him because he was Willie's younger brother. At the end of the day, when they were kids, he'd always be out looking for Willie and steering him home. Since Richard was one of the Publics, though, one of the kids who went to Otis Elementary and then to Wells High School, none of the St. Columbkille kids really knew him. When he came around they all averted their gazes and talked quietly among themselves, trying to look like altar boys, trying to hide their shame for the kid with the crazy brother. Or maybe they were trying to cover up their own guilt over having harassed Willie earlier in the day.

When Victoria first met Willie's brother at the beginning of that summer, he introduced himself using his full name, Richard Kazenko, which struck Victoria as odd. But he was polite and thanked Victoria for walking with his brother—Willie had mentioned her name over dinner—and he was especially grateful because he'd been away all year at the University of Wisconsin in Green Bay, and he wondered how Willie would manage by himself. Willie apparently knew how to reach home when he was hungry, but without Richard, he'd walk all night. It didn't take Willie long, however, to realize that his brother wouldn't be there anymore, and he soon learned to read the sky for signs of darkness.

Willie called his brother Richie and clapped with a fury every time he saw him. The clap was virtually silent, the palms coming together, the fingers remaining splayed and rigid, but the gesture never failed to move Victoria. Before long, she began calling Willie's brother Richie, too.

Looking at them, no one would ever guess they were brothers. Richie was lanky with a long face and a strong jaw with big teeth. Like Willie and most of the other boys she knew, he wouldn't look you in the eye much, but he had what Victoria considered patient eyes. She'd never seen that quality from a distance, and maybe the patience wasn't there until recently, but up close his eyes told her what years of watching out for his brother had done for him.

The three of them had spent a good part of that summer walking. Richie would slow down and Victoria would drop back, too, and together they'd watch Willie gain distance between them and she'd let Richie take her hand. A few times they'd gone out without Willie and stopped for a hamburger and a Coke and talked about college or what it was like to lose a brother. There was more than one way to lose a brother, and Willie had been lost to them from the beginning. She told him about Benito and the fever, knowing he'd understand. And for that entire summer there was never a mention of a backseat and no tough words to impress her and no standing on the street corner. Most of the guys she knew had a talent for standing on the corner. But Richie wasn't one of them. With Richie there was only restraint. Victoria assumed he had a girlfriend back at school, someone to whom he was trying to be faithful. Probably some agreement had passed between them. Victoria never pressed him about this and he never offered explanation. For now she'd be satisfied with the hamburger and the Coke and the walking.

Richie waited for her outside the small frame house his family rented at the corner of Ohio and Marshfield. He fidgeted with the snaps of his windbreaker and examined the lining, looking everywhere but in Victoria's direction, as if he wanted to be surprised by her arrival. When he finally looked up and saw her he ambled over and they made their way to Jimmy's Beef on Ashland.

She imagined them sipping out of the same straw like she'd seen in a movie, but they sat across from each other with separate paper cups and separate straws and picked at the remaining fries in the basket between them.

"I don't think I've ever met anyone who's gone to college," she said.

He puffed his chest in mock pride and reared back as far as the booth allowed. "Well, you know," he said. "They don't just let anyone in."

"Oh, shut up."

"A little respect here maybe?" He tried his best standing-on-the-corner voice but sounded more like some constipated movie gangster.

She'd hoped for more serious talk, their last night together. Tomorrow he'd be back in some dorm room scrubbed down with powdered detergent that came in enormous gray boxes. This is what she thought about when she thought about college, tiny rooms and mildew. In time, she imagined, the room would start to smell like him, an outdoor smell that brought to mind turned dirt and sun.

She looked up at the menu board above the order window. "So, will you write?"

He chewed on a fry and swallowed and took a slow sip from his drink. "You would bring that up. I was hoping that maybe—I'm just not very good at, you know, and if I say I will and I don't, I'll feel bad and you'll think . . . so I don't know what to say."

He definitely has a girlfriend, she thought. And she came the closest she would come to asking about her. But this was his last night. She didn't want their first argument on his last night. "Well, if you get a chance," she said. "If you remember. I won't expect anything." She tried to keep the hurt out of her voice.

After a while he fingered a fry and brought it up to his eyes. He shook his head and said, "I'll miss these fries."

Victoria tightened her lips into a smile.

"What's wrong?" he asked.

"Nothing."

"What?"

"It's nothing. Really."

"Did I say something?"

"No."

"I'll try. I will. To write."

"No, really. Don't worry about that. I'm not good at writing either. I know how that is."

"So nothing's wrong? You sure?"

"I'm sure."

"Okay."

"Okay," she said. She rubbed her oily fingers on a napkin and listened to the traffic on Ashland. "I was thinking about Willie. He's used to you being around again."

"Yeah, I talked to him some."

Willie was safer ground, and she felt the tension drain out of her. "What did you tell him?"

"I showed him a picture of the school and told him I'd be living there and he said something about yellow pencils and I told him I'd bring him home some yellow pencils. Just for him."

All summer she'd held back. She'd forced herself to take her Richie-thoughts and temper them with the knowledge that he wouldn't be around that long. They'd have their one summer together—she'd take that, let those memories buoy her for a while, and then let them slip away like a firefly bursting out of her hand. But now, on his last night, she heard a screaming voice in her head. *So! You'll bring home pencils for Willie. What about me? What will you bring me? And while you're at it with the pencils, sharpen one of them and write me a goddamn letter. You can write me how much you miss those fricking fries.*

"Pencils," she said.

"I thought he'd be upset. But all he wanted to do was listen to the radio."

"Maybe he was more upset than he let on."

"I don't know."

"I mean, he understands everything. Well, most things. Sometimes . . ." She waited for him to look at her, and when he did, she said slowly, "Sometimes people don't know how to tell you what they really want."

He looked out at her over his straw and worry crossed his eyes. He knew they were no longer talking about his brother.

"Sometimes," she said, "when you tell someone what you really want, you ruin everything. You know what I mean?"

"I think."

He sipped through his straw until the sucking sound came up from the bottom.

"But other times. Other times you only get a single chance to tell someone what you want, what you really want."

When they first met, Richie had been quick to joke, maybe safe in the knowledge that Vicki was younger, that his real girlfriend was waiting for him back at school. Nothing would come of their jokes and their walking, he must have thought, especially with Willie tagging along. As the summer unfolded he remained his usual distant self, rarely planning when they'd meet again, yet something changed. His voice became softer, filled with hope, at least that's how Victoria heard it. A trace of uncertainty crept through the edges of his sentences, and he was no longer as in charge of his emotions as he might have thought. Now, sitting across from Vicki at Jimmy's Beef on an early Sunday evening, he'd been trying to regain some of his early confidence but was failing miserably.

"So what is it that you want, Richie? What do you really want?"

"You mean aside from world peace?"

"Yeah, aside from that."

"I don't know. It's not something that I . . . put into, you know, words." He glanced at the door. "What would *you* say? What do *you* want?"

"Maybe just peace. Plain old peace."

He'd sidestepped her, but the question still hung in the stale air. She reached for her cup and let it swivel between her fingers and she waited. "So?" she said finally.

"What do I want? Let's see . . . I want . . . so many things." He shifted in his seat and looked hopeful suddenly. "The problem is that it's kind of like the letter thing. If you say 'I want this' and you don't get that thing, then—"

"If you don't want to tell me, that's okay. But tell me you don't want to tell me. I can get a straighter answer from your brother."

He hung his head and chewed on his straw. "Sorry," he said. "You're right. I'm not being—" He looked at her. "What is it you want to know?"

"I just want to know if you're going to miss me. That's all. If there's a small part of you that's going to miss my company. I don't need any letters or promises of letters . . . or, or any *things*. I'd just like to know . . ." She worried she might cry, but she kept her voice steady and refused to give in to any tears.

"Of course I'll miss you," he said. He broke into an assured grin. "You're—why, yeah. Why would you think . . ."

"Oh, I don't know. Because I'm younger, I guess. That's one thing. And I don't know what *we* are. And that's okay. I don't need to know. I'm not saying I need to know. I definitely don't. But it would be nice to know that there's a chance I'll be missed."

"Well, that's an easy one."

"Because the summer flew by. I don't ever remember a summer flying by so fast, and now you're going back to school."

"It did fly."

"And like I told you, I don't need a letter with a stamp on it and all that. But it'd be nice to know you had the thought of a letter in your head, that you had the idea of . . . that you had things you wanted to say to me even if you don't end up saying them. And I'm sure I'm making absolutely no sense right now."

"No no. I get it. I do. And I promise—"

"No promises—"

"I promise I'll have the thought of a letter."

"Stop. Please. Because you were right. Once you promise an actual letter I'll be waiting. If there's no promise I won't expect anything."

He considered this for a while. "So I was right? Now there's a scary thought."

"Oh, shut up."

"I tell you I'm going to miss you and you tell me to shut up!"

"You know what? I'm glad you're going away. 'Cause you're a real pain in the neck."

"Better than a pain in the ass."

"I have to go."

"Let's go."

"My mother's going to kill me."

He walked her to the end of her block as he'd done many times before, and they said their good-byes on the corner. For the first time he held her and kissed her, and if they hadn't been standing on the corner, Victoria thought, they might have done more. She walked away and forced herself not to look back, and her thoughts drifted back as they sometimes did to Eddie Milano. She was certain that the kissing brought Eddie to mind since those were the only Eddie-thoughts she had anymore, the mad, pulsing thoughts about the physical. She still savored the long slow kissing in the alley behind Eddie's house, the way he pulled her toward him. Even the two times in the backseat hadn't been terrible, just hurried. And Eddie had never gone further than she would allow. All the physical warmth between them, though, never sustained her. When she got home after seeing Eddie she still felt alone. She still felt a gaping hole in her heart over losing Benito. Maybe it was unfair to judge Eddie on those terms. Maybe they'd met at the wrong time. But she never felt *better* with him. The only thing Eddie provided was raw, short-lived passion.

With Richie, she felt a sense of renewal, and she wasn't sure whether to trust the impulse, but she gradually surrendered to it. Richie made her laugh, really laugh, like she hadn't done in so long. He made her believe there were things to look forward to in this life. He helped her understand her grief. What he hadn't given her at all until now was the physical. Walking away from him, she imagined Richie's warm breath and his hands searching. She imagined his scent pressing up against her. She wanted to inhale that scent and lock it away for safekeeping and when she took it in again his scent would become her breath. She turned into the gangway of her apartment and swallowed and wondered what she would do now with this new yearning.

For weeks Santo had avoided going anywhere near the A&P. Just about anything he needed he could buy at the corner dime store that smelled like polished wood and sawdust. But then Vince sent him out one day. He needed an emergency bottle of vermouth—the delivery guy never showed up last week, Vince cursed—so Santo had no choice, leaving him to wonder whether the vermouth was a Vince or a store emergency. If Ella was working, he decided, he'd put down a ten spot for the bottle, grab his change, and exit without a word.

When he got to the A&P he stepped on the black rubber pad that automatically swung open the heavy glass door, leaned in to eye the registers, and breathed relief when he saw that Ella wasn't there. He zoomed past canned vegetables, cereals, paper goods, dairy, and nearly stumbled over Ella in the pet aisle. She was transferring twenty-pound bags of Purina from a flatbed cart to a low shelf and stopped when she saw him. Down on one knee, she peered up at him.

"I'm looking for vermouth," he said.

She pointed. "Last aisle."

"I know. Thanks."

When he got to liquor, he spent more time there than he needed picking out a thirty-two-ounce bottle of dry vermouth. Finally, he set the bottle in the crook of his arm and walked back toward the pet aisle. There was another route to the registers, but he decided it wouldn't hurt to say good-bye. He slowed down some but not so she'd notice. "Found it," he said.

"Good," she said, and hefted the last bag onto the shelf. She straightened up and blew away a strand of hair that had fallen over her eyes. She kept her dog-food hands away from her sides.

Each time Santo saw her she seemed changed in some small way. She hadn't gotten her hair set in a while. She wore no makeup that he could detect and her brown eyes appeared startled and smaller as a result, which made her seem vaguely remote, almost feline, but harmless, too. She sighed and Santo thought he detected an invitation to say more.

"Dirty work, the pet aisle?"

"Somebody's gotta do it. Isn't that what they say?" She looked spent, disheveled.

"Don't they have stock boys or something to do that?"

"They only come in on Fridays, so we double up."

"Ah." He shifted his weight to his other leg and decided to cut short the conversation before he kept asking more questions he didn't need the answers to. "Well, I'll see you around maybe."

He turned.

"Wait. Before you go. I wanted to tell you—I felt I—you know, like I was pretty rough on you last time. And I tried to think why you deserved it, but I couldn't come up with anything, not really. Anyway, I wanted you to know, I'm sorry. I'm not usually—"

"Don't worry—"

"Or maybe I *am* usually . . . I don't know. Anyway . . ."

"It's all right."

She looked like she wanted to wash her hands.

"I better go," he said. "My uncle's waiting for his vermouth."

She nodded and he turned again.

"And . . ." she said. "This is going to sound—not stupid but . . ."

"What?"

"I think maybe I owe you five minutes."

Santo didn't know what to say. He didn't know whether he'd just had his five minutes or whether she was proposing five more.

"Don't worry about it," he said. Over the last couple of weeks he'd built up his own resentment and found it hard to cut through that now. He motioned with the bottle. "I have to get this back."

"Sure," she said. She pulled the bottle from his arm. "I'll ring you up."

She led him to an empty lane, wiped her hands with a paper towel, and punched a few keys on the register. "Identification?" she said. The other cashier peered over, going right on tapping in prices.

He reached for his wallet and remembered he'd left everything from his pockets on the ledge near the sink at the store. Vince had handed him the car keys and a ten. Even as this dawned on him, he continued patting his pockets. "I think I may have left everything back at . . . I do have money, though."

"I was kidding."

"Really?" *A first*, he thought.

"I guess that's hard to know with me sometimes. That's all I do at home with my mother and she never . . . she doesn't get it."

He handed her the ten and watched the numbers rise up

like toast inside the cash-register window, gold numbers on black tabs. The drawer slid open and he studied her fingers as they moved adroitly from one money compartment to another, as if she'd been working there her whole life. He waited for the change to be deposited into his open palm, considering what he might say next. If he walked out now, he knew he wouldn't return soon. He took his change and cleared his throat. "Thanks," he said. "You didn't have to open a line just for this."

"No big deal."

He glanced over his shoulder, then back at Ella, and spoke more softly. "And thanks for what you said back there. I never meant to upset you."

She nodded and tightened her lips as if embarrassed by her old anger. "I know."

"Anyway, take care," he told her.

She nodded again.

"And Joey, too," he added. "Take care of Joey."

That night, a Wednesday, Uncle Vince's night out with Carmel, Santo told his dad he needed an hour break. Agostino looked out at him with his lazy eye that Santo could never read and waved him away with a shrug. A few minutes later Santo slipped out through the back, feeling his father's steady gaze on him, wondering for the first time whether Ella had been right about the father moving in first and then the son . . . The thought disturbed him enough that he altered his route to the A&P several times, passing at corners and even doubling back once before moving ahead to the grocery store.

He waited in the parking lot without his uncle's Cadillac, hoping Ella got off at seven and that no one else would show up to pick her up and that she'd offer a trace of a smile when she saw him waiting. He leaned against a light pole that hummed with electricity at his back. An old woman with a tight babushka filed out, pulling her two-wheeled shopping basket behind her. A mother hand in hand with her son followed, her other hand hugging a large brown sack with a loaf of Gonnella threatening to sag out the top. By seven-fifteen he'd counted fifteen other customers and debated leaving. There'd be other opportunities, other emergency liquor he'd need for his uncle. Five minutes later she finally appeared, looking even more forlorn than before, a small bag in one hand and her smock crimped in the other.

She didn't see him until she was nearly upon him, and a question formed in her eyes, as if she couldn't immediately place him. "What—" she muttered.

He remained rooted there, leaning against the light pole with his arms crossed. "Hi."

"Hi," she said.

She seemed more puzzled than pleased, her usual state, and a surge of panic flashed through him. Her kind remarks earlier, he feared, had been a momentary lapse, a fluke, and he felt his confidence already slipping. Besides, he had to get back to the store—the last thing he needed was his father snooping into his affairs. Papa was generally passive, but he'd erupt over this craziness. And Santo couldn't blame him. His persistence here was beyond comprehension.

He blurted out what he'd rehearsed, and as the words left his lips he regretted them instantly. "I thought I'd cash in," he said.

She retreated a step.

No, he thought. His thoughts hurtled back to the first time they met, how he had to convince her he wasn't a stalker. Now here he was, back on his heels again. He pushed himself away from the pole. "Five minutes," he said quickly. "You said, 'I owe you five minutes,' and I thought I'd cash in. On the five minutes."

She looked to the parking lot.

"Well, I don't have my uncle's car, but I thought—"

"You thought you'd cash in today while she's in a good mood, huh?"

Cash in dripped off her tongue like hot tar.

"I didn't mean to make it sound like that." He wanted to move toward her but inched back.

And then he saw it. The resignation. The scowl. And he understood that look. He saw behind the scowl. All her life she'd been the dutiful daughter, bitter in her role but isolated in her bitterness. The more she did, the less she was appreciated, so she cooked and cleaned and obeyed out of spite. The one time she ventured out to please herself ended in trouble, not the ordinary trouble that could be swiftly brushed away, but trouble of a magnitude that convinced her that nothing good would ever come to her. Others would get their fill while Ella suffered quietly. And while her son, conceived in shame, would offer joy, a brief respite from the harshness of her life, he was also a burden, a reminder of her shame, another reason to barricade outsiders from her world like Santo, especially Santo. When the years passed and her son finally left, not able to properly express the gratitude Ella deserved, she wouldn't be surprised. Just like she wouldn't be surprised if Santo marched away from her at this very moment with barely a nod. That's what she expected. Maybe that's what she wanted, for him to turn away before he could *cash in* as everyone else in her life had done and would do.

She looked off down the block and muttered to herself. "He didn't mean to make it sound like that, he tells me . . ." Then she turned and took a step toward him. "So tell me, how was it supposed to sound?"

"Innocent, I guess."

"We're way past that, I'd say."

"I guess I thought—"

"What is it you want from me?"

"I'm not sure. A chance maybe."

"A chance for what?"

He needed to be careful here. "I guess I'd like a chance to be disliked for my own stupidity."

Her stern glare told him he was succeeding.

He looked at his hands and said, "I know we haven't gotten off to the best start. But I would've put money down that you wanted me to come back today."

"Does everything with you have to do with money?"

He suddenly remembered the bank receipt in Uncle Vince's strongbox and the talk about cashing in and he felt stupid all over again. Maybe he did deserve her disdain. "Sorry," he said. "I'm nervous, I guess. And I guess I misread you by a mile in the store. The fumes from the dog food maybe . . . threw me off. Anyway. What did you mean when you said you owed me five minutes?"

She loosened her grip on her smock and draped it over her arm.

"What you thought," she said.

He considered this. "What I thought. What I thought . . . But?"

"But I changed my mind. I talked myself out of it. What good are five minutes? What possible difference could five minutes make? And then you come along wanting to cash in."

"I don't want to cash in. Really. I don't. Forget that. Please. I just want to talk."

She moved toward the bus stop. "Okay," she said.

"Okay?"

"We'll talk."

"Well. Good. We'll talk."

He walked with her toward the bus stop, lagging a step behind, shuffling quietly. He craned his neck, looking for a bus, hoping for a little time, not sure whether he would hop on with her when the bus arrived.

"How's your son?" he asked.

"He's good. He's really good. I don't know what I'd do . . ." She pulled a stick of spearmint gum from the hip pocket of her smock, placed the gum on her tongue, then pushed the crushed foil wrapper back in the pocket. "He makes us laugh."

"Us?" He pictured her with another man, a stab of worry gripping his chest.

"Me and Mama." Ella told him about her father passing away nearly two years ago, how her father would never see his grandson. Which may have been fortunate. Since learning about Joey would have pained him. "I don't think I could have faced him," she said. She peered down the street, searching for a bus as she talked. "Anyway, now it's just me and Mama and Joey in that small house. That's why I started working. To get out."

"I know what it's like to be cooped up like that. Nowhere to turn to." He looked at his sneakers. "You and your mother get along okay?"

"About as good as you might expect. I'm still an embarrassment to her, I think, with her friends. When they're over for their coffee cake she'll fuss over her grandson and show him off, but he's always her grandson, never my son. I'm nothing when they're over. I'm the dirty stain on the carpet that no one looks at." She tried to make a bubble with her gum, but it wasn't the right kind for that. "So yeah, me and Mama get along swell. Everything's A-OK. Couldn't be better. Every day's like a vacation on the Riviera."

They didn't say anything for a while.

"And how is your family?" she asked. "How are you all getting along?"

They were two people waiting for a bus, discussing their lives. A surge of relief and something like elation coursed through Santo, followed almost immediately by a flurry of concerns that dampened his excitement. Was she really asking about his father? Did she have feelings for him still? Had she softened toward Santo in order to become closer to Agostino? Or did she want her own money now? The mother moves in for $10,000 and then the daughter . . . She *had* started working. She could use the money. Who couldn't? Who wouldn't take an easy ten grand if it were laid out on a platter? She'd earned it, deserved it. Uncle Vince had always warned Santo about owning a business and the vultures who circled for their cut. After all, Santo didn't know anything about Ella. He knew her wary eyes. He knew she could be shrewd. He knew she was the only child — more importantly — the only daughter of a first-generation European couple who would manage her life and breed the contempt required to give rise to thoughts of extortion. Beyond that, he knew nothing.

"Why do you ask?" he said.

"It's not a trick question," she said.

"Oh."

"I meant, how are they dealing with, you know, your brother's passing?"

"Oh."

"You don't have to—if you'd rather not."

"No no. It's okay." He thought about this for a few moments. "Everyone walks around it, I guess. I'm hoping this year will be better. We got through the first year, and that was tough, the first Thanksgiving without him, the first Christmas. He was only a baby, but it's hard to remember how we celebrated before him. I'm thinking this second year will be better."

He wanted to add that his father was particularly haggard. He wasn't entirely sure why, but he wanted to hear regret pouring from her lips. He'd seen her anger, her mistrust and bitterness, but never any trace of regret over her little affair with his father. Not that she'd caused his father's sorry state. Santo didn't want that on her shoulders. He just wanted her to realize she'd gotten involved with an old man, his *father*. In some sense, Ella had betrayed Santo, too, his entire family. He wanted to hear regret over *that*. Santo had long ago resolved his bitterness toward his father's repeated betrayal to the family, mainly because he felt powerless to feel otherwise, but with Ella, Santo held out hope for raw, anguished regret.

She looked off toward the ash trees reaching across Ohio Street and shook her head.

"What," he said.

"I just had a crazy thought."

"What?"

"I was just thinking . . . about Joey. And how he sort of saved us after my father was gone. He gave us something to laugh about. We hadn't laughed in that house for so long. And I was thinking that it's too bad you don't have — this is crazy — that it's too bad you don't have another baby in the house. I don't mean to replace your brother. But to give you someone to care for. It's a crazy thought, I know."

She hugged her smock nervously.

"That *is* hard to imagine," he said.

Three or four blocks away, a bus finally emerged.

"So Joey saved you?" he said.

She reached for the purse slung over her shoulder and unsnapped the pocket inside and retrieved two coins. "Maybe *saved* isn't the right word. I don't know. Maybe it is. I guess maybe he did."

The bus was moving now, looming larger, its giant headlights carving a path in the dusk.

"So without him . . ." he said. He dug into his pocket for a dime but didn't have any change. "Do you ever, you know, regret — "

"Every day," she said. "Not a single day goes by — but then I look at Joey, my little boy, and feel this shame that's so black my insides hurt. How can I think about regret? I wonder. When I feel like that I usually go over and hug him and pretend and forget about what I've done with my life, but the regret always comes back. Like one of those jackhammers that rip up the sidewalk."

The bus clanked to a stop in front of them. It was one of the newer, more streamlined buses that didn't run on a trolley line. The double doors hissed open, and the driver gazed down on them, two more passengers on a slow Wednesday evening in September. Ella looked at Santo, and her eyes asked, *What do we do now?* With a slight nod, he motioned for her to step on, then followed her up the three short stairs, knowing he had no dime to drop into the driver's open palm and that he'd be late getting back to Mio Fratello, but none of that mattered much to him right now. If he could whistle, he thought, that's what he would do. He'd whistle and let the airy tune guide them through the narrow aisle to their seats at the back of the bus, apart from the others. He'd whistle, and the others would pull in their bags to let them pass. But he couldn't whistle and Ella had to lend him a dime and they sat up front near two chattering old women who looked at them disapprovingly, the smell of dog food and stale liquor from their work rising up between them. They both stared at the back of the driver's head. The bus chugged along, Santo and Ella rocking quietly to the rhythmic jostling of the bus, surrendering to its sway and pull.

7

⁂

ngela Rosa gazed out at the tall stand of cypress trees lining the base of the Apennine hills and wondered how she could have forgotten this remarkable view. She'd been gone twenty years, of course, and the trees may have been mere saplings then, but even the hills themselves, ice-capped and cobalt blue at their peaks, ridged and runneled from centuries of rain and snow, seemed more magnificent than she remembered. How could she have forgotten? And how could she ever return to Chicago?

Though it was February and cold, she walked each day to this spot before the hills just beyond her family's fields so she could escape the stale air of the old farmhouse where she, Lupa, and Victoria would reside for the rest of the winter and spring. The farmhouse, rough-hewn stone walls and mortar, had been abandoned by Angela Rosa's family shortly after her father died some ten years ago. Her mother couldn't keep up with the farming, so she sublet the land to a neighbor and moved the two kilometers to San Salvatore. The village was nothing more than sixty or seventy squat houses along three winding roads that all led to a cobblestoned square of storefronts—a food market, two bars, a seamstress, a barber, and a tiny post office with a telegraph. Angela Rosa's mother invited the three of them, the three Americans, to stay with them in the village, where they at least had electricity if not indoor plumbing. But Angela Rosa insisted on the rustic farmhouse. She told her mother there was no room in the house in the village, what with Angela Rosa's widowed aunt and her kids living there. Besides, she wanted to teach Victoria about hardship, real hardship. She wanted to knock out all the American nonsense that filled her head. Victoria's time in Italia would be hard, Angela Rosa said. Only then would Victoria realize how good she had it on Superior Street in America, and only then would she learn to obey.

At the farmhouse, they had a fireplace, cooking supplies, candles, basins for water, and a deep well. Only Lupa complained about the conditions, as if she'd forgotten where she came from. She agreed that Victoria needed to be taught some lessons, but why must Lupa sacrifice, too? Why should Victoria's wildness translate into Lupa's punishment? she argued. Angela Rosa invited her sister to leave. She didn't have to come along, Angela Rosa reminded her. Only two tickets had been bought—originally intended for Angela Rosa and Agostino—with Lupa's airfare added at the last minute at her own insistence. No one had shoved a ticket in her face. Lupa would always back down, of course, because her sister was right, but she couldn't hide the fury building inside her. She would pace the four rooms of the farmhouse muttering to herself, cursing one thing after another.

Victoria largely ignored her aunt's ranting and remained, in Angela Rosa's eyes, remarkably calm. Maybe their trip was already doing some good, she thought. Victoria padded around each room mostly silent, either tired or repentant, Angela Rosa couldn't tell which, completing chores that hadn't yet been doled out to her. Having seen her mother's village and the square and the clapboard schoolhouse, the only clapboard building in the entire village, Victoria even had questions about her mother's childhood.

Sometimes, with the day's chores done and with bread baking in the fireplace, the three of them would sit before the flames and forget their squabbles, an air of domesticity descending upon the room unexpectedly, as if the three of them had always occupied this space. Angela Rosa would lean back then, aware of her contentment, and recount the stories of her youth to her daughter.

In Italian she told Victoria about the old schoolhouse, not the clapboard one built after the war but the solid two-room fortress of a stone building that housed all the grades. She'd only completed seven grades because she had to help around the farm, feeding chickens, shelling peas, small chores that, if not backbreaking, made her bone weary by the end of the day. When she was in sixth grade, her teacher, Mrs. Alligretti, would lead Angela Rosa to her home at lunchtime and make her sweep and scrub the floors, threatening her with a failing grade if she ever told anyone. She didn't fail. She got down on her hands and knees and scrubbed, counting the minutes until the lunch hour ended so she could get back to school and push down a few bites of the sandwich her mother had prepared for her.

Angela Rosa looked at her daughter. She hadn't intended to convey some lesson or evoke the pity she saw in Victoria's eyes; she was simply telling stories, the only ones she knew. In their kitchen on Superior Street, such stories elicited blank stares, even anger if they were followed by moral directives. But here in her native land, the tales resonated. Victoria shook her head and rubbed the side of her face, and in that moment Angela Rosa saw how her daughter would look in five or ten years. For the first time, she saw her daughter as a woman.

Victoria turned to her and asked about coming to America, how she came to adjust.

Those first few months, she said, were burned in her memory. Lupa nodded but didn't interrupt. She didn't know the language, she didn't know how to act, she didn't even know her husband. She walked around like a shell, afraid to let anyone see how afraid she was. She'd stand before the mirror each morning practicing a big American smile to face the world, but that kind of smiling didn't come easy to her, so she lowered her head and kept to herself. Thank God for Lupa, who stayed with them that first month. She did like how Americans always moved, not slowing even at midday. This she could do. Work was not foreign to her. She walked twenty minutes each day to the Zenith plant because she worried about getting on the wrong bus. Everyone there spoke Spanish or Italian, which was reassuring, but where would she learn English? She retreated further into work, putting in overtime—she enjoyed the piecework—then washing and painting the apartment on weekends. "It feels like I've never stopped."

She and Lupa took turns removing the bread from the fireplace, lightly fanning the blue embers. Reaching for the pan, her face flush from the heat, Angela Rosa wondered how she could miss those hard days, struggling to please her husband, learning a new job, fending off yearnings for home. Agostino did his utmost to please, courting her, reassuring her with his questions about what she wanted. In bed his touch was tender and patient, though she would have been content to lie next to him. She knew she couldn't refuse him, though, and learned how to please him, Agostino making efforts to learn the same about her. But then he'd fall fast asleep, and she'd be alone again.

She began waking earlier, at first because she was restless, but then because she wanted to stop at St. Columbkille before work to light a novena candle and sit in solitude. There were other women, but their eyes were downcast and their mouths solemn. One morning when she forgot her rosary, she prayed directly to Jesus and Mary, crafting her own prayer, pleading for strength. Why such a simple gesture would mark for her the bedrock of her faith, she couldn't say. Maybe she was fatigued and prone to seek meaning in any misstep. Maybe the other women, curled around their rosaries and scapulars, inspired devotion. Maybe her loneliness had become unbearable. Or maybe, and she was most inclined to believe this notion, the light pouring in that morning from the high windows fell so softly upon the oak pews, illuminating the rich grain and honey brown, that she had to believe in God. A shaft of light held motes of dust that went ordinarily unseen. She'd seen such a constellation of light and dust before, she'd learned rudimentary science in school, she knew that things unseen do exist, but the enormity of that possibility hit her like revelation. The next day she remembered her rosary and prayed the beads, but the words seemed less rote. She came to recognize the beauty in repetition, in ritual. She came to believe that religion was nothing more than that, an acknowledgment of all the beauty in the world. Which is why mass sustained her. The slow flurry of ritual—the purple vestments during

Advent, the raising of the chalice, the incense shaken from gold canisters, the ointment pressed onto foreheads on Ash Wednesday, the, solemn chanting during Holy Week, the genuflecting, the kneeling, the crossing, the dipping of fingertips into holy water—all this was proof of God to her. She wondered if these ideas had been unwittingly passed on to her through her grandfather, who in winter, when he couldn't plant or plow, painted landscapes of fertile fields on stone walls. Maybe her staunch faith, her rapture with beauty, was merely an expression of love and longing for her grandfather, whom she would never see again. When Benito passed, she suffered doubt about all this, of course. How could God take such beauty from her? And she refused to see light anywhere. But to refuse God like that meant abandoning her son as well. Battered, she forced herself back to church, losing herself in ritual. Nothing else could comfort her.

When they sat down again, Angela Rosa wondered if she could adequately express any of this to her daughter. She looked to the hills and told her instead about Mussolini. Her class had been assigned an essay that was to be entitled "Believe, Obey, Fight," and the winner would get to carry an effigy of Il Duce in a torchlight parade in his honor. Angela Rosa had seen the metal placard at the entrance of the school with the same three words stamped on it, and she'd seen the identical sign at the post office. But the words meant nothing to her. She asked Lupa, who understood fascism better than she ever would, to write the essay in her name. She won first prize, of course, and got to lead an entourage of local villagers and some Black Shirts from Naples around the school and to the main square. She'd felt phony and hapless the whole march, worried she'd be found out, this new child leader of the Fascist world.

Angela Rosa's father, Victoria's grandfather, seemed worried, too. He frowned and scratched his chin when he read the essay. After the Black Shirts returned to the north, he tried to help her see through all the nationalistic chest-thumping. Mussolini may have improved some things now, he told her, but in the end he would ruin Italia with his brutal tactics. At the time, Angela Rosa didn't understand most of what her father said, and she wanted to ease his worry, but she couldn't tell him that Lupa had written the essay. Years later, when Agostino showed up looking for a wife, she finally understood her father's concerns. And she understood why he was willing to let her go to another continent. They'd all seen too many young men and even women being torn from their families by the secret police. Her marriage to the Americano would be his daughter's escape.

Believe, Obey, Fight. Angela Rosa still didn't understand entirely what those three words together meant. She didn't understand the single-mindedness it required to live a life devoted to such a collective cause. She had a hard enough time worrying about her immediate family.

There were other stories, of course, and Lupa joined in, too. But there was one Angela Rosa wouldn't share. Even Lupa knew only sketchy details. The story reminded her of what it was like to be a girl and gave her hope that Victoria would turn out all right. When she could no longer stand her daughter's obstinacy she remembered this story.

Having won the writing contest in its inaugural year, Angela Rosa, wearing a black sash and waving a miniature Italian flag, became its celebratory masthead. The parade was all show to her, but she came to look forward each year to dressing up and preparing for the day's events. In the parade's fourth and last year, when she was seventeen, she met

Giuseppe Conti, one of the Black Shirts from Naples. While all the other young men marched stoically as they'd been trained, Conti wiggled his eyebrows and stepped with a clownish hitch whenever he passed a group of children. Angela Rosa marched three columns ahead of him and wouldn't have noticed any of this if it weren't for the children's giggling and their eager pointing. She widened the scope of her waving so she could turn and glance back at the source of all the amusement. Though he was several years her senior, when he saw her studying him, he stopped clowning immediately. She read remorse in his sheepish grin. If this was the girl who represented fascism in this hill country, he wasn't about to fly in the face of that. The other uniformed men behind her were so regimented in their gazing that Angela Rosa realized that she and this young man with the bright eyes could privately exchange glances. She lifted her arm abruptly in a high wave to catch his attention and shot *him* a clownish look that at first astonished him then pleased him so much that he began to roll his eyes and stretch his grin for her entertainment.

Milling around the sweet table later, Conti kept a respectful distance from her, but as he reached for a pastry he leaned into her and muttered wild things in her ear. What loveliness to lead a parade, he said. He had been in Rome, in Milan, throughout France, but had never witnessed such loveliness before. If they could disappear for an hour undetected he would take her on a picnic up in the hills and they would pick berries and find a stream where they could dip their feet—away from the parades and the Black Shirts and talk of Mussolini. He spoke this way, he said, because his patrol would depart within the hour, and because there was no other way to talk amid such beauty. Who was this Salvatore for whom they named the village? They should have named it after her. He spoke quickly and with such playful animation that she couldn't object or take offense or even try to temper his praise with staged humility. All she could do was smile and try to contain her pulse.

He left with the other men, of course, but said he'd meet her at one o'clock next Sunday afternoon a kilometer outside the village along the north road that led to the Appian Way. She never agreed to meet him—how could she respond so quickly—but when Sunday came she walked along the north road for twenty minutes until she finally felt so foolish that she simply stopped and sat down and waited without hope. The sun baked the back of her neck and the wind kicked up great swirls of dust all around her. After a while she began to make her way back, already resigned to never seeing again her impassioned suitor with the long lashes and straight nose. She didn't get far. Behind her she heard the rumble of a truck and two friendly honks, and before she could fully turn around he was out of his little jeep and running to take her hand.

They met nearly every Sunday for the rest of that summer, sometimes just driving, sometimes pulling off to a grassy field for an afternoon picnic. Most often they drove to a neighboring farmer's shed where enormous tobacco leaves were strewn about for drying. They discovered that a pile of these leaves, though initially pungent, provided ample cushion for their heads. Conti seemed content with the limits she placed upon their touching, and she was happy just to be lying next to him. She didn't allow herself to fall in love with him because she knew he'd be gone, and she couldn't begin to imagine explaining this Black Shirt jester to her father. She couldn't keep this promise to herself for long, though. She would have defied her father, she would have run away with him, but those urges, finally, only drove Conti away sooner than he would have left anyway.

Sitting on the edge of a hard-backed chair, forcing down a few bites of breakfast, fried egg whites and some kind of steak, Victoria stared at the brass hands of the alarm clock on the fireplace mantel. When she'd gotten up twenty minutes ago, she wound the clock as tightly as it would go, and she now imagined the little windup tab on the back loosening with each tick. The loosening wasn't something she could see, but she could feel it. She could hear it.

She spent most of her days now calculating Chicago time, subtracting six hours and imagining the intensity of the Midwest sun or the brightness of the moon illuminating the streets so familiar to her. The things she longed for sometimes surprised her—the sight of a mailman, cracks in the sidewalk, the scent of newspaper ink on her fingers, pushing clothes through the ringer washer in the basement, the sound of coins jingling in her father's pockets, his Brylcreem scent. These things would flash before her without warning and she'd have to stop and catch her breath, and for those few moments she could block out the faint but persistent scent of salami and mortadella that seemed to have permeated the farmhouse walls. That smell she could bear, but there was another odor, too, that she couldn't quite place when she first arrived, a stench from the cellar, where, she later learned, butchered meat once hung from iron hooks. She ventured down there once, the bloodstained hooks still hanging from the ceiling, and had to turn and race outside, where she let loose her breakfast in the frozen field.

She pushed her eggs away and glanced at the clock again without realizing she was doing so. She counted back to when she'd last seen Richie, around Christmastime, and then counted back further to September, five months and four days ago, an ordinary Tuesday evening. She'd been walking around after dinner, hoping she would run into Willie, that maybe he'd have some news about his brother back at school. Richie had been gone nearly three weeks, and her heart still fluttered when she thought about him. But she hadn't gotten any word from him, not even a postcard. After walking around aimlessly for a while, she began to make her way to Darlene's, and she remembered now the sense of clarity that overcame her about this minor certainty. Knowing where she was going, she began to move more deliberately, as if she were gliding across a slick sheet of ice. And that's when she saw him, felt his car creeping up alongside her. His aunt's car actually. He was still driving his aunt's boat of a car, the copper-colored DeSoto. He nodded his crooked nod and leaned into the passenger seat and called through his far window.

"Hey, good lookin'," he said.

"Hey, Eddie."

She kept walking, and the car inched alongside her, a slow creep.

"Need a lift?"

"Not really. I'm just going to Darlene's."

"Need a smoke?"

She knew he could be persistent, and Darlene wasn't expecting her this early, and she *could* use a cigarette. She could really use a cigarette. Getting cigarettes most nights was a game for Vicki and Darlene, the two of them taking turns guessing where the night's cigarettes would come from. Lately the game was getting old, though, and Vicki was tired of the scheming, and here it was, a cigarette right in front of her, an easy invitation. So she nodded and went to his car and pulled open the heavy door, listening to the deep click of the latch as she pulled the door shut behind her. She took the cigarette from Eddie's extended hand and let him light it with his chrome lighter, the butane flame licking the air blue. Suddenly the lighter was closed and tucked away in his pocket, but she couldn't remember the precise movements that made this happen. In one moment the flame danced before her eyes and in another the flame was gone with a thumb click.

His arm rested along the top of the seat, his body leaning toward the middle. He looked her full in the face with his blue eyes, nearly the color of the flame, she thought. And that smile. She remembered licking the corners of his mouth, one side and then another, the warm taste of his lips.

"I don't see you around much anymore," he said.

"Yeah. My mom got me a job at Zenith. Secretary stuff."

After a few deep puffs, she already felt more relaxed. She watched his foot ease off the brake, and they began to move.

"You can drop me off by Darlene's," she told him.

"Exactly," he said. "Whatever you say."

They both blew smoke out their windows, Victoria grateful for the cigarette, grateful for the ride, glad that Eddie was being so agreeable. She watched the houses glide by her window and heard the whining of tires under the car. Then, without warning, Eddie's hand reached for hers, his fingers lacing around her fingers.

"Remember this?" he said. "Holding hands, cruising? Seems like a long time ago, huh? Whatever happened?"

She could have taken her hand away, but he got her thinking about their cruising, and for a few minutes she was back there again, more naive maybe but still in charge, even then. She remembered the thrill she felt when she discovered the power she could have over men by letting them take her hand or smell her hair, small gestures that turned them into boys. She decided to let Eddie hold her hand for a while and have something to talk about when she got to Darlene's.

"I don't know what happened with us," she said. "Maybe it wasn't meant to be."

"Your asshole brother didn't help."

"That's his job, I guess."

"What? To be an asshole?"

"Yeah. I guess so. In a way." Santo hadn't bothered her about Richie, and she'd been feeling generous toward him lately. "He means well," she added.

Eddie took his hand away and rested it loosely along the top of the steering wheel. He stayed leaning toward the middle of the seat. "Yeah, he meant well when he slugged me in the face. He meant well all right."

"I shouldn't have gone there that night. Or I should have left when I saw him at the club."

"Oh, so it's your fault I got slugged?"

She gave him her best pout. "Poor Eddie."

"Exactly. Poor Eddie. So how're you going to make it up to me, Vicki?"

She knew this was a line, a rock-solid Eddie bullshit line that he knew wouldn't get him in trouble with her. She wouldn't ask him to stop the car so she could storm out. But she might, she just might come back with her own line. He was exploring possibilities, Eddie possibilities. And though she realized all this, though she heard the hollowness of his *exactly—whatever you want,* she still felt a faint stirring somewhere within her that she couldn't ignore. Here was the man or the boy she'd been most intimate with in her short life, an arm's length away, the smell of night descending upon them, his cologne scent making her feel light-headed, and here she was aching to hold someone—there would never be enough touching in this life—with little chance of ever hearing again from the one she really wanted to hold. A sense of unfairness gripped her for an instant, but she was used to that by now. She expected unfairness. No surprises there. She refused to hold on to that, though. Not this time. She wouldn't gripe. She wouldn't let her true desires interfere with the heat rising inside of her. She felt light. She felt a restlessness in her legs.

"So?" he said.

A low laugh rumbled from the back of her throat. A devious little chuckle.

"You're bad," she teased.

"Who? Me?"

"Yes, you."

"What did I say?"

"It's what you didn't say."

"You see. I didn't say anything."

They went back and forth like this, both of them waiting for the night to envelop them more fully so they could park and follow through on what they knew would happen now. She didn't recall the driving to the woods or the parking or how they got in the backseat, but she remembered the trembling and the warmth she felt on her upper lip beforehand.

She remembered the anxious tugging of clothes. This time she pushed him below her, determined to take her time, riding him slowly, building up to what she wanted until she let herself go in final hungry thrusts and desperate gasps. She felt primitive and powerful all at once.

Two days later she got Richie's letter, the Wisconsin postmark emblazoned across the top, mocking her. In the letter he offered a sweet apology for not writing sooner, light but direct. He said he'd been thinking about her a lot and that he missed her more than she could imagine, and he told her when he'd be home. He said they could walk to Jimmy's and have a beef and fries and that he really did miss the fries but not as much as the company.

She hadn't promised him anything when he left but believed now with the letter in her hand that she'd betrayed him in the worst way. She could have waited, she told Father Ernie in the confessional later that week. She spent fifteen minutes in there one morning asking her priest friend if there was any difference between two times and three times in the backseat. Was the third time worse for some reason?

"I won't condone any of this. You have to know that," he said. "I'm not going to attribute different values to different sins."

"Don't pull that on me now. Isn't that what you do? Three Hail Marys versus five Our Fathers. Isn't there some chart you use?"

"I *would* have you consider this. Did you believe you loved the boy each time?"

She felt Father Ernie's warm breath float across the dark curtain now.

"That's the big question, isn't it, Father? How can I answer that? How am I supposed to know about love?"

"Given that, maybe you should have waited. But you've already said that."

His words always sounded more priestlike in the confessional. She should have tried to catch him outside.

"Yes, I did say that," she said. "And I could have. I could have waited. Don't you think I know that? What's worse . . ." Her voice broke as she knew it would, just as it did when she explained everything to Darlene.

"What's worse?" he whispered.

"I didn't love him. I guess I know that. It was a selfish thing." She wrung her hands together. "What's worse, though . . . is that, at the time, I cared for someone else."

"I see," he said gravely.

"You must think—"

"It doesn't matter what I think."

She heard the strain in his voice, the measured restraint, and this restraint was her reprimand. She wiped her eyes.

"It *does* matter what you think," she insisted. "That's why I came here."

"If what I thought mattered," he said, "you would have come to see me before you did what you did."

"Don't be angry, Father. Please. It's not something I planned."

"Yeah, well, planning would be an interesting consideration."

She felt herself sinking into the padded kneeler. He'd never been this cold toward her. Only later did it occur to her that he might have been struggling with his own affection, that maybe he was remotely jealous in a way even he couldn't understand. But in the confessional, all she heard was his sternness. And it was the first time she felt regret over coming to see him. For the first time she had to endure long patches of screeching silence in the confessional.

She heard him sigh and shift around on his chair. He whispered some Latin incantations to himself that struck her as soothing if unintelligible.

"Listen," he told her. "Listen to me. I'm sorry if I got you upset. I shouldn't have let my disappointment interfere with . . . with my sacred duties here." He cleared his throat, a sign of his discomfort. "I won't disguise my disappointment in you. We've been through all this before. You're an intelligent young woman with strong convictions, but you're human, too, and you make mistakes. What's important here is that you recognize your mistakes. You do, I think. And it seems to me that you want to learn from those mistakes. God forgives mistakes — if that's what you want."

She cared less about God's forgiveness at that point than Father Ernie's. She'd settle for simple understanding. But he'd barricaded himself, hunkered himself behind his little sermon.

"Pontificate," she said. "Isn't that the word you hate? Isn't that what you said to me one time? You didn't want to pontificate, you told me. Because I wouldn't listen anyway. I guess that doesn't apply anymore, huh?"

He didn't answer.

"I guess I better go," she said. "Someone else might need to get in here."

She heard his door open and then close. He sat back on his stool. "No one out there," he said. "But if you need to go."

"I hate to leave with, you know, you being disappointed in me and all."

"My disappointment is nothing compared to your own."

"Do you hate me?"

He chuckled. "Vicki—"

"Because this hasn't exactly been my favorite time at confession, let me tell you."

"Confession shouldn't come easy."

"So do you hate me? And please, no more priest answers."

"Actually . . ." He sighed, and she could make out his hand rubbing his brow. "You make me laugh, Vicki. Gladys, the secretary at the rectory, she says she can always tell when I've been talking with you. No, Vicki. I don't hate you. That is farthest from the truth. In fact, I love you. Not only as a priest but as a friend."

She couldn't speak for a few moments. "Thanks," she said finally. "I guess I needed to hear that. What should I do now?"

He waited. "Maybe you should talk to—"

"No, I mean about penance. What prayers should I say?"

"No penance this time. Just talk to this person you care about. Tell him everything. Find out what he's made of."

"I'd rather have the twenty Hail Marys, thank you very much. Nothing's easy with you, is it?"

He sighed, the old Father Ernie sigh that told her everything would be okay between them.

"If you weren't a priest," she muttered, which surprised her, this line that held no teasing this time, only acknowledgment.

"If—" He couldn't finish. With the back of his hand he wiped the corner of his eye, which stirred her own tears. "That's my line," he managed, bringing the two of them safely back to what they'd always been to each other. Though she was grateful, she had no regrets about blurring that line. She knew their friendship could withstand this tiny jolt. There would be no shame over this.

"Talk to him, Vicki," he urged again.

She walked home a bit more assured about her troubles. Confession had done her good. But mostly, Richie was over two hundred miles away, and she wouldn't have to face him until Christmas.

Angela Rosa missed her husband. She woke up one morning after two months of being away and ached to hear his voice and take in his musk scent. And with that ache came the quiet realization that she'd been missing him since Benito's passing, for nearly two years now. In that time he had reached out to her, but she'd resisted each time. She didn't have the energy to look at him. After a while she forgot how to respond.

Theirs had been a marriage of regularity, set patterns built up over years of familiarity. They'd allowed their grief to generate its own routine, by stepping around their sadness. They never mentioned Benito's name. They allowed his room to be filled with Agostino's odd clutter, which took on a shape and a breath of its own. Vince had driven her and Agostino to the cemetery several times after the funeral, but the silence in the car and at the grave site was maddening. The two of them, the two men, were lost among the markers, and so she began to take the trolley alone each week. Looking back now, she wondered whether she should have taken along her children, whether they needed to go, but she'd been too intent on shielding them; the idea of walking around the graveyard with them never remotely occurred to her. She did hug her sons more, especially the two younger ones—she made a point of doing that—and she would have done the same with Victoria if she would have allowed it. She saw the pain in her daughter's eyes and wanted to lift that from her.

But Agostino she resisted. She knew he felt punished—and she wondered sometimes how she could be so cruel to her own husband. It wasn't that she blamed him. Lately she'd been thinking that her son's death was no one's fault. But she did punish Agostino. She punished him, finally, for his drifting, for his callousness, for his thinking she was stupid enough to believe his late-night excuses. She'd never confronted him and didn't care to spy, preferring to know as little as possible, but she remained confident always that he would curb his straying once Anthony was born, then once Alfredo was born, then after Benito arrived. And as far as she could tell, she was right. The birth of each child unleashed a paternal side to him that she always found endearing. And he *had* been mostly faithful throughout their twenty years together. He came home each night, which was more than one could say about some of the other fathers in the neighborhood. He came home sober. And never raised a hand to her. This was something. She felt she couldn't complain. Besides, who would listen?

She wondered how her life would be different if Agostino had not come along, if she had married a different man. Would the same questions of fidelity still plague her? She assumed that most men were like her old black-shirted friend, Giuseppe Conti, who had a passion for wandering. But unlike Conti, most men concealed their lusts and confined themselves in threadbare prisons that barely kept them. Conti once told her that he'd seen and heard too much of the baser side of human nature—how Mussolini ordered tailors to take

clothes from the dead and refashion them into military uniforms—that Conti would dedicate himself to spreading joy instead. She knew that this joy he spoke of was grounded in his
own selfish pleasures, but she admired his passion nonethe-
less. She asked him if he could ever be a father. Could he ex-
perience this boundless joy he spoke of within the confines of
a marriage? He wasn't sure, he said. But he knew that all mar-
riages involve great lies; both partners had to perpetuate the
lie. They had to pretend.

Conti was right, of course, she knew that now, but she preferred to view marriage as compromise rather than fabrication.
Lately, though, she couldn't give Agostino even that. They'd
burrowed themselves away from each other for so long that
they barely looked at each other. But she was determined now
to come back to him, to give him what he needed. She only
hoped she wasn't too late.

Another sharp pain. *Respiri*, they said. Breathe. And then
their incessant whispering. Half prayer, half curse. She understood a quarter of what they said and didn't care to know
even that. If they would only shut the hell up for five minutes.
What could any words from their mouths possibly matter?
Especially Lupa. She never said anything. She talked without interruption now and never said anything. Say something.
Say some thing. The pains were more frequent now. *Respiri*.
Shut up, she thought. She thought it and thought it and said
it finally. *Shut up!* But that didn't stop their whispering. They
couldn't stop. Nothing could make them stop. She would lie
in this bed forever with the two of them hovering over her

like a bad dream. She closed her eyes and felt herself drifting away. When she opened them again a third woman appeared who took Victoria's hand but didn't say a word. Victoria didn't think she could stand a third voice in this room. *Sforzati,* the woman said. Push. She squeezed the woman's hand, this woman without features who suddenly appeared at her bed. She was older than Mama, a paisley kerchief holding back her iron-gray hair. *Respiri,* the woman said. The voice was soothing, without rancor or apprehension. If only Mama and Lupa would stop, if only she hadn't shown Mama the swelling back then, another lifetime, if only she had waited she could have waited she was good at waiting. Only if. The woman waved at Mama and Lupa, and they moved from the bed. They moved away from her. But their whispering. Incessant like fire. They sat on the far side of the room, but she could feel their hot breaths. *This will ruin her,* they agreed. Ruination. Damnation. This will ruin her, they said again. They couldn't let that happen. They whispered like fire, their words lapping the gray walls, the dry sibilance of their whispering unhinging her. Damnation. Ruination. They both agreed. She felt a tightening below and arched her back from the bed. *Sforzati,* ordered the woman. Push. They were at her side again, Mama taking her hand. *Respiri,* the woman said. *Respiri.* Lupa with her broad shoulders towered over the foot of the bed now. She gripped the mahogany bed frame. She gazed at Victoria, strained benevolence iced on her face. *Noi auitiamo,* she said. We will take care of you. *Can't you see I can take care of myself? I don't need anyone except this woman who holds my hand and doesn't whisper. This pain is mine not yours this pain is mine and all you have is your whispering and this pain is* —Sforzati. Sforzati con forza— *how much longer if only I hadn't if I hadn't . . . I want to go home. I'll tell her, I'll tell the woman I want to go home I'm through here. This pain is mine not yours I'm done here I can't I won't how much longer this can't go on much longer if only I hadn't if only why does it hurt back there a new pain think about the new pain I can do this the new pain where is she where is the woman with the warm hands who is going to stop all this I need a hand I need I'll take any hand I'll take your hand Zia Lupa squeeze my hand Zia squeeze my hand Mama squeeze* —Sforzati sforzati—*I'll do anything you say just stop this I'm finished why won't you end this . . . there, there she is. The woman. At the foot of the bed now her bloody hands oh God let this be over God I'll obey I'll listen I'll pray just end this* —Respiri—*I can do that one breath then another easy* respiri *the skies back home are they blue today six hours six hours I need to see the clock someone bring me the clock what time is it back home subtract six can anyone is there anyone who can feel this pain get it out I need it out why doesn't he just come out* —Sforzati con forza—*her hands the woman's hands strong now firm the same hands that earlier or did I imagine that the same hands that had lit a match and thrown it in a glass and covered it with a cloth and then placed the glass on my swelling that must have been a dream these barbarians with their superstitions let me go home but it wasn't a dream because the glass and the match are there on the table Mama and Lupa were right damnation ruination stop this and I'll do anything they say.* The woman's hands were not so soothing anymore. They were forceful, pushing and prodding inside her. *Sforzati,* she ordered. She pulled something like forceps from a pot of water next to the bed. She disappeared, prodding and pulling inside, her fingers frantic. *Aspetta,* she shouted suddenly. *Aspetta.* Wait wait. Victoria thought she might pass out then. She let her body go slack. *It's over,* she thought. She could have her body back. *Sforzati,* she heard again. *Sforzati,* the woman ordered. *Go to hell* sforzati, *I'm done.* The woman showed

Victoria her eyes. *Sforzati!* She heard a finality in the command and drew up all her remaining strength for one last push. One last tug. She thought she felt tearing, a ripping. She heard a baby's cry and felt a ripping still and wet warmth and then the woman told her, No more. Stop. *Respiri. Respiri.* They told her not to move, to relax. Mama carried the bloody baby away from the bed while the woman pulled more instruments from the pot and some kind of thread. Victoria didn't want to look. She refused to look. She just wanted to see this baby. *Mama, come here,* she thought. *Mama.* But she felt more tugging and pulling and couldn't get the words out. *Mama, I need to see. My baby,* she wept. Zia Lupa placed a cold towel on her forehead and told her to relax. It's over now, she told Victoria. It's all over. But it wasn't over. She needed to hold her baby. *My baby,* she finally managed to say. Zia Lupa told her to relax. Mama has the baby, Lupa told her. We need to take care of *you* right now, she said. *But the baby. My baby.* She felt herself trembling, turning cold. Delirium must have set in because she heard Zia Lupa telling her that everything would be all right and she was soothed by her aunt's voice. Pure delirium. Everything would be all right, Zia Lupa told her. She heard the woman, still working beneath her, bellowing instructions, and Lupa disappeared. It would be over soon, the woman told her. But Victoria had to keep still. Lupa raced back and handed the woman something and Victoria soon felt another tug and then a burning and she screamed from the burning and the heat surged through her and she screamed *My baby my baby I want my baby.* The woman with the soothing hands came up from beneath her and wiped her hands and slapped Victoria across the cheek. It's over, she told her. All over. Victoria was afraid to move. She turned her head and wept into the pillow, hard sobs she couldn't contain. She wanted to stop her tears, though. She needed to stop. She needed to talk with them, reason with them. They'd dragged her to this farmhouse to steal her baby. That's what all the whispering was about. She wasn't stupid. And they believed they were helping. Damnation. Ruination. She'd be damned if she would let them steal her baby. She'd carried that baby for thirty-eight weeks, felt him kicking inside her, felt him tumble and grow. *I want to see my baby,* she sobbed. The woman gave her something then, made her drink it and told her the baby was a boy. She packed away her things. After a short while Victoria felt drowsy and closed her eyes and slept without dreaming.

When she awoke they let her hold and feed her son. Afterward, they spoke calmly about what would happen. While they talked she stared at her baby snuggled in her arms and wondered about a name, something she hadn't even begun to consider. They told her they would have to return home in the next several weeks and that they'd find a way for her to secretly feed the baby. Agostino and the others, they scoffed, wouldn't notice if she fed the boy in front of them, that's how foolish they were. They, the three of them in this birthing room, would all act as if the baby was Angela Rosa's, but in a couple of years, once Victoria was ready, married hopefully, which they would pray for, then other arrangements would be made. Angela Rosa would feign sickness and tell everyone she couldn't care for the baby any longer. She'd tell everyone she was too weak, too old. Who would object? Everyone would think, the baby is in good hands with Zia Victoria. And if Victoria got married sooner, all the better. This is a temporary arrangement, they reassured her. Victoria would be in the same house with her son. She'd feed and care for him. And when she was ready, she would take him. *Why should you ruin your life now?* they said. *Who would want to marry someone with a child?* In the meantime, Lupa would go into the village and order formula for the baby to take with them, to be used only when necessary, while driving home from the airport, for instance.

Barely listening, still pondering a name, Victoria muttered, "And the woman?"

"The midwife? She is like a priest in confession," they said.

They'd worked out all the details, these two most reasonable sisters. They'd devised a foolproof plan to save Victoria. They'd even taken care of the paperwork, documents from this backward country that Victoria would rip to shreds. But what they really wanted was to avoid disgrace. That much was clear. Victoria kissed her baby, wondering how such a perfect little package could possibly lead to disgrace. She could deal with disgrace, she thought. She'd perfected disgrace. But she also knew that right now she needed her mother and Zia Lupa, if only to bring her her baby. So she remained calm and focused her attention on the baby and told them she'd like to call her son Nicholas.

A week later, Victoria awoke to a quiet farmhouse at early sunrise and wondered if what she saw in the middle of the night had been a dream. She'd seen Mama's stout frame creeping from one end of the kitchen to the other, all gray shadow and moonlit silhouette, and she'd seen Mama lift Nicholas from his bassinet and tuck him in the crook of an elbow and bring him to her breast. In this dream or nondream she heard her mother whispering to the baby, softly crooning a sweet

Mediterranean melody. But after a while, the baby was no longer Nicholas but Benito. And Victoria couldn't be angry.

Victoria had gone to sleep the night before enraged at Mama and Zia Lupa. She wondered how she'd fallen asleep at all. And she was shocked now that this watery image of Mama feeding her baby failed to stir up some of the rage that had filled her just hours ago. Roller-coaster emotions. That's what Darlene would have called her moodiness. Wild emotions that controlled her every thought. She'd be angry one moment and crying the next.

The day before, Mama and Lupa had orchestrated an open house. Victoria was able to get around better now, so they'd invited friends and family from the village. The women swooned over the baby and cooed and lightly pinched his warm cheeks, and when they finally got around to seeing Victoria, they called her *bella sorella,* beautiful sister. The men looked over the women's shoulders and offered their deep-throated congratulations to Angela Rosa. As these blood relatives and their neighbors paraded through the house all day, Victoria watched the clock, convincing herself that none of them mattered. She'd never see any of them again. What they believed was unimportant. They lived in a different world, and she didn't know how to even begin to set the record straight with them.

She sat up in her bed and walked to the kitchen and found Nicholas sleeping. Because he would grunt all night they'd moved the bassinet to the kitchen so they could all steal a few hours of sleep; if he cried outright they'd all hear him, Mama assured her. She watched him breathe, good strong breaths that made her weak with pleasure. She glanced outside at the cherry tree and hoped Lupa would ask D'Innocenzio, the neighbor who sublet the land, to pick another bushel for them. She slipped outside and followed the gravel path until she could see the Appenines. She couldn't wait to get home, but she knew she'd miss these hills. The sun coming up over the hills and the dew at her feet gave her a sense of renewal.

After yesterday, after the rage of watching strangers paw at her baby, she welcomed anything that restored her. She'd been burdened so long by the physical demands of a baby inside her, and she'd been trapped so long in the farmhouse to hide that fact, that she embraced the odd sense of liberation that swept through her this morning. She felt finally that she had options, real options. She could fight Mama and Zia Lupa and bring disgrace upon them all, upon the entire family. She'd feel comfortable in that role. Or she could remain silent and let their incredible scheme unfold. Nicholas, after all, *would* be with her. She'd treat him like a son, even feed him. She didn't give a rat's ass whether others saw her as Nicholas's mother. Except for Richie. He was the unknown in all this. His reaction mattered. If a baby was going to scare him away, then . . . She hated thinking this way, giving in to what he might think, but this weighed heaviest on her mind. She recalled her desolation after he left, dark thoughts replaced soon enough by other worries. But Mama was right; what man would want her with a baby? She could deal ultimately with isolation, she'd proven that, but why should she ruin her entire life?

After Richie left she remembered seeing couples everywhere, holding hands, nuzzling each other's necks. She had the awful sense then that her life was on hold. And then she found out she was pregnant and imagined her own versions of damnation and ruination—pushing a stroller around the neighborhood, fielding the sneers from her mother's friends, retreating to the apartment. She walked around aimlessly for weeks, sullen and listless, her listlessness interrupted by attacks of panic that gripped her chest and constricted her throat. *I am pregnant,* she would think. In the midst of her panic black thoughts swept through her. She could end this business swiftly, she thought. She'd heard stories. She could go somewhere and have it done. Arrangements festered in her mind. Hours later she'd berate herself for such selfishness. What kind of mother could think of bringing harm to her own child? What kind of monster was she? And if she went through with this pregnancy and had this baby, her baby, would she grow to resent the child for stealing her life away? Could these sinister thoughts of harming her child resurface? She'd never believed that such darkness dwelled in her, but now she wasn't so sure. Someone as unstable as she was didn't deserve a child; she shouldn't be trusted alone with a baby.

Having cradled and fed Nicholas with her own milk, she knew now he'd be safe with her. The moment she'd heard his little cry and laid eyes upon him, she knew. She knew that much. But she still wasn't sure whether she could be a good mother to her son, to give him all he needed. She thought some sort of maternal instinct would blossom in her, but so far she'd felt nothing but confusion. The midwife had to come over more than once to teach her how to breast-feed her own baby.

But Mama. She'd grown to admire Mama in the past week. Everything came easy to her. The way she swaddled and enveloped Nicholas in her arms made Victoria believe that a baby belonged there in Mama's soft cradle. When Victoria tried to swaddle him, the loose tucks flopped out and she feared he might slip out of her arms when she moved him from side to side. She *had* become more confident each day, but every movement still felt strained and deliberate.

Mama, on the other hand, wasn't playing at being a good mother. She *was* a good mother—or a grandmother. Victoria had never seen her so alive. Or maybe because she'd seen her mother only through her grief for two years now, she'd forgotten. She imagined trying to describe to someone the change that had overtaken Mama, but she knew words would be inadequate, like trying to describe the birth of her son. Mama had gone through her own rebirth, and Victoria didn't know whether she had the heart to take that away.

8

⚜

When Agostino received the first telegram he
didn't know where to turn. He fumbled around
the store for two hours until his brother returned and then he showed him the paper. In Italian the telegram read: "Agostino. Wonderful news. Doctor visited. We
will be blessed with another baby. Angela Rosa."

Agostino and his brother offered each other embraces
and opened a bottle of champagne they'd dusted off from the
back, thoughts of Benito underlying everything they said to
each other. *Is she okay?* Vince asked. *Is everyone healthy? How far
along?* Agostino shrugged and looked helpless. Vince pointed
to the telegram. *Is that all?* Agostino shrugged again, almost
apologetically. He only knew that he needed to get his wife
home. He calculated how long it would take for a telegram
to arrive from Chicago to Naples to the village and for someone to deliver that message to the farmhouse. Days at the very

least. Nothing was urgent to those civil-service workers in the hills.

Three days later Lupa called and told Agostino that everyone was all right. There was no need to panic. They would make arrangements as soon as possible. Calls and letters went back and forth like this for weeks, Angela Rosa insisting ultimately that she didn't want to travel in her condition. Agostino suggested he fly to her instead, that Vince and Santo could take care of the store. He got a terse letter back from her explaining that Santo needed to watch out for Anthony and Alfredo, that Santo couldn't mind them and the store at the same time. Not wanting to upset her, relieved finally that she seemed to be her old self again, Agostino agreed.

Months passed. And then, on a Thursday morning, the second telegram arrived. Delivered again to the store. More hastily written than the first. "Baby born. Nicholas. All fine. Home soon." Agostino had to sit. He read the two lines over and over again. *Baby born.* He tapped the table, counting, figuring and refiguring. Baby born? Whose baby? There'd been only a single time in bed, that once when she'd awoken him in the middle of the night just days before her departure. While he slept she'd pushed herself onto him, her body already bare, her warmth penetrating his nightshirt. The episode was like a dream, blissful and bittersweet, both of them tearing at each other, inhaling the other's scent. They couldn't breathe deeply enough. They couldn't touch each other enough, as if making up for time spent apart. But that was a mere six months ago.

His hand shaking, he lit a cigarette and stared at the telegram. He could smell deception better than anyone, he thought. Six months. Ha. *So this is what my life has come down to. My own wife deceiving me, adept at my own game.* He needed air.

He glanced at the clock behind the bar and walked out the front of the store. Vince was upstairs asleep. Santo would be in shortly. He'd wait for one of them. Then he'd go. Maybe take in a movie, stop along the way at Lucca's market for a sack of ripe peaches from his bushel baskets. That was all he could think to do. His own wife. He thought he'd be more angry. He ran through a mental list of men Angela Rosa encountered in a day but couldn't stomach those images for long. And what difference did it make now? Agostino was reaping finally all he'd sown; how fitting, then, that Angela Rosa had delivered this baby on her old farmland. He deserved this, he thought. And he could bear this.

The thing he could not bear, the thing he knew, even then, that would destroy him, was the stinging memory of their love-making that night six months ago, how she'd climbed onto him with no other intent than to deceive, to plant her own seed of illusion in his mind. As if he couldn't count. She'd been cold and calculating, and this, this would be the thing that would eat at him. Worse, she had pulled their own daughter into her plan. Victoria would take *his* ticket because Angela Rosa couldn't bear to have this baby with Agostino watching. She needed to have this baby on her own, in the privacy of women. She needed to study the baby for a while, make sure he didn't resemble the father, make sure no one would detect a flaw in her scheme. He understood now why Lupa tagged along as well; while Victoria took care of her mother, Lupa could tromp to the village telegraph office and put off Agostino with her false reassurances. He only wondered if Lupa had been told everything. All this, this scheming, his wife's calculated actions, would gnaw at him. In her calculating, she'd forgotten to ask Agostino for help in the naming of this baby. She probably couldn't bear to lay this final insult on her husband. In any case, not asking Agostino for a name confirmed what he already knew, and he felt as if a vault door was pressing in on him.

He lit another cigarette and waved to an old woman walking across the street. Later he'd show Vince and Santo the telegram, as if it had just arrived. He'd feign exuberance and let their excitement shadow his bruises. He'd play along, just as Angela Rosa had played along for nearly twenty years now. And he'd become proficient at forgetting.

He had no destination in mind, but when he arrived at the church that afternoon he knew why he'd come. The heft of the great mahogany door caused him to stagger for a moment, bringing him back to Benito's funeral when everyone scurried to open doors for him and his family, kindly ushering them around. He pulled again at the door. The church was empty, the only movement the flicker of candles in crimson jars near the altar. His breathing labored, he sat in the middle and waited, dozing off in minutes.

He heard the light footsteps first, intruding on his dream of being trapped in a small room, the steps growing louder and vaguely ominous. Then the voice.

"Mr. Peccatori?"

He woke and gazed up at the young priest wearing his long black cassock and stiff collar, a striking contrast to his ruddy cheeks. Is it possible the priest had gotten younger?

Agostino couldn't speak. He couldn't move. Still hazy, trapped in the room, he held his gaze on Father Ernie, comforted by the placid eyes. Agostino blinked, glad not to be rushed, understanding why people were drawn to these pews.

"Father," he said finally. As if he were in his own bar, he

motioned with his head, and Father Ernie sat two pews in front of him, turning to face him, listing to the left. Agostino liked this view that held both altar and priest, his own private mass.

"Did you come for confession, Mr. Peccatori? Because we can go in there."

Agostino looked to the curtained booths.

"Or if you just want to talk, we can sit in the sacristy. Or my office." He glanced back at the altar. "Or. We can sit here. Here is fine."

Agostino wondered how to begin, knowing he could derive no satisfaction here. He was a fool to have come. "This life." He put out an empty hand, searching for words. "Is hard."

Father Ernie nodded, fingered the lobe of his ear.

"I make mistakes."

"You want atonement."

Agostino knew this word. He'd looked up the word, spoken it, though never to another. The roundness of the middle syllable, sorrowful and pleading, seemed to hold its meaning, though he couldn't explain why. "Yes," he said. "I need."

"Why now?"

"I think I—maybe I see better."

Father Ernie waited.

"Ah, mio padre. Forget. Non importa." It doesn't matter. He began to rant in Italian before catching himself. "When I come to America I try to learn everything. Every day I read newspaper. I look by dictionary. I talk. But I'm buffoon. I no understand Americano." He gripped the pew in front of him, searching again for words that would not come. He detested his stilted English, the halting starts, yet he often found himself *thinking* this way. How could he make himself understood if he couldn't think? He plodded ahead, the words torturous on his tongue. "In Italia, when dog"—he put up a level fist—"how you say?"

Flushed, Father Ernie turned away. "Mount?"

"When dog mount other dog, we no say bad dog. Is not bad. Not good. *Naturale.* For a little time, they feel good. No sin, hey?"

Father Ernie lifted his chin, about to speak.

"I know, I know. With man is different. But still *naturale.*" He paused, inviting response now.

"There's nothing sinful about the act itself. Is that what you're getting at?"

"Yes."

"I'm afraid it's not that simple. You can't possibly believe—what if you found out that—"

"What?" Agostino couldn't believe his good fortune. He'd meandered to this church to ask about his wife's wandering, whether she'd ever confided, outside the confessional, of course, a question he wouldn't dare pose, and here the priest was raising that very possibility. Just as Agostino could not voice the question, he couldn't bear the answer. He simply needed subtle affirmation, and then the matter would be dead to him.

Father Ernie waved away his what-if. "No, nothing," he said, a slight quiver in his voice, affirmation enough for Agostino. "The act alone, the natural act of two people—a husband and a wife—joining, is certainly not a sin. The circumstances dictate the sin." He seemed on firmer ground now.

"If two people do, and one marry, they make sin? Always?"

"Yes."

"If they do one time, and no mean nothing?"

"It means something to God," Father Ernie said. "It means something to the other spouse."

This last remark pierced Agostino, stirring loathing for himself, and pity for the ones he'd hurt, especially Ella. In his weakness, he'd taken advantage of the poor girl. There was no sidestepping this. *If no mean nothing?* He was referring to the times before Ella. He'd merely wanted to cleanse himself of those earlier transgressions at least, to return to a time when the world was young, when living and breathing and staring full into the afternoon sun possessed order.

His eyes swept the church. Maple carvings capturing the Stations of the Cross surrounded him. A mortal Christ bearing the weight of the rough-hewn timbers always moved him. Pure suffering. "I know one a thing," he said. He waited for the young man to look at him. "When you lie is sin."

He bowed his head, closed his eyes, and brought his palms together. "Bless me, Father. I have sinned." He waited. "Please. Make bless for me."

He basked in the Latin unspooling from Father Ernie's lips, some of which he understood. *In nomine Patris, et Filii, et Spiritus Sancti.* The sign of the cross. Words passed down through centuries of suffering. Like a child, he prayed. He muttered the only prayers he knew, his whispers cushioned by Father Ernie's steady incantations. To his surprise the words came back to him whole. *Padre Nostro, che sei nei cieli, sia santificato it tuo nome.* His brother would have called it poetry, the joining of Latin and Italian, rising like song. He wanted not to think, to listen only, but flashes of thought pressed through. He'd lie no further. He'd tell Angela Rosa everything. *Sedet ad decteram Dei Patris omnipotentis.* But he couldn't. Hurting her would be the greater sin. They had to bury the past. Their lies had caused enough pain. Why let them fuel more? *Ave, Maria, piena di grazia.* He'd never find true absolution in denying the past. But this is what he deserved. Benito's face appeared to him. At the funeral he vowed not to stray, a promise he'd kept. His celibacy, as it turned out, proved easier than he imagined. It seemed just and right. In the middle of the night, when he couldn't sleep, he'd visit Benito's room, click on the lamp light, and reaffirm his vow. One time, without reason, he left a clipping from the newspaper on the bureau, a photograph of Sophia Loren standing outside a theater. As the months passed he left more and more, never thinking of why, and felt as if he were losing his mind. But in prayer now, his delirium became clear. Or maybe he'd known all along. The artifacts were constant reminders of what he could no longer have, of the shame he'd brought to his family, designed to cause him suffering, and this it never failed to evoke in him.

Father Ernie's last prayers trailed off. Everything was still.

"Grazia, padre."

An automobile horn sounded in the distance. A single bird chirped with little insistence.

"Any word from Italy?"

Agostino pulled the telegram from his shirt pocket and held it out like a communion host. *Another immaculate conception,* he wanted to say, and nearly cried.

Father Ernie opened it. "This is wonderful news." He looked into Agostino's eyes. "You must be—" He rose and took Agostino's hand in both of his. "Another son." He sat next to him, handing back the telegram, but before letting go, tightened his grip. They held the paper between them for a breath. Agostino could feel the pulse in his thumb.

"You got this today, Mr. Peccatori?" He released the paper.

"Yes."

"This must—you must have. You came here for atonement. On this day." As if trying to regain his balance, he added quickly, "But who am I to—I imagine this day brings back painful memories. Or maybe I can't imagine. All you must be feeling."

Smile, Agostino told himself. *Begin now.* But he would need to grow into this. "I make happy when everyone come home," he said.

"When will that be?"

"Soon."

Agostino stood, a cue for Father Ernie to follow, yet he didn't move.

"Maybe we talk again, hey?"

On his way out, he dipped his fingers into the porcelain bowl of holy water, crossed himself, felt his pocket for the telegram, and without turning back, marched into the bright afternoon.

Santo hated the word *estrangement.* When he was a boy and he'd overhear the blue-haired women on their lawn chairs gossiping about this or that uncle they hadn't seen in fifteen years, the uncle who ran off without explanation or forwarding address, Santo shook his head along with the old women. Why would anyone abandon their families like that? The old women filled in their own explanations, of course, and these explanations eventually became truth. Uncle Louie drank. Cousin Millie stole other wives' husbands. Vivian was a common whore. And Santo. What would they say one day about Santo?

Though he hated the thought of being estranged from his family, especially now with Mama bringing home the new baby, he feared he might have no other options. A part of him believed that his leaving might be noble. He would leave to keep his family intact. He would leave to bring peace to Ella's family. Ella had already begun to convince her mother that Santo was in fact Joey's father, that Agostino had simply been trying to cover up for his son, who was young, with a promising future ahead of him. Ella's mother, always practical, would accept this lie or risk not seeing her grandson again. And the lie was more palatable, something she could pass off to her friends with relatively little shame.

There was only one person in the family he could talk to, so he stopped at the store that morning before his father arrived. He knocked on the apartment door upstairs and waited at the sewing machine, pumping the pedal, the silver needle rising and falling in rhythmic clicks. His father used to tell him that sewing was a lost art but never bothered to teach him a single stitch. When it became clear that Vince wasn't going to answer, he let himself in and poured some milk in a glass. After downing the glass, he lit up one of his uncle's cigarettes and focused on nothing more than each puff and the sunlight pouring through the front window. A trolley wheezed by, and his uncle finally appeared.

Vince stopped midstride. "Listen," he said. "Outside. You hear? Pretty soon you no hear no more. They make new bus. All gasoline. Somebody make rich, eh? No me."

"You do pretty well for yourself, Zio."

"No complain." He lit a burner on the oven and set a pot of coffee over the flame. "Coff?" Santo shook his head, and Vince poured a shot of whiskey into a cup. He waited at the stove, and when the coffee began boiling he topped off the whiskey with the steaming brew. He sat down and sipped. "Ahh."

"Nothing like that first cup, huh, Zio?"

Vince's eyes were rimmed a bruised purple and the whites were shot with blood lines. "Why you no drink coff, eh?"

"Someday maybe."

"Some a day. Always some a day *con mio Santo*."

Santo poured himself more milk. "Sometimes 'some a day' comes sooner than you think," Santo told him.

Vince sipped his coffee and peered at his nephew over the cup's rim.

That pensive stare. That shrewd glance. Vince always seemed to know when Santo had something on his mind.

"*Ah, mio Santo.* Is early."

"It's past eleven."

"Ha. 'Leven. Pretty soon make dark."

Santo let him joke around awhile, let him wake up. Vince asked how the old Caddy was running. Rather than trading in his old car and getting nothing for it from the bastard dealers, Vince had given the Caddy to Santo, the only other Peccatori with a driver's license. When he handed his nephew the keys he announced, "Now you have two Cs, the coin and the car." At the time, Santo didn't mention that he'd had his share of the third *C*, which was what he needed to talk to his uncle about now. He'd been saving, really saving. Not just talking about it. And Ella had more put aside than he did.

Yesterday's cup and saucer were still on the table, and Santo pulled the saucer close to him and tapped it with his fingernails. "I'm getting married," he blurted. The words sounded strange spoken, and Santo could barely believe what he'd said.

Vince lifted his cup in a toast. "Bravo," he said. *"Salute!"*

"I mean it, Zio."

"Who marry you?"

"I don't know. Probably lots of women. But there's one . . ."

"One, eh?"

"Well, that's the thing. It's not easy to say."

"Marriage no easy."

"No, that's not the problem. The one I want to marry . . ."

"Brute?"

"No, she's not ugly. Believe me. She could be in a movie."

"Trouble," Vince said. He told Santo about his old wife, how beautiful she was, how other men constantly eyed her, nothing Santo hadn't heard before.

"That's not it either. This one dresses plain. You wouldn't notice her unless—"

"So no trouble." He shot a sudden look over to his nephew, then rubbed his broad belly and asked, "No trouble?"

"No. No trouble. Nothing like that."

"Good. No trouble. So when you make twenty-five, you marry, eh?"

How could he explain? *You see, Uncle. She has this kid, this two-year-old who needs a father around, and if you could just see this kid, this nephew of yours you've never laid eyes on, which is a shitty deal, believe me, you'd fall in love with him on the spot guaranteed. But that's not the problem. If you and Papa don't care to see him, you won't see him. No sweat off my back. The problem is this, the problem is his mother. I know you don't want to see her either; I can understand that, but I do. I definitely do. I want to marry her. But how do I—it's not like I can bring her around at Christmastime or Easter or Mama's birthday. And I don't see how I can live a normal life in the neighbor-*

hood like this, you know . . . I mean I can keep this, I don't need to be blabbing to everyone, but what would Papa say? I need to work this out with Papa. Maybe if you talk to him, break it to him.

Vince offered him his placating half grin.

"The thing is, I don't want to wait. I love her. I want to marry her now."

Vince rubbed his eyes. "Then why you wait? No wait. Call priest. Order cake. Make honeymoon. Buy house. Work work work and die. Hurry. No wait. Go. Make wedding."

Santo laughed and went on laughing, louder and longer than he might have if his nerves weren't so tangled because in the middle of his laughing he decided he would drop his little bombshell in Vince's kitchen and wait for the inevitable eruption. He wouldn't say he derived great satisfaction in disrupting the even disposition his uncle had worked years to master, but he did feel a surge of blood, a quivering pulsation in his chest and in his arms and down through his legs.

"The problem . . . this is the problem, Zio. You see, she — her name is Gabriella Paolone."

Vince grumbled, his half grin smeared across his face, plastered there. Santo could read his uncle's thoughts in that grin. *You little prick. Gabriella Paolone. That name is like a curse to me. I give you my Caddy and you throw that name in my face.* The grin broadened and his eyes widened into a crazed stare and then the ranting began. Full-fledged, deep-throated, ruddy-faced ranting that aroused admiration in Santo. He wished he could become that incensed about something. His uncle sprang from his chair and unleashed his usual lamentations while Santo sat back and waited for the inevitable calm. He watched the clock. The roar was so loud he never heard the creaking of the stairs or the footsteps just outside the door or the turning of the doorknob. He only saw the light from behind him shift slightly as the porch door swung open and his father appeared.

"What is this noise?" asked Agostino.

Santo's heart seized up. All his bravado left him. Here was the man he most feared, a thought that struck him with a fullness he'd never felt before. He'd never fully articulated in his mind the fear he had of his father. Not until that moment, Gabriella Paolone's name still ringing in the air.

"*Tuo figlio,*" Vince said.

"Yes, my son. But what is all this screaming?"

"Gabriella Paolone," Vince shouted, as if this name would explain everything.

Agostino winced as if slashed from behind. His jaw muscles worked. "What does she want?"

Vince pointed to Santo, accusing and dismissing him at the same time. "*Tuo figlio.*"

"*Che?*"

"*Lei vuole tuo figlio.*"

"What do you say?"

"*Gesù Cristo. Tuo figlio. Tuo figlio primo.* She want this son now. Santo."

Agostino looked puzzled. "Santo is in trouble?"

Vince stopped and pointed to Santo again. "He. He want to make wedding. With that *putana* Paolone."

"Wedding?"

"*Sì*, wedding."

"Santo make trouble?"

Santo rose from his chair, and the three of them stood around the table now. "I'm not in any trouble," he shouted. "I'm not in any goddamn trouble."

Agostino looked at his brother and shrugged. "Then why—"

"Is that all you can think about?" Santo screamed. "Trouble? Getting rid of trouble? Covering things up? I'm tired of all the whispering around here."

"What whisper?" Agostino shouted. "Nobody whisper. Everybody scream."

"Don't play dumb with me, Papa. I'm tired of that, too."

"What dumb?"

"I know you have a son."

"I make four son." He crossed himself and asked God to bless Benito.

"And Nicholas," Vince added.

"And Nicholas, yes."

"I know you have another son, Papa. I can bring him here tomorrow and show you. He looks like us. He looks like all of us. It's time to quit pretending."

"I no pretend. You crazy."

"I'm not going to tell anyone if that's what you're worried about. Gabriella's not going to tell anyone. I just want it out in the open between us."

The two brothers exchanged tired glances.

Vince shook his head, his eyes downcast. "America," he said.

"This has nothing to do with America," Santo shouted. "We make our own goddamn troubles."

"You want wedding?" Agostino asked.

"Yes, that's what I want, dammit. That's what I want." He banged the table with the heel of his hand.

"With that *putana*?"

"She's not a whore, Papa."

"Why you do this to me?"

"I'm not doing this to you, Papa. I'm not doing this to hurt you." But Santo knew this was exactly what he was doing to his father, inserting daggers. And in his screaming, in his killing, he felt remorse.

"If you marry," Agostino said, pointing a finger, "if you marry this *putana*, you leave my house and you leave my store." His voice was firm, his jaw steady. *"Capisci?"*

Santo glanced at his uncle, who seemed to be pinching his hip to secure it in a certain position. Agony lined his face. Santo felt remorse over his uncle's pain, too.

"I don't need your blessing," Santo said, more evenly now. "I just want this out in the open."

The two brothers turned to each other and began rambling in Italian, their voices echoing off the kitchen walls, their hands gesturing wildly. Agostino cut Vince off finally and turned to his son.

"If you marry, you leave," he said gravely.

"Please, Papa. Don't talk that way."

Agostino stepped from the kitchen and walked to the front window. He pulled aside the curtain, leaned down into the window, and gazed outside. He tucked his other hand in his back pocket and remained frozen like that for a while. And then it happened. Not ten feet away from him, his father unraveled. He began talking to himself. Santo had seen signs of this solitary give-and-take since Benito's passing, but it had grown worse since Mama left. The talking always started slowly with mild reprimands to himself, but then the pacing and the gesturing would begin and before long he'd be slapping his forehead and berating himself with fierce hard-edged whispers. And that's what disturbed Santo the most, the whispering, as if his father imagined that no one could hear him, or worse, that his father believed all the whispering was happening inside his head, for when Santo glanced at him, hoping to embarrass him into silence, Agostino showed no signs that anyone was near.

Santo looked across at his uncle for help, but Vince seemed lost somewhere, too. He held his hip. Apparently he'd heard the talking before and didn't seem at all fazed by his brother's fury. And so they waited. They waited for the pacing and the whispering to spin itself out. When it did, Agostino returned to the window, his back to them. He fingered the bottom of the paper shade, pulling at it, then easing his grip so that the shade would slide up with his hand. He let the shade rise to the top and seemed satisfied. He turned and looked toward the kitchen.

"If you marry, you leave."

All the sternness had drained out of his father's warning. He couldn't even meet Santo's gaze. His eyes were suddenly glassy and distant. He would deliver the admonitions he thought he needed to give, but his thoughts were elsewhere.

If you marry, you leave. Standing stock-still in Vince's kitchen, his arms folded now across his chest, Santo knew these words were his destiny. These words his father couldn't take back. With his awful pride, he wouldn't be able to see past this. Santo knew he'd crossed some line, broken some code, and there was nothing left to salvage. Even if he gave in now and agreed to forsake this marriage, even this would not matter anymore.

For the first time he saw his future clearly. He and Ella would be together and maybe have children. He'd venture into the neighborhood now and then to visit Mama and his brothers and Vicki. But he'd never set foot on this spot again.

He'd never work with Uncle Vince again. Maybe he and his uncle would meet for coffee somewhere, maybe mornings at some regular time. He'd like that. But he wasn't sure when he'd ever see his father again.

"Bye, Papa."

Agostino turned to the window.

"I'm sorry, Papa," Santo called. "I'm sorry I have to leave."

He wanted to touch his father's shoulder before he left, press and hold it there for a moment, he wanted to leave him with that, but he knew he wouldn't. He turned and trudged down the stairs, one plodding step after another, allowing each footfall to become stamped in the same memory trace as the whispering, to which he could already hear the echoes.

When she saw him again, looking about as forlorn as she'd ever seen him, her husband of over twenty years, she let out a muffled cry. "Agostino," she said. She breathed in her husband's name as it rang in the air. She hadn't said his name in so long she'd forgotten the sound of it. "Oh, Agostino."

They embraced and held the embrace.

"I've missed you," he said.

"It's been too long."

"And the others?"

"Your brother dropped me at the door. They're coming. They're sorting luggage. It was so good to see Anthony again. He was a big help with the bags."

They stepped apart, wiping their eyes. He was glad now that he'd closed the store for a few hours so he could properly welcome everyone. The last time they'd closed Mio Fratello was for Benito.

"You look good," he told her. "Do you feel all right?"

"Yes, everyone is fine."

"Are you happy to be home?"

"Happy, yes. Finally home." She scanned the apartment for signs of her other sons. "And Santo? Alfredo?"

"Alfredo's out playing. He'll be in soon. I warned him."

They heard the heavy thud of footsteps and Vince's voice booming in the stairwell. "Delivery *speciale*," he shouted. He came into sight step by crooked step, holding Nicholas as if he were a log of hard salami. "I present to you, *mio nipoto*," he said. My nephew.

Agostino took the baby because there was nothing else to do, but he couldn't find any words. He could barely breathe. He kissed the baby on the forehead without looking at him and watched them all emerge from the stairwell, Anthony, Lupa, and lastly Victoria, who appeared both gaunt and bloated. Still holding the baby, he kissed each one in turn and retreated to the couch behind him.

They all followed and collapsed into sofas and chairs, catching their breaths. Lupa filled the apartment with chatter about planes and shuttle buses and the conditions they'd had to endure these past months, while Agostino gazed at this baby. Nicholas. A good name. A name a young person might choose. He wasn't sure what to feel. This boy could be his son. There was nothing to distinguish him otherwise. His complexion was a shade lighter perhaps but only a shade. The baby began to fuss, and Victoria was there to take him.

She paced about the room with the baby on her shoulder and patted him lightly. The odor of the eight-hour flight was still on her, jet fuel and carpet disinfectant, along with cabin handbags filled with Romano cheese and provolone. That, and the rumble of the engines at the back where they sat in the last few rows, had made her queasy. She still felt light-headed, off-center. She thought the short ride home in Uncle Vince's new Cadillac would steady her, but she felt a different sort of dizziness then. The neighborhood looked compressed, one tiny block pushing onto another. The tight grid of city streets she'd walked along for hours on end her entire life no longer seemed like hers. Even the apartment seemed smaller—the stairwell, the landing, these couches. And now with Nicholas on her shoulder, his anguished wail of hunger pushing out from his tiny lungs, she knew through her grogginess that her old life was over. She slipped down the hallway to her bedroom.

Angela Rosa couldn't sit. She followed Victoria, grateful for Lupa's ranting behind her. She went to the refrigerator, carried back a dish of antipasto that Agostino had left there, then caught up with her daughter in her bedroom.

"He make hungry?" Angela Rosa whispered.

Victoria sat on a chair near the foot of the bed. "Yeah. He must be starving."

Angela Rosa took her daughter's face in her hands and kissed her hard on the cheek. "My daughter," she said. *"Ti amo."* I love you.

"I know, Mama."

Angela Rosa sat across from them on the edge of the bed and watched her daughter feed this new arrival. She prayed to God they were doing the right thing. She hoped the rash plan they'd laid out wasn't born of selfishness or self-pity, all designed to ease her own lingering grief. Now that she was back in the apartment, one certainty struck her, though—this baby would thrive here. Early on in their European sojourn, she and Lupa had discussed the possibility of leaving the baby behind with Cousin Serafina in Naples. She shuddered at the thought now and felt shame for not including her daughter in these considerations. She felt then that she couldn't trust Victoria to be reasonable, especially with Lupa around. But Victoria had been nothing but clearheaded and able. And she'd proven to be agreeable, if grudgingly so.

"Welcome home, Nicholas," Victoria crooned.

Angela Rosa glanced at the door to see if it was closed. *This is how we will live,* she thought, checking doors, speaking in hushed breaths. At least for a while.

Victoria finished her feeding and handed Nicholas to her mother. After each feeding she had to remain immobile for a minute or two until the pain in her nipples subsided. Mama told her that each day the pain would become less severe, but she hadn't noticed any signs of that yet. She'd endure this, along with the birthing pains in her pelvis, which were healing, because she had to. But she didn't think she could endure Lupa's shrill cackle for another day. Her voice carried from the far reaches of the apartment to the bedroom like a scratchy toy trumpet. Fortunately, Lupa would depart soon—she made it abundantly clear she wanted to get back to her house—but this was small consolation because Victoria knew she'd be visiting more frequently now to see Nicholas, her favorite because she'd been there from the start. And Lupa would pretend not to despise Victoria because they had this secret between them now. Lupa would whisper—Victoria could hear it now and feel the dryness of Lupa's breaths—and her aunt would offer conspiratorial winks to remind Victoria of the link they'd forged. Victoria felt weak to her stomach; she knew she wouldn't be able to avoid these sweet and severe endearments.

A few minutes passed and she and her mother slid back to the living room, Victoria thinking they'd need to be more discreet about disappearing together like this. And she hoped no one would detect the yeasty scent of milk on her.

Uncle Vince got to his feet, preparing to leave so he could drop off Lupa at home and return to open the store. But Lupa didn't move. She talked about the deep well outside the farmhouse. She looked at her sister and without pausing for breath said in Italian, "Every morning, I was telling them, every morning I would bring in six or seven pails of water and the water would be gone by noon, what with soup and washing —"

"Lupa," Vince pleaded.

"Yes, yes, I know," Lupa said. "Let me look at him once more, this beautiful baby. Where will he sleep, this little one? All the bedrooms are taken here. Let me take him with me."

Victoria's heart jumped.

Vince and Agostino exchanged glances. The apartment, they knew, wasn't as full as the women thought.

"Where is Santo?" Angela Rosa asked.

Vince moved to the door, waving Lupa on. "We go, eh?"

"Let me put him down to sleep," Lupa insisted. "Five minutes. If I can't have him, I can at least put him down. Then we will go."

"Please. We go now, eh?"

Lupa pried the baby from her sister's arms. "Where will he sleep? Show me."

They all looked at one another. No one wanted to mention Benito's crib, stored away in the cellar shortly before he'd gotten sick, nor his room, buried with tawdry trinkets. And Agostino wouldn't volunteer Santo's bare room. Not yet.

Victoria broke in. "I'll make a temporary bed for him on your floor, Mama. We'll borrow a bassinet from Irene next door later."

"Good," Angela Rosa said. "You make good . . . girl."

For a second, Victoria yearned to hear that she'd make a good mother, it's what Mama wanted to say, but she let that yearning pass. It would do her no good to dwell on those kinds of thoughts.

In Mama's room she found a quilt, laid the quilt on the floor, and spread white linen over it. *My old life is over,* she thought. She would be a mother to this child, but she would be no mother at all. Her life would be nothing more than play-acting, one exclusive role, day after day, with no one to guide her.

Lupa brought the baby in and placed him on his makeshift bed. She kissed him three times, patted Victoria on the back of her head, spouted off hurriedly about the wisdom of keeping secrets, then left. Victoria watched her go out, she wanted to savor her leaving, and sighed deeply when those broad shoulders disappeared from her sight. She remained crouched on the floor, her legs tucked under her, studying Nicholas. She wanted to savor this, too, these quiet moments alone with her son when it didn't matter what anyone called her. Another thought occurred to her then, a new thought: this secret would also rob Mama of her role as grandma, a title she knew her mother would have worn well.

Later that night, alone in their bedroom, Agostino tried to console Angela Rosa over Santo's leaving. Sitting there on the bed, his arm around her, her skin cool against his own, he felt he'd gotten his wife back finally. She'd moved away from him and toward another, thinking it would alleviate her grief maybe, then traveled back to her motherland, separated herself from Agostino as she had to, but now she was back. He'd welcome her and this baby and teach himself how to forgive. And through his actions each day, he'd ask Angela Rosa for *her* forgiveness. They could begin anew, he thought.

As for Santo, he couldn't bear to look at him. Dozens of women to choose from—girls were always interested in Santo—and he had to pursue this one. Agostino would never understand this betrayal.

He handed her another tissue.

"He's nearly twenty," he told her. "He was ready."

"I wasn't."

"Well . . ."

"But why so suddenly?"

"Young people today."

"He didn't leave an address? A phone number?"

"Yes yes. Vince has it all. He said he would come by after you arrived. You will see him tomorrow. I am sure of it. There's no need to cry anymore. Leaving is natural. You were younger than he is when you left your mother."

She glanced up at him and their eyes held, both of them recalling their first days together, awkward and thrilling. He pulled her in and took her hand. Sitting on the edge of the bed like that, leaning into each other, they could have been sixteen again, innocent and hopeful.

"Promise me one thing," he said. He gripped her hand. "Promise you won't leave again."

She forced a smile and nodded.

"You promise?"

"I do."

"Never again."

"Yes."

"And I will not—" Agostino said. "Never."

And then they made love again, only the second time since Benito's death, taking their time, exploring with slow touches, giving in to each other like waves into a shore, their sins laid bare and silent before them and beginning to recede.

Three weeks home and she had to tell someone. How could she keep this any longer? After feeding Nicholas and swaddling him—the very word made Victoria ache with delight—and placing him in his crib for what she hoped would be until midnight, she ambled down the block on this Friday evening in July to find Darlene, already feeling with each step that she should get back. She brought along a photo of Nicholas, but—unlike Father Ernie, who immediately recognized the mother in this boy but who remained staunchly silent about it—Darlene detected nothing. And when Darlene realized that Nicholas did not automatically evoke in Vicki painful memories of Benito, she seemed almost wholly disinterested—Nicholas was simply another of Vicki's brothers—and wanted to resume their quests for cigarettes and a car for the night. They made their way to St. Anthony's and sat on the school steps.

Cigarettes. Cars. Pushing curfew. How could any of this have mattered? Despondent, Victoria claimed she had to get back and nearly managed to break free but couldn't stem the hot tears, which sprang forth with little warning lately. Darlene took hold of her arm and pulled her back to the stairs, apologizing for saying the wrong thing, for not asking what was wrong because she knew, she could see, but was afraid since there hadn't been any letters or calls.

Victoria saw the hurt in her friend's eyes. "I could have written. You're right. I had time. I know what it's like to be waiting for a letter. I'm sorry. It feels like—like my life's been on hold for a while."

Later, thinking back on the next few moments, Victoria wondered why she'd told her friend anything at all. Victoria didn't want entrance back into her old life. She wasn't seeking pity, nor did she feel she owed Darlene for not having written. Even the release she yearned for, the unburdening that talking would bring, would turn out to be short-lived. What she wanted most, she admitted to herself during dark moments, was a display of common human frailty from her friend, Darlene taking Victoria's solemn secret and trusting *another* with it, the truth spreading until Victoria could no longer defend the lie. She'd already relinquished her desires; why not let others continue to forge out her future? Darlene, however, would remain faithful to her promise, perhaps less out of loyalty than pity, for when Victoria told her about labor in the cold farmhouse, Darlene looked like she'd been stabbed, remaining rapt, stifling any shock she might have felt until Victoria told her of the manufactured birth certificate. Darlene's sudden outrage caused Victoria to view the last few months again from her old defiant self. How calculated they were, Mama and Lupa. How resourceful.

To her surprise, Victoria found herself defending them. She could have resisted, she told Darlene. She could have howled until Lupa had given in, for Lupa was the key architect of the plan, she suspected. But, and she spoke now with measured calm because she needed Darlene to soften, she had to ask herself a simple question: *What would be best for my son?* She wasn't sure how to answer this but felt certain that bringing Nicholas home as her son would serve only her own desires. Victoria could barely acknowledge, even to herself, the other selfish thoughts, the ones Darlene in fact might understand; that is, if she didn't have a son she might be able to recapture seventeen again, though that no longer held much appeal to her at this instant. And what a gift for her mother, another boy to care for, after all she'd been through. "I only want what's best for my son," she kept insisting between tears, more to herself, as Darlene, brushing her back in wide circles, tried to comfort her.

Angela Rosa needed to set things right. They'd been home three weeks, and other than the middle-of-the-night feedings when she'd often sit with Victoria, taking delight in how she gazed upon her son, they'd had no time alone together. She waited now before the black screen of the television for Victoria to return from her walk. Every few minutes she sauntered to Santo's old room and remained rooted there until she could hear Nicholas breathing. Was there a more beautiful sound? she wondered.

An hour later, Agostino still at the store and the boys helping there tonight as well, Angela Rosa barely heard Victoria pad in from the back porch.

"Sit," Angela Rosa said.

"Let me just check on him."

She listened to her daughter's fading footsteps, the slight creak as she neared the bedroom, the movement toward the kitchen, the clink of a glass, the faucet, the sweet sound of her daughter's steps returning to her.

"Why so dark in here?"

The only illumination filling the apartment came from the overhead bulb on the porch that spilled its weak rays inside, the night-light in the kitchen, and the table lamp on a stand in the living room, where they sat.

"Where you go tonight?" Angela Rosa had to check her annoyance. She'd been waiting over an hour for what she expected would be a short walk.

"I ran into Darlene."

Still the short answers. Still the resentment.

Angela Rosa had never learned how to subtly broach difficult matters—she bluntly announced the concerns that weighed on her—but now she found herself asking about feedings and the next doctor appointment, insisting they try to find someone closer. Finally, she turned and said, "Victoria—" She thought she'd attempt English, but she couldn't find the words. In her own tongue she said, "You have suffered. I see that plainly. And when I see you like this, I suffer, too. In my head, I tell myself—I hope—that if I suffer I will swallow yours."

She looked away from her daughter and down at her hands and said in English, "I make shame."

They let this thought settle for a while, the July street sounds blanketing them.

"I'm not suffering, Mama."

"I no believe."

"I'm just—sad, I guess."

"Sad."

"I was reading about it. In the paper. Sometimes women become sad after a baby."

Angela Rosa nodded. "I rememb."

Her daughter's gaze swept from the television to the carpet to the end of the apartment, as if deciding, then she finally asked, with clear reluctance, "Shame for—why shame, Mama?"

"In this house," she began. She took in the apartment, waving her hands as if to curse these rooms. "Nobody make—nobody tell—everyone make hush-hush. *Penso che,* maybe better if we tell"—she faced her daughter and whispered hoarsely—"maybe better if we tell everything."

Victoria began to weep, she wept all the time, so Angela Rosa crept closer and took her hand, began to stroke her hair.

"Papa *è* Santo. They no talk. Nobody say to me this. But I know." Angela Rosa had to suppress her own weeping now. *"Pero,"* she said. *"Non voi lo stesso per tu* and me." I don't want the same to happen to us. "Right now. Every day. I regret. You believe? I regret. But no more. I do what my daughter want. I mean." She cradled Victoria's chin in her palm. "I do what you want. You want I tell everything? We tell."

Angela Rosa had intended to make some grand gesture to bring them closer, but she hadn't planned on going this far. But that no longer mattered. Nothing else mattered. She would find a way to honor her daughter's wishes. "Tell me how you want," she said.

"I want what's best for Nicholas."

Angela Rosa nodded in agreement.

"How? How you *make* best? For *you,* too."

"I don't care about me."

"No no no."

"Here's what I've been thinking, Mama. I don't know if this makes sense. But right now, it doesn't matter who knows the truth about any of this. The whole world could know. The whole world could not know. Either way, Nicholas still gets fed and held and loved. If I wake up tomorrow and decide

this is too complicated and my son is worse off because of—
because of what we say or don't say in this apartment, well
then . . . I'll do what I need to do. For my son."

The world was harsh, so Angela Rosa had always demanded much of her children, especially Victoria. One day
they would have to get along on their own. But she realized
with stark suddenness that Victoria no longer needed her. For
the first time, she viewed her daughter as another woman, as a
mother. To take that from her—

There was another concern weighing on her, unspoken and
lurking in the cellar of her thoughts, the chance that Nicholas
was her daughter's blessed offering, compensation for her
great loss, their loss. She recalled that last night, waiting for
the doctor, clutching her baby, though she couldn't bear to utter his name now, she couldn't bring herself to talk of such
matters.

"Please, what you want—" she said. "*Figlia bella,* I give you
what you want."

Victoria bent down as if to kiss her mother's hand,
but merely squeezed it, tightening her grip. "I want to be
godmother," she said. "Tonight, this is what I want. To be godmother to my son."

October 1978

NICHOLAS PECCATORI

I gaze out my bedroom window, and I can't stop thinking
how Mama's death brought us all together for a while.
Just before she passed on, exactly a year ago, the dining room on Superior Street was teeming with Mama's friends
and neighbors and a handful of old coworkers from the factory who wanted to say their last good-byes. I'm not sure who
told them to come, but they brought casseroles and soup and
pasta and pies and other dishes I didn't recognize and couldn't
pronounce. Mama was miraculously lucid that night, as if she
knew this would be her last time with them. She wanted them
all to believe that no one else was more important to her at the
moment of their good-byes. She fixed her gaze on them and
smiled placidly, intent on putting *them* at ease.

They wouldn't have guessed that weeks before she'd been
coughing up black tarlike phlegm, the sight of which upset

her more than the pain. She trudged around the apartment with a towel, hunched over with her wheezing, the rattling cough tearing her apart inside. She'd gone to the doctor a few times, but when he sent her for X-rays and they told her she had a tumor lodged beside her vena cava, she refused to go back. The matter was out of the doctor's hands.

Papa's health began failing, too, for a while, as if he yearned to take her place. But it wasn't his time. He finally realized, I think, that she needed him. Pale as he was, he put aside his own ailments and followed her around the apartment collecting towels, telling her stories about the old country, as if he were courting her. He even found the strength to finally clear Benito's room of his clutter, as if to restore for everyone the pure memory of Benito's short time with them, hauling boxes to the basement, insisting that no one else help him. Mama was too sick to appreciate much of this, but there were moments when her eyes would glaze over and I could look at her without turning away, and I imagined her off somewhere on her mother's lap or feeding a mountain goat or in a green field running on little-girl legs. I wanted to ask her where she was. But her reverie wouldn't last, and she'd begin to yell at Papa. *I can't have two minutes alone,* she'd say. *Just go make me some chamomile tea.* He ignored the yelling and made the tea. The apartment smelled constantly of chamomile. He couldn't have seen that she was pushing him away because she worried about him, how he'd get along without her.

After the last of the visitors left, some of them bellowing out final farewells on the stairwell as they descended—*Angela Rosa, we will pick tomatoes in the summer*—others wailing uncontrollably, I wanted to pull them back in. It seemed that as long as they were there filling the apartment, Mama would continue to breathe and smile and utter her small instructions to all of us. We would have done anything she asked. But her friends did leave, the last of their voices sealed away, it seemed, in that stairwell, and then only the family was left. Papa, Uncle Vince, Aunt Lupa, Santo, Vicki and her husband, Anthony, Freddy and his wife, and me. An odd silence descended upon the apartment after the door closed on the last visitor. We paced around, we gazed at the trail of food, bowls and dishes on every table, we stole furtive glances at one another, maybe looking for someone's lead, we picked up napkins off the floor, we did everything but look at Mama. We wanted her to rest, she needed to rest, but more than anything, we wanted to preserve a semblance of normalcy for a few moments. We didn't want to admit that there was a hospital bed in the middle of the living room, where Mama had lived for the past week. She'd fought the idea of the bed at first, but when she barely had the strength to sit up anymore, we pushed aside the chairs and the sofas and placed the bed in a spot where she could see everyone.

Vicki finally pulled everyone back into the living room and asked Anthony to lead us in prayer. We all held hands in a circle around the bed, Mama seemingly at the head of the circle. Papa held her hand on one side, and Vicki held the other. I don't recall much of what Anthony said, but I remember his first few words: "Lord, as we gather here . . ." I squeezed Zia Lupa's hand on one side and Uncle Vince's on the other and imagined everyone else tightening their grips, too. *As we gather here.* I didn't need any other words. These were the people who mattered most to me and we were together, sharing in something sacred and final. We'd all be at the head of the circle one day, and Mama was teaching us not to be afraid.

The praying ended. We sat. We all looked off somewhere, alone in our thoughts. Then each of us took turns standing before Mama. She'd been drifting in and out of wakefulness without warning, her strength waning each time, and we wanted to say our farewells while we could, while she still knew us. Santo stepped up first. He clasped Mama's frail hand in both of his and breathed deeply, forcing back tears, not saying anything. He bent down close to her, their faces almost touching, and whispered something to her. It seemed then as if no one else was in the room, as if no other breaths filled that cramped space. *Thank you,* he said. *Thank you for understanding.* I barely knew Santo, but I could see that something passed between them, a tacit avowal that Santo was her first, a secret glance between a mother and her oldest child that spoke of generations and history.

But there was also apology in his eyes, though I'm not sure why. No one ever talked about Santo. He'd done something shameful, that much I gathered, but his sins were never fully disclosed, at least not to me. I remember overhearing fragments of conversations across back porches on summer nights when I was a kid. We'd play ring-a-levio, hiding out in dark corners behind trash cans, and the neighbors always talked freely, unaware that we were soaking in their adult secrets. Santo stole some money from the bar, some claimed. He married a woman twice his age, others said. He had a fistfight with his father, the poor man. Agostino had lost one son to fever and another to rage, they said.

Santo did stop by the apartment now and then, but his visits were always brief and unexpected. He never appeared for birthdays or Christmas or Thanksgiving. And when he did show, he never brought his family. I did meet his oldest son one time, which seems almost like a dream now. I was sitting on the school steps with my softball and bat one morning, waiting for friends, when he pulled up to the church next door. He and his son got out, and I saw Santo pointing up to a classroom window and the iron fire escape. I didn't recognize him until he got close. When he saw me, he smiled broadly, and I wondered what shameful thing he could have possibly done. He introduced me to his son, Joey, who looked maybe a little older than me, eleven or twelve, then the three of us threw the ball around awhile. There was nothing extraordinary about any of this, other than the fact that this was Santo. But a couple of things have stuck with me all these years. This son of Santo, this cousin of mine, he looked like what I imagined Benito would look like at that age, stocky and quick, with dark, alert eyes. The other thing that struck me was that Santo seemed thrilled about this meeting, as if he'd been planning it, in fact, and that he thought Joey and I would be great friends after this. But I never saw Joey again. And when I ran into Santo again a week later at the apartment, having lunch with Vicki and Mama, as if he'd been living there all along, he never mentioned our game of catch.

Just as I've searched for evidence of Benito's passing, I've tried to discover the reasons for Santo's exile. Having lived in his room my entire life, I've examined every crack and corner. But he left no hidden letters beneath a loose plank of floorboard, no riddles inside a discarded toy, no ripped photos tucked away in the closet, no clues of any sort anywhere. But watching Santo comfort Mama, Papa clearly pleased, I didn't need answers about the past. While little would change — Santo wouldn't be breaking bread at Sunday dinners, there would be no conciliatory demonstrations of affection — the bitterness they'd harbored for so long now washed pale.

Anthony and Freddy approached Mama next. They seemed at ease, smiling and talking to Mama as if they were sitting at her dinner table. Anthony handed her an ebony rosary he'd gotten blessed by the bishop, and Freddy showed her the recipe book he and Mama had been working on, a recent project that had given Freddy an excuse to come around more often. Mama became more excited about passing on the recipes than anyone would have imagined. Though feeding everyone was a priority, she always downplayed her abilities as a cook.

Mama began to cough and everyone looked ready to leap to their feet, but Anthony and Freddy remained composed. They waited for Mama to stop and talked about what they would miss most. Her whistle. When they were kids, she'd step onto the back porch or crouch down by the front window and call them in with her two-note whistle they could hear from blocks away. Freddy backed away from the bed and whistled then. He could barely get it out, but he whistled, Mama's whistle, a long high note followed by a shorter, lower one, to show that he would use those same notes to call in his own children. I could see that Mama was tired, only her eyes moving, but the corners of her mouth curled up when she heard that sound.

Aunt Lupa and Uncle Vince said their good-byes next, both of them praying over Mama in Italian. They spoke of faith and heaven. Their prayers seemed glib and manufactured, but a visible calm spread across Mama's face. I imagined that the prayers called up memories for Mama, sent her back to the catechisms of her youth and the innocence of those times.

I stepped up next, not knowing what I'd say. I touched her hand. For the first time, Mama's bottom lip quivered and if she had the strength she would have begun to cry. "It's okay, Mama," I said. "I'm going to be okay." But suddenly I wasn't sure that I *would* be and crimped the end of the bedsheet with my free hand. Vicki came up beside me and pulled me into her. She reached over and pushed Mama's white hair away from her face, stroking the hair with her fingers. The hair looked smooth and soft and I wanted to touch it. With great effort Mama turned her head so she could take in her daughter more fully, and she said the last words I ever heard her say. *You make,* she started, and caught her breath. Her voice was raspy and hoarse and barely audible. *You make sacrifice,* she said. Mama's spatulate fingers moved and Vicki let the fingers find hers. She placed her hand inside Mama's, and Mama's hand tightened. *My only daughter,* I imagined her thinking. I felt Vicki's hand at my shoulder and then her fingers combing my hair.

When it came Papa's turn we all moved into the kitchen so that the two of them could have a few moments alone. I sat in the wood-rail chair and thought about all the meals Mama had served for us, her solitary complaint being that we didn't eat enough. We probably didn't need to leave the living room. We could hear Papa speaking softly to her, a steady cadence of prayers and reassurances to Mama that everyone would be okay. He knew this would be her main concern, everyone else. I had a strange thought then: this was the first time I'd ever heard Papa talking to Mama. She was always *Mama* to all of us, but now, in the privacy of her living room, amber lamp-light casting long shadows along the gray-green carpet, she was a wife, too, Papa's wife.

He talked awhile longer, then called us back. We sat around, silent mostly, waiting for Mama to give us some sign that she wanted us to stay or go.

Father Ernie finally came by. Vicki had called him at his South Side parish, but he'd been delayed and worry lined his face when he walked in. He raced straight to Mama and breathed a sigh through his mouth when he saw Mama's chest rise and fall. Despite the gray around his temples and along the back, Uncle Vince and Papa still called him the young priest. He had a shyness about him that I liked right away, that reminded me of Anthony. He took his time greeting each of us, consoling us with his earnest eyes and boyish grin. He spoke softly, as if he were weighing each word. When it came time to administer last rites though, he took charge. He told everyone to gather around the bed as he blessed Mama and applied his oils to her forehead. He said his prayers and then asked us to pray along with him. Our Father and Hail Mary. Our chorus of voices reciting those prayers in the living room chilled me. Mama's eyes opened only briefly, and I'm not sure she recognized Father Ernie at all.

He took his time saying good-bye to everyone, and Vicki walked him downstairs. Through the window I could see them below on the front stoop of the apartment. They talked for ten or fifteen minutes, and when she came back up, she looked away from us and dabbed her reddened eyes. She walked to Mama's bed and patted her hand. Papa joined her, taking her other hand, and they whispered back and forth to Mama. Like heavy shades, the lids of Mama's eyes slid open. Her mouth was permanently open now, as if gasping for a breath that wouldn't come. *"Tu ci lasci,"* Papa told her. You can let go now. Mama showed no sign that she understood, but I wanted to believe she moved her fingers, that she squeezed Papa's hand.

I never marked the precise time of Mama's passing, but I know it came shortly after this. In the middle of the night.

We buried Mama next to Benito, her granite stone next to his sun-bleached marker, her mound of fresh dirt shading his small patch of earth. Over fall and winter, the dirt settled, and in the spring grass grew over the dirt, and day by day the summer sun baked her gravestone. Over the course of a single year, the two lots looked like one, as if Mama and Benito had always been together.

Papa didn't wait long to sell the apartment on Superior Street. Mama died in October, and two months later, he was living with his brother above Mio Fratello. I think Mama believed she'd be abandoning Benito if they moved, and she wouldn't let go. For over twenty years she wouldn't let go. But Papa couldn't see staying, not after Mama was gone. He'd pace half the night, muttering to himself, the TV on low and the lights blazing, as if he couldn't wait for morning. Still, I'm not sure Papa would have acted so quickly without Vicki's urging. She cleaned up the apartment, discarded everything in storage in the basement, including all the Sophia Loren memorabilia, contacted the realtor, and assured Papa that everything would be okay. I'd already begun classes at Northeastern, living with Papa and commuting each day, so Vicki insisted I move in with her and her husband, where I could come and go as I pleased and where I still live to this day.

They treat me like a son. Which makes me wonder why they don't have children of their own. Vicki's only thirty-seven. They've been married five years now. Happily, it seems. Her husband has a stable job teaching at a junior high in the south suburbs. Vicki works as a secretary in an office three blocks from home. But her eyes seem always wary, as if she's waiting for some inevitable collapse in her good fortune. After all, she was married once before, to a Richie somebody from the neighborhood. But that didn't last long. I picture the crying, Mama trying to console her but admonishing her at the same time, because whenever Mama talked about the failed marriage—never to me—she always cursed in a low, fierce whisper, insisting that wives don't have to tell their husbands everything. My guess is that Vicki married him too soon and too young, that her marriage was a way for her to get her out of the house, though I'm not sure.

I'm not sure about a lot of things.

In fact, as I gaze out this bedroom window a year after Mama's death, and take in the vastness of the starlit sky, I marvel at all the things I don't know—the patterns of the constellations, the source of their illumination, how blackness can seem so bright. I don't know anything, it seems. Some nights this vastness embroils me with frustration. Yet tonight I'm filled by it.

I look across at the swell of rooftops and think about the old neighborhood: playing kick-the-can in front of St. Columbkille; sneaking into the side door of the Hub theater on Saturday afternoons; eating french fries dipped in beef gravy at Jimmy's; lighting firecrackers at the feast; searching for empty pop bottles and cashing them in for potato chips and chocolate milk at the A&P; climbing the apartment stairs on Superior Street; sweeping the floor at Papa's store, thinking I owned the place.

The smell of fall is in the air. I imagine everyone else at their windows tonight, too—Papa, Vince, Lupa, Santo, Vicki, Freddy, Anthony—looking up at the same roiling sky or maybe staring down at the same river of rooftops, all of us thinking about Mama, and then Benito, each of us alone yet together.

I'm the one who came after. But not so innocent anymore. I know they've kept things from me, things I'll never know, but in the keeping they've taught me how to be a Peccatori, how to endure, and I've come to realize, finally, that I am more than just an afterthought.

Acknowledgments

I am deeply indebted to friends who offered invaluable support and unerring advice: Gary Anderson, Kevin Brewner, Jay Ferrari, Daniel Ferri, Dean Hacker, Billy Lombardo, Maria Mungai, and Edie White. A special thanks to the best reader I know, Henry Sampson, who was there at the first reading and who always has a kind word; the kindness means everything. I also want to thank inspirations Fred Gardaphè, the first editor to take an interest, and Tom Bracken, a wise and generous teacher. Many thanks to Julie Mosow for her valuable suggestions, and to Michael Radulescu for his encouragement and frequent assurances. Thanks to everyone at HarperCollins, particularly Claire Wachtel, a brilliant editor who knows how to nurture more from a writer. Finally, I can't thank enough the person who took a chance and brought this book to publication, the best agent any writer could hope for, Marly Rusoff.